SECOND
WIVES

BOOKS BY CAREY BALDWIN

Her First Mistake

The Marriage Secret

THE CASSIDY & SPENSER THRILLERS SERIES

Judgment

Fallen

Notorious

Stolen

Countdown

Prequels

First Do No Evil (*Blood Secrets Book 1*)

Confession (*Blood Secrets Book 2*)

SECOND
WIVES

CAREY BALDWIN

bookouture

Published by Bookouture in 2023

An imprint of Storyfire Ltd.
Carmelite House
50 Victoria Embankment
London EC4Y 0DZ

www.bookouture.com

ISBN: 978-1-80314-944-8
eBook ISBN: 978-1-80314-318-7

For Scout
who brings me so much joy

PROLOGUE

Lake Tahoe, California

My favorite winter sport is staying home and cozying up by the fire with a good whodunnit and a cup of hot apple cider. You won't catch me on the bunny slopes at Lake Tahoe, much less its treacherous black diamond runs. I steer clear of this fabled California resort in winter.

But August is a whole different bonfire on the beach.

In summer, I'm drawn to Lake Tahoe's storybook blue skies and mountain-ringed waters.

Some of my best childhood memories are from the time my parents found seasonal work down the way at Camp Richardson. On their off days, we'd head to the water, living it up, breathing the same air as the tourists—only it tasted that much sweeter because of how little we had. Even now, it's easy to pretend Mom and Dad are up ahead, just out of sight, sprawled on a beach blanket, enjoying a picnic of pimento cheese sandwiches and peaches—leftovers from the lunches they served up in the camp kitchen.

I like coming back to Tahoe in the summertime.

I like pretending I'm happy.

Take now, for instance.

I'm indulging in a late-night wander near the water. A fierce wind scrapes across the sunburned skin on my cheeks, my arms, my legs, setting my body ablaze like an out-of-control wildfire; but I laugh, and then I throw back my head and open my mouth to savor the taste of damp, woodsy air. They say the heat, earlier today, set a record high, and with the sun blazing down on my kayak, I'd thought I might spontaneously combust. At nearly midnight, it's still hot, but I can't resist the pull of the lake.

It's eerily quiet out.

The unexpected winds have erased the children's sandcastles. The sportsmen have dragged their canoes ashore, and the revelers have long since packed up their umbrellas and coolers and headed to the nightclubs that litter South Tahoe.

The beach is all mine.

I startle at a loud "gurk" followed by the hollow, rushing sound of a duck taking flight.

Make that all mine and the night creatures'.

At the edge of the water, I abandon my flip-flops and wade in. My bare feet sink in wet sand, while wind-generated waves stir around my ankles, cooling my scorched skin. Lifting the skirt of my sundress, I pad on until the water reaches my thighs. My gaze stretches across the lake, past a small island, to find the blue-black shadows of mountain peaks, and then descends onto moonlight shimmering atop the water like sequins on a ball gown.

I follow the path of light, until I see movement.

An arm darts above the water; ghostly white against inky waves.

A strangled cry, and then the moon drifts behind the clouds, leaving me in utter darkness.

I shiver—the water suddenly too cold.

Did I imagine that disembodied arm, that hand grasping for air, that ungodly scream?

I strain my ears, listening for the sound of a human voice, but there is only the gentle whoosh of the waves against the beach and the rasps of barn owls.

Then a plea for help drifts toward me, a whisper braided into the strains of wild, avian conversation.

I push on, parting the flowing water with my arms, gingerly putting one foot and then the next forward, always reaching for the bottom with my toes. Even though my feet drag the sand, the midnight lake feels bottomless. Now that the clouds have stolen every bit of light from the sky, there's not so much as a canopy of stars to guide me.

But then, the clouds break apart, the moon emerges, and my breath catches.

I see a figure dressed in black. The night has disguised its form well, but its movements, its actions suggest a human, not an animal. I think it's a man—no, maybe a woman—no, surely a man. Whoever it is looms waist deep in the lake, hunched over, forcing something... or someone underwater.

Then a head juts above the surface, and the figure wraps his elbow around his victim's neck.

Silence.

Even the birds go quiet.

I have to act quickly.

I have to stop him before it's too late for that pitiful soul in his grasp.

But my chest is frozen, my heart paralyzed beneath my ribs. I feel the absence of its beat, a burning in my shriveled lungs. Like a drowning woman, I am desperate for oxygen.

I gasp in a trickle of air and will my legs to kick, to carry me forward.

The victim disappears below the black water.

I'm out of time!

I lunge toward the spot I last saw the head above water.

The man's arms drop to his sides.

He straightens.

Turns.

A pair of eyes, glowing from an indiscernible face, fix on me, transforming my anemic heart into a full throttle engine.

With powerful strides, he charges through the water—coming at me—coming *for* me.

I whirl, setting my sights on the shore and the forest beyond. The wind-churned waves are my enemy. I fight them, slipping and struggling back toward the beach, not daring to look behind me until, at last, I stumble face first into sand that seeps into my pores, my mouth, my eyeballs. I push myself back up off the beach. My muscles, sore from the day's kayaking, scream as I catapult off my knees and bolt. When I reach the edge of the trees, rocks and sticks shred the soles of my tender, bare feet, but they do not deter me.

I keep running.

I am fleeing for my life.

ONE

Cielo Hermoso
North San Diego County, California

Brigid Templeton's heart broke long before she found out about the affair. It wasn't one quick, powerful snap. Instead, a slow drip-drop of tiny, erosive affronts, each one seemingly powerless to do much damage on its own, eventually carved out a channel. That channel became a crack. That crack widened and, finally, it split her heart in two.

The damage began quietly.

Her husband, who used to drink up her conversation like nectar from the gods, stopped paying attention when she tried to tell him about her day or ask after his. On their regular Friday date nights, when he didn't cancel on her, he spent more time looking around the restaurant than into her eyes. He began coming home in the wee hours of the morning, three, maybe four, times a week, though always with a legitimate excuse.

But how many bona fide reasons could there be before the sheer number of them became implausible?

Brigid was no fool, and she didn't believe in playing ostrich.

"Are you having an affair?" She greeted him at the door with the inquiry at 4 a.m. one morning.

Leveling his eyes with hers, he raised his right hand. "I fell asleep at the office. I swear on my mother's grave I've loved you since we first met, and I love you more every day. I've never so much as looked at another woman—not in that way. I would never do anything to risk losing you."

Maybe a sociopath could pull off a whopper without so much as a telling twitch or flush to the face, but Brigid knew a good, decent man like her husband could never lie that convincingly. Not to mention, he always stroked his chin and stared at the floor when he was hiding something from her.

In that moment, his gaze didn't falter.

He must be telling the truth.

And yet, that didn't make her nights less lonely.

"I think we should try marriage counseling," she said.

"Count me in." He pulled her close and dotted her forehead with kisses, filling up her heart with hope.

The next day he brought flowers, but then had to rush off to put out a fire at the office—a fire that burned until long after she fell asleep, curled up on the sofa, listening for the sound of his car pulling into the drive.

But true to his word, he went to therapy with her, where he hulked, arms crossed over his chest, jaw clamped tightly shut, week after week, month after month, until, at last, it became impossible to deny the truth—her husband didn't love her anymore.

If she stayed, she had no doubt she'd spend the rest of her life pacing the floors, worrying that he'd been in an accident, asking herself if it was time to start calling the hospitals and wondering when or *if* he'd come through that door with his perfect excuse at the ready.

Unless *she* found the courage to leave, they'd *both* be trapped.

So, after listening to Bonnie Raitt's heart-wrenching song, "My Opening Farewell", at least a thousand times, she threw back her shoulders and told him it was over.

Even after the divorce, he claimed he'd never cheated, and she continued to believe him, lost yet more sleep wondering if she should've stuck it out longer, tried one more round of counseling.

But then, mere days after the final decree, he eloped to Las Vegas with Charity from Supper Club!

The pair claimed they'd started up only after he and Brigid split, but that simply didn't ring true.

So why now, with her eyes finally open, did she keep on going along *pretending* to believe him?

Dr. Tanaka, their marriage therapist, told Brigid she was a peacekeeper, and the way Dr. Tanaka said it didn't sound like a compliment.

But her daughter's feelings were Brigid's main concern.

Off to college or not, it would devastate Tish to discover that her perfect saint of a father had cheated on her mother. For the sake of their only child, Brigid desperately wanted to keep things amicable. She hated it when divorced couples put one another down in front of the kids, each making the other the villain.

Divorce was never one person's fault, was it?

Even if she could no longer *actually* give her ex-husband the benefit of the doubt about an affair, she made a choice to *fake* doing so. There was a lot to lose, but little to gain, by confronting him with his lies.

It was over between them.

He was getting on with his life; therefore, she ought to do

the same. And there was another person who'd been just as blindsided by that fast-track Vegas wedding as Brigid.

Charity's ex-husband.

Everyone, from Brigid's hairdresser to Charity herself, cautioned Brigid against getting involved with him. They all called it a double rebound, and maybe it was. But after years of being ignored, Brigid couldn't resist the sweetness of him gazing into her eyes, avidly reaching for her hand, craving her company... and her body.

And so, less than a year after Charity married Brigid's husband, Brigid married Charity's.

Then they pretended things were perfectly normal between them.

After switching husbands, they carried on in their same social circle, even attending their monthly Supper Club. After a period of initial awkwardness, which Brigid and Charity, by tacit agreement, ignored, things seemed to be working out fine.

It was all very cordial, very civilized... until one fateful night.

TWO

"Well?" Charity asked. The light from the dining room's newly installed chandelier danced off her golden-brown eyes and made her jet-black hair, with its spectacular Cleopatra cut, gleam like polished glass. "You haven't said anything about the makeover, and I'm *dying* to know what you think. Be honest."

The skin on the back of Brigid's neck prickled, and she rubbed it hard, reminding herself to play nice. This wasn't the first time since "the switch" that Charity had hosted their supper club in Brigid's former home, but it was the first time since the renovations.

Charity pivoted on her richly upholstered chair and aimed her knees and her conversation toward Brigid. Then, informally, she rested her elbows on the table, which had been lavishly set with a Chantilly lace cloth, fine, bone-white china, and crystal goblets. Majestic white orchids, their centers freckled with purple, towered from squat, square porcelain vases, perfectly punctuating the place settings. To celebrate the completion of her home makeover, Charity had broken with Supper Club tradition. Usually, the host prepared the meal for the group, but tonight, a for-hire chef was putting the finishing touches on the

ιu vin, according to the hand-lettered menus
)assed around earlier), and every time a
bounded through the pocket door between
and the kitchen, mouth-watering fragrances
whooshed in along with them. Currently, one uniformed server busied herself refilling wine glasses while another gathered up salad plates littered with the remnants of roasted artichoke and remoulade. At the far end of the table, Nash and Jackson raised their voices, talking loudly over each other in a show of friendly one-upmanship, their bravado sounding only slightly forced.

Farrah Benedetti and Darya Oladipo, the women seated on either side of Charity and Brigid, reprimanded their husbands, Roman and Jamal, for scrolling on their phones, then excused themselves for a powder break. Directly across the dinner table, Rollin and Aiden Martine-Watteau seemed to be having some kind of marital tiff, and that left Brigid with a choice. She could either sit stonily beside Charity, simmering in silence until Farrah and Darya returned to act as a buffer between them, or she could do what was expected: pretend everything that had happened was water rolling off a duck's back traveling swiftly under the bridge.

Her mind flashed on that woman in Texas who'd had an affair with her friend's husband and then chopped that friend into little pieces with an axe. Had she and Charity really buried the hatchet or was her hostess merely hiding it in the kitchen?

Charity curled her lips into an intimate, eager smile, as if nothing had changed between the two of them. As if that ginormous hand-blown blue-glass Chihuly chandelier descending from the twenty-foot ceiling—a gorgeous, one-of-a kind piece of art—hadn't taken the place of a small, milky fixture that had been a wedding gift from Brigid's father and cost him a month's wages.

"What's the verdict?" Charity beamed conspiratorially.

Charity seemed to think Brigid would be pleased she'd

replaced the furniture in her former home—that she'd replaced *Brigid*.

"Oh, come on. I can't read your mind."

Brigid almost swallowed her tongue from... what? Nostalgia? Envy? Had her ex-husband doubled his real estate sales? Finally found his way back from all those losses he'd suffered in a volatile stock market? "Wow. Just wow."

"So, you approve?"

How could she approve of such extravagance when Tish was entering her sophomore year of college? The University of Southern California came with a price tag to match its prestigious reputation, so unless there had been a drastic change in her ex-husband's finances, he couldn't afford his half of USC *and* all of this.

She took a breath and forced her shoulders out of their hunched position.

Charity was obviously contributing to the household expenses, and even if those funds came from Charity's divorce settlement—in other words out of Brigid's new husband's pocket—that money was Charity's to spend as she pleased. As long as this house-beautiful project hadn't depleted Tish's college fund—something that both she and her ex had made a priority to protect throughout the ups and downs of the economy—Brigid had no right to complain. "It's mind-blowing. Stunning."

"I realize it's not your typical southern California motif, but the Cielo Hermoso town council can't dictate what we do with the *interiors* of our houses. So, I thought why not bring a taste of the Orient to North San Diego County? These murals are hand-painted." Charity swept her arms wide to indicate the larger effect. "They call this style Chinoiserie. Doesn't it feel like we're in a garden?"

Indeed. The walls were a fantasy in bloom. The base color the palest of greens, as if someone had photographed grass, and then left that photo outside to fade under a hot summer sun. In contrast, vividly colored birds and flowers had been painted on with a delicate hand, resulting in a dramatic, yet tasteful, effect.

"East meets West. Outdoors meets indoors—that's the goal." Charity inhaled deeply, happily.

Brigid tilted her chin, gazing up at the blue-glass chandelier dripping into the room—a vortex of escaped sky. "Mission accomplished."

Charity had done an undeniably beautiful job of redecorating—and in the process wiped away virtually all evidence that Brigid had ever lived here. In contrast, Brigid had never occupied Charity's old house at all. She had occasionally acquiesced to spending an evening in front of the television there, but she couldn't have lain in that bed without cringing at the thought that it had once been Charity's boudoir. Nor could she stomach the way Charity used her house key to enter unannounced, leaving behind little bombs in the form of Post-it notes stuck everywhere.

I notice you've been neglecting the lawn. There's nothing healthy in the refrigerator. Does she want you to have a heart attack? This place is a pig-sty. Please have Brigid do a deep clean.

That last missive had settled things for Brigid, and she'd insisted that when they married, they move into a new house—one where Charity had never reigned supreme.

Brigid made her choice, and Charity made hers.

Neither woman wanted to live in a house with constant reminders of her predecessor. They'd simply gone about achieving the same ends by different means. There was no reason to take this redo personally.

And that chandelier was truly a beauty. Brigid could hardly take her eyes off it... until she noticed the dinner table shaking, dishes first sliding, and then clattering to the floor. When a server dove under the table, Brigid realized what was happening—it must be a small earthquake. She'd been through enough of these California mini-quakes to know better than to panic, but something seemed different this time.

"Guuun!" Nash's voice boomed out, followed by the sound of more plates clattering.

What?

Brigid turned and stared, uncomprehendingly, at Nash and Jackson struggling, rolling around on the table, faces red, spittle flying from their mouths, another man she couldn't quite see in the middle of the fray.

"Get down!" This time it was Jackson shouting.

Pop. Pop. Pop.

Heart thundering in her chest, Brigid jumped up, reeling from a stinging sensation in her neck. Her ears rang.

Looking down, she discovered a layer of shattered blue glass frosting her arms, and bright-red blood spurting onto the lace tablecloth, puddling into strange designs. Her head felt light, and then, suddenly, she wanted to laugh because the table looked like a giant Rorschach card and wasn't that just too rich?

Freud would have a heyday psychoanalyzing this bunch.

Then her fuzzy gaze slid from a bloody blot, resembling a dancing bear, to something shiny lying on the hardwood floor.

A gun.

The kind with a cylinder that spins.

Charity's going to be very, very angry about this mess.

Hot sticky blood dripped from her neck. Her legs felt tenuous beneath her heavy, heavy body. Did this kind of stream of consciousness portend death? Instead of her life flashing before her eyes, maybe all she was going to get was a bunch of loosely connected thoughts scrolling across her brain.

No! No! No! Do not die! Tish needs you!

Brigid reached for her burning neck, wanting to stop the bleeding, but her fingers didn't land.

Around her, mouths, on blurred faces, gaped. Voices shouted, but she couldn't pin down the words. She saw a man's hand grip her arm, but despite the way the thick fingers dug into her skin, making her flesh blanch around them like a glove, she didn't feel his touch.

If only the room would stop spinning, if only she could breathe...

More shouting.

More spinning.

Fade to black.

THREE

An alarm went off in Brigid's brain, and she awoke, shivering and kicking like a bear emerging from hibernation. From the top of her head to the tips of her toes, she felt stiff and disjointed, like someone had disassembled her and then tried to put her back together again without the benefit of an instruction manual. Blinking against an abusive, overhead light, she fought to focus her vision and pulled at scratchy sheets that smelled of bleach. She could barely resist the urge to tug them over her head and hide.

"Brigid, honey, can you hear me?" A man's voice—a voice she knew she knew—directed her gaze.

The comforting scent of stale coffee wafted toward her as he bent closer.

Then, slowly, the jut of a strong jaw, the smear of salt-and-pepper stubble on a dimpled chin, the warmth of plain brown eyes, aligned themselves into a face that made her heart settle down into a less erratic rhythm.

There's nothing to be afraid of.
Everything is going to be okay.

"N-nash." His name seemed to stick to her thick, dry tongue. So hard to speak—and nearly impossible to swallow. The lining of her throat stung as though it had been scrubbed with a steel wool pad. "W-water."

"She's awake." Nash straightened, speaking over his shoulder to a second individual. His voice sounded high-pitched and excited.

A pretty young woman in blue scrubs materialized, pressed a button that raised the head of the bed into a sitting position, poured water from a plastic pitcher into a paper cup, then stuck a straw in it and put it to Brigid's lips. "Just a sip or two to start—your gut's going to need a minute to get going again."

Brigid sucked greedily despite the advice and the way the water shocked its way down her throat. "Thank you," she croaked.

"You're welcome, but try taking it a little slower, okay? I'm Sarah, and I'm your nurse." Sarah pointed to a dry erase board near the door. Her name was spelled out in red marker. Sarah, with her delicate features, bright-blue eyes, and silky blonde hair looked more like she belonged on the cover of a teen magazine than in hospital scrubs, but her tone held confidence and authority. Brigid decided, on the spot, that she trusted her. "You're my nurse."

"That's right." She gently tapped Brigid's arm. "You've been out for a while—Dr. Banner had you heavily sedated—but you're doing great now. I'm going to give you some time alone with your husband. Would you like that?"

Brigid nodded, and the motion alerted her to the presence of a bulky bandage below her jawline.

"Don't touch the dressing on your neck. Buzz if you need me."

.   .   .

Once they were alone, Nash took the cup from Brigid and placed it on a tray-table. Then he clasped her hand in his, stroking her wrist with his thumb as he spoke—a sweet habit that always made her feel special. "The doctors said you might be disoriented when you woke up. Do you know where you are, sweetheart?"

Her gaze drifted over white walls, tile floors, and the television mounted to the wall. A monitor stood at the bedside, and a tube taped to the back of her hand—the one Nash wasn't squeezing the life out of—snaked across her body, connecting her to a bag of clear liquid that hung from an IV pole. She had "doctors" as well as a nurse named Sarah. Her thinking might not be razor-sharp, but she wasn't brain dead either. "I'm in a hospital."

"You remember what happened?"

She closed her eyes, and at first nothing came back to her, but then, she recalled Supper Club—a gun lying on the floor. Blood pooling onto a lace tablecloth. Her stomach lurched at the memory, and she took a few quick breaths. The nausea soon passed but she couldn't escape a sense of impending doom. "Someone brought a gun to the party. They tried to kill me."

Nash lifted her hand to his lips, pressed a kiss into her palm, and then his eyes filled with moisture. "No, no, my love. No one tried to kill you. It was a terrible, terrible accident."

"But I remember a gun and blood and screams. What happened?"

"The important thing to know is that you're going to be fine. They've been watching you closely, but you've done so well they've demoted you, kicked you out of the ICU into a regular room."

Nash's reassurances were making her worry more, not less. Why wouldn't he give her a direct answer? "But how did I wind up in the hospital? I remember a gun. I remember seeing blood. But then, I must've blacked out."

"Someone did bring a gun—a revolver." His eyes cut away but soon returned to meet her gaze. "It went off and a round hit the chandelier. Then the chandelier crashed and sent shrapnel flying."

He made it sound like a war zone, not their regular supper with friends.

"*Who* fired a gun? I deserve to know what happened, Nash."

"I thought we could go into it all later, but I can see you're impatient as ever." He cracked a smile. "Good to know you're still you."

That tight feeling in her chest eased up. Nash was teasing her. He wouldn't have taken off his kid gloves if the news was too bad.

"Like I said, after the gun *accidentally* went off, the chandelier crashed onto the table, and a piece of glass, from a broken plate, we think, flew up, punctured a muscle in your neck, and 'nicked the anterior jugular'—I'm quoting your trauma surgeon. But, luckily, they were able to successfully repair the wound and stop the bleeding."

My jugular.

Her head lolled onto the pillow. Her mouth wouldn't form the question her mind was asking: *If my jugular was cut, then why didn't I die?*

"If Roman hadn't acted so fast, they say you might've bled to death. We were all impressed with how he leaped to your aid, so quickly, so decisively. He rushed to put pressure on your neck, and that saved you. You did lose a lot of blood, though. By the time the paramedics got there, you barely had a pulse." He paused, and his Adam's apple worked in his throat. "I'm not going to lie—you scared the devil out of me—out of all of us— but the doctors say you're going to be absolutely fine. It's one of those things where, had circumstances been slightly different, the laceration even a millimeter deeper, it would've been fatal.

Instead, they expect a complete and quick recovery. As a precaution, they want to watch you one more night in the hospital, something about a 'neck wound protocol', but the plan is to let you go home tomorrow, and then you can go back to full activity after another day or so of rest."

"I wish you could take me home right now. I want to see Tish," she said, her voice sounding hoarse and low. She withdrew her hand from Nash's to reach for more water. Just one more small sip—she remembered her nurse's warning not to take too much at once, but her throat was so dry. "Why isn't Tish here?"

"You'll see her soon."

It was a simple enough response, and yet, Brigid was struggling to comprehend its meaning—or lack thereof. It was like there was a missing piece of information floating around in her brain that she couldn't quite grab hold of.

"Are you sure we can't go home, now?"

"Believe me, honey, there's nothing I want more. But I'm afraid that's not possible."

"Tomorrow's soon enough." She managed a smile for him. She wasn't a child; she would do what the doctors recommended and follow their orders. And she was feeling very, very tired. She wouldn't mind going back into hibernation for a bit, only... "You still haven't told me who brought the gun."

"We'll rehash the rest later. Nurse Sarah warned me not to stay too long, and I really should go. But there is something else I feel I *must* say before I do." His thumb stroked her wrist again. "I can't leave your side without telling you that this awful accident really opened my eyes. When I saw you lying on the floor, bleeding, my heart stopped. And all I could think was that I wished it were me instead. You're the love of my life, Brigid."

His words, spoken so soft and low, so poignantly, made her feel the need to respond in kind. He was her husband, and he deserved nothing less. "And you mine." She wiped away unexpected tears, and took a deep breath, not understanding the sudden upheaval in her stomach. Maybe it was because she'd drunk too much water too fast, or simply because she still had unanswered questions. "Nash, *please* don't leave me hanging. Who brought that gun to the party? And why?"

"Don't get me in trouble with Sarah—she's meaner than she looks. I think you should rest now."

"But I can't sleep. Not until I know who brought the gun."

He stepped away and threw his hands up. "I surrender. It was Roman Benedetti."

But he'd just said it was Roman who'd saved her life. She was groggy and growing more tired and more confused by the minute. "I don't understand why Roman would do such a thing."

"Please don't worry, honey. The police are investigating. They questioned everyone right away, but they didn't arrest Roman. I don't think they will unless you want them to press charges. But I don't think your focus needs to be on Roman right now. You just concentrate on getting well."

When she shook her head, the bandage on her neck tugged uncomfortably. "I'm exhausted. I admit it. But my head is swimming with questions. Explain it to me one more time, and then I promise to rest."

"Do I have your word?"

"I promise."

He nodded. "All right. We had just finished appetizers when Roman started talking under his breath. I thought I heard him say something about being worth more dead than alive, or that he couldn't go on—honestly, I'm not sure exactly what he said because he was muttering. But the next thing I knew, he'd pulled a revolver out of his jacket. Jackson must've seen it at the same time I did, and the two of us tackled him. We were rolling around on the table, trying to wrestle the gun away from Roman, when it went off."

Get down!

Pop. Pop. Pop.

She covered her ears with her hands. It was all coming back. Her heart kicked like it might jump right out of her chest.

Jackson!

"Nash, please tell me, where is Jackson? Is he okay?"

FOUR

Charity hustled down the hospital corridor wrangling a giant vase of exotic flowers in her arms. Burying her nose in the blossoms, she reveled in their delightful fragrance.

Mission accomplished.

To find a floral shop that was up to her standards, she'd driven more than thirty miles from her home. Then, she'd personally selected orchids, ginger and birds of paradise. She'd handpicked each individual stem before overseeing an arrangement by the florist that was fit for a queen. A lot of people would say she'd gone to *way* too much trouble over flowers for her husband's first wife, but Charity took pride in going the extra mile.

Living up to the beautiful name her parents had bestowed upon her was something she took pride in.

And she didn't mind taking credit where credit was due. Virtue might well be its own reward but only fools hide their light under a bushel.

If you do a good deed, you ought to point it out.

Anyway, Brigid was her best friend, and she deserved something really special. If the tables were turned, Charity would expect Brigid to do the same for her. So, no, sorry, but an ordinary vase of roses simply wouldn't do. She held out her arms, surveying the flowers for the umpteenth time.

These will prove how much I care.

A deep sense of satisfaction welled into a smile—but then, an image of Brigid lying prone, bleeding all over the floor, popped into her head. Charity shuddered, and a bird of paradise dipped its beak.

Charity had been truly terrified that night, and she was still struggling to figure out what went wrong: Roman pulling the gun, and then later acting so fast to undo the damage he'd wrought. It was all a horrifying blur.

Poor Tish had almost lost her mom.

Random tragedy is a sharp knife—one that carves deep wounds and leaves the soul forever scarred.

The thought struck quickly, showing her no mercy. Caught off guard, she backed against the cold tile walls of the hospital corridor, out of breath and fighting back tears.

Not today, Charity.

Slowly, deliberately, she filled her lungs, breathed through the moment and waited for her chin to cease quivering. Then she straightened her shoulders and strode down the hall, head high, heels clacking.

Tomorrow was Hope's birthday—the one day out of the year Charity indulged her grief.

Today, however, was just an ordinary day, one meant for looking forward not backward.

Today, Charity would show Brigid her commitment to their friendship.

Brigid had survived... but if she hadn't, Charity would've been there to comfort Tish. She would've wrapped Tish in loving arms and, in time, Tish would've grown to love Charity just as she loved Brigid—as her mother.

Every cloud has a silver lining.

Brigid was so lucky to have Tish. If Tish were Charity's biological daughter, she'd be on the phone with her every day. In fact, as her stepmom, she called Tish daily to check on her. Brigid would do well to follow her example, work harder to keep the lines of communication open. Charity would be more than happy to teach Brigid how to be a better parent. Naturally, she'd have to broach the subject tactfully, respectfully. And before Brigid could improve her parenting skills, she had to regain her health. Charity would first focus on doing whatever was necessary to help her friend get well.

Everything had happened so fast, Charity hadn't had time to come up with a plan for that... but once they released Brigid from the hospital, she'd surely need follow-up doctor visits.

Charity could drive her to all her appointments, pick up her meds at the pharmacy, bring over meals... if Brigid would let her.

Charity worried that Brigid seemed to be holding a grudge at times—and while that would've been understandable had she known about the affair, she hadn't. Not really. In order to cause the least amount of hurt to all parties, Charity had decided to deny, deny, deny. And without a confession, with no actual proof of the affair, Brigid should have given Charity the benefit of the doubt.

Innocent until proven guilty—that was the law of the land.

So, clearly, Brigid was the one in the wrong on that count.

Besides, Charity hadn't made a fuss when Brigid married *her* ex. In the end, since they'd simply swapped spouses, and everyone was happy, there was no justification for any lingering resentments.

All's well that ends well.

Only Brigid hadn't gotten over the sting of coming in second to Charity—and she could understand that must be hard. Charity had never come in second to anyone, nor did she plan to.

She sighed.

If she just gave her a little more time, Brigid would come around.

In fact, a near-death experience might be just what the doctor ordered to snap Brigid out of the mood she'd been in ever since the divorce. Charity shifted the flowers, peering through the stems at the number on the hospital room door in front of her.

Wrong room.

Lost in thought, she'd walked straight past Brigid's room.

She pivoted and, under the camouflage of flowers, made her way back to room fourteen, slowing her step at the sound of Nash's voice. She wasn't eavesdropping. The door to Brigid's room was slightly ajar, and Charity couldn't help but overhear snatches of conversation.

This awful accident really opened my eyes. When I saw you lying on the floor, bleeding, my heart stopped... I wished it were me...

Charity stumbled, nearly sending her beautiful arrangement crashing, and then backed against the wall, hiding behind the flowers, her mouth agape.

A long pause ensued before she heard Brigid say: *and you mine.*

What the hell did that mean?

A strange, gurgling sound escaped Charity's throat, and she covered her mouth to silence it.

If only she'd heard the entire conversation.

You heard enough, didn't you?

No. She hadn't. As she skulked outside the door to the hospital room, Nash, her husband, of little more than a year, continued his urgent, emotion-wrought whispering to his ex-wife, Brigid—Charity's best friend.

And that's when the thunderbolt struck.

As terrible as it would be for Tish to lose her mother, as

awful as it would be for Charity to lose her best friend... everyone's life would be easier, in the long run, without Brigid around.

Oh no.

She mustn't think like that, mustn't succumb to the kind of dark thoughts that had a way of sneaking up on her around the time of Hope's birthday—and her accident.

Nash and Brigid have been through a trauma, that's all.

Charity shouldn't say or do or even *think* anything rash... although, of course, she'd be foolish not to take note of the potential threat to her marriage.

When Brigid had still been Nash's wife, Charity had a distinct advantage over her—after all, there's nothing sexier than forbidden love. But now, the tables were turned, and it was Charity who found herself wrong-footed.

Now Charity was the wife-in-the-way, and Brigid the alluring, off-limits lover—at least potentially.

I wish you could take me home right now, Brigid's plaintiff voice carried clearly.

Nash's response was too low for her to catch.

Still under camouflage of flowers, Charity sidestepped closer to peer around the door frame. Brigid sat propped up in her hospital bed, face gaunt, big blue eyes fixed on Nash, her tussled blonde curls adding to a waif-like innocence. She could've been a pale angel... or one of those heroin-chic supermodels.

Pathetic and yet seductive.

Charity covered her mouth to stifle her gasp—Brigid and Nash were holding hands.

Gagging on the cloying scent of the flowers, she slunk back against the wall before those two realized that she'd seen them. She wanted to smash this vase and stomp the blooms to bits. Maybe another piece of flying glass would take Brigid out for good this time. Too bad there was no way to pull the plug on her, because the way Charity felt right this second, she'd damn well do it.

Stop!

The blackness of her own thoughts jolted her back to her senses. She would never do anything to hurt her best friend. The whole idea was absurd, and absolutely meaningless since Brigid wasn't on life support, and there wasn't any plug to pull. She was breathing on her own, sitting up in bed, flirting away with Nash. Thank goodness there was absolutely no opportunity for Charity's dark side to win out.

And she could understand, since Nash and Brigid had been married so long, how a scare like this might stir up old feelings. It was only natural for Nash to be protective of the mother of his child. She need only recall that Nash had chosen Charity over Brigid.

Charity had nothing to worry about.

It was best not to overreact.

In fact, it might be wise to come back later when she was feeling more composed. She turned on her heel and headed back the way she'd come in. She'd almost reached the exit when she spied an older woman sitting up in her bed, alone in her room—crying.

The poor thing.

With the back of her hand, Charity dabbed moisture from her own cheeks, shifted the flowers in her arms, and knocked on the open door of the woman's room. "Special delivery! These gorgeous flowers are for you, dear. Someone must love you very much."

FIVE

The door to Brigid's hospital room stood slightly ajar, open just enough to allow various sounds to drift in: sneakers squishing; unfamiliar voices rising and falling; wheels rattling over tile whenever a nurse trundled by with a pushcart. Then, quite suddenly, the door flung wide, and, as if a director had yelled "action!" on a movie set, Jackson burst into the room.

His straight, silky hair, cut just beneath his jawline in a style his barber aptly referred to as *rock star*, needed a wash. His brown eyes were puffy and ringed with red. His shirt looked like he'd just grabbed it out of a hamper or maybe slept in it, but despite his bedraggled appearance, Brigid's heart lost its place, forgetting its rhythm, the moment his eyes met hers.

One look from Jackson Templeton could heat you up and turn you inside out like a sock in the dryer.

Everyone knew Jackson had *it*—that special something that had made him a star in his youth, and no doubt would again if he ever chose to go back into show business.

"You're awake!" Jackson barreled past Nash, shoving him aside in the process. "Why didn't anyone call me?"

Nash stepped back, clearing his throat. "I-I thought the nurse..."

Brigid grabbed the rail of her bed. Less than an hour ago, she'd awoken in a hospital room, disoriented, yes, but as unperturbed as one could be under the circumstances. Because the first face she'd seen, the first voice she'd heard, had belonged to a man she'd loved most of her adult life.

Nash.

He'd been there, watchfully waiting, hovering protectively.

When the nurse had said she'd give Brigid time alone with her husband, Brigid had accepted the situation at face value. And why wouldn't she?

After all, Nash hadn't corrected her.

Why not?

He'd also been circumspect when she'd asked about Tish, failing to remind her that Tish had moved to L.A., and that, furthermore, they hadn't been getting along as of late. Brigid hoped that wasn't why her daughter wasn't here at the hospital. Surely, there was some other reason for her absence.

An important exam, more likely.

That had to be it. Nash would've explained to their daughter that Brigid was out of danger, and that she wouldn't want Tish to miss school. Which was correct. But why, when Brigid had said she wanted to go home together, hadn't he told her they were divorced?

Surely that had been the right moment to set the record straight.

To be fair, he had asked if she was disoriented, if she knew *where* she was. But, apparently, that was the wrong question—he should've asked if she knew *who* she was.

Then, she would have answered "Brigid Clarence".

But now she would answer correctly, "Brigid Templeton".

How that clarity came about, she wasn't sure. It wasn't as if, in the past few seconds since Jackson burst in, she'd shuffled through the days of her life like cards and cut the deck on the memories of divorcing Nash and marrying Jackson. It was simply that one moment she was Old Brigid, propped up on pillows in a hospital bed, gazing up into Nash's loving eyes, and the next, minute she was New Brigid.

As New Brigid, she could access her relevant history; all her memories seemed well within reach.

But this updated version of herself didn't feel *real*.

And though she certainly remembered getting married to Jackson, though she definitely felt a magnetic attraction to him, she had a huge knot in her stomach.

Jackson Templeton was her husband.

She absolutely *knew* that to be true.

So why did she *feel* like Nash Clarence's wife?

SIX

The sun had risen. Now, only the barest hint of pale pink infiltrated the blue horizon. Clouds climbed from the ocean into the heavens in little white puffs clustered like footprints. Charity closed her eyes, desperate to believe that Hope was among the angels whose feet had smudged the sky this morning.

That she was nearby, watching.

Miss you, my darling girl.

Charity inhaled deeply. The scent of eucalyptus leaves would now and forever be bound with memories of her daughter. Charity and Jackson had chosen this cemetery, high on a hill, overlooking the Pacific Ocean, for its expansive views, and because among the umbrella trees and cedars, a rainbow eucalyptus grew. The first time Hope had seen such a tree with its peeling bark, its trunk striped in neon purples, yellows, and blues, she'd rushed home to her easel and painted a landscape filled with them. Hope had inherited so much creativity from her father—like Jackson, Hope sang and played guitar—but her adeptness with a brush came from her maternal side. Charity's mother, Hope's grandmother, had been an artist—of the immensely talented but starving variety. Charity had envisioned such an amazing life for Hope: an artist's loft in Paris, a record deal, finding true love...

You laugh and the wind dances.
You weep and the rain falls.
You smile and the stars shine.
What would the world do without you?
What would I?

Jackson's tender song carried on the wind, and the way his voice broke at the refrain made Charity's chin quiver, her chest ache. She crept forward, closing in on him at Hope's graveside, then slipped behind the rainbow eucalyptus. They'd paid a premium for a site under its shade.

The magnificent trunk barely concealed Charity's slender form, but it didn't matter because Jackson kept his gaze heavenward as he strummed an acoustic guitar. From this distance Charity couldn't see the scratches that marred the guitar's red spruce soundboard, but she knew they were there, beneath his palm, as he paused to caress the wood.

Hope's old guitar.

The vintage, embroidered psychedelic strap was a dead giveaway. Besides, she knew whenever he visited Hope's grave, he serenaded her with it. Usually, Charity stayed out of sight, but this morning, she wanted him to see her.

She *needed* him to see her.

What would I? What would...

Jackson's song ended without finishing, colliding with his pain. He ducked his chin and wiped his cheeks with the back of his hand.

Charity took a deep breath, pasted on a bright smile, and strode out from behind the tree, waving. "I'm surprised to see you here."

Jackson turned.

Sunlight streaking through the billowing eucalyptus leaves dappled his cheeks and brought out the gold highlights in his

ash-blond hair. Despite his furrowed brow, the lines fanning
around his eyes even when he wasn't smiling... or frowning... he
looked incredible. That magnetic look in his eyes reached out,
pulled you in and held you until you could hardly breathe. Or
maybe the real reason she couldn't catch her breath was that he
reminded her so much of Hope.

Hope's features and coloring were more like Charity's, but
her mannerisms, the way she'd held herself, the look in her eyes,
were all Jackson. In truth, ever since Hope died, Charity hadn't
been able to bear to look directly at him for more than a few
seconds at a time—much less live with him. "You could still do
it, you know."

"What?"

"Have your own television show. Cut a hit record. Be a
star."

He turned his back to her and faced Hope's tombstone—an
angel standing tall and proud as any warrior.

Charity went to his side. "Have you considered doing a
Songbirds' series sequel? You could suggest it—that kind of
thing is all the rage these days, and you still have fans who'd love
to see how Stone Songbird turned out, all grown up, with a
family of his own." Though it was not her intent, her voice went
wispy. "What kind of a father he turned out to be."

She saw his back stiffen, sensed his anger.

"I'm not going to have this ridiculous conversation with you
again. Certainly not today."

"Okay, but maybe you could try not to snap at me." Being
near him like this, the fresh smell of his spiced soap floating
around in the air, standing in front of their daughter's grave-
stone, wrapped in a shared blanket of pain, nearly made her
break down, but she'd be damned if she'd let him see her cry.
Her grief was like a razor blade scraping across her wrist. The
less she acknowledged it, the more superficial the wound. But if
Jackson, or anyone, ever saw how much she was hurting, if she

allowed anyone to see the true extent of her grief, she feared the blade might cut so deep she wouldn't survive.

Now he was looking at her directly in the eye. She turned her face away.

Do not let him see.

"I'm sorry," he said softly. "I shouldn't have been sharp with you. It's a rough day, but that's all the more reason for me to think before I speak."

"It's a hard day for both of us." She sighed. "So, let's not bicker. Not here. What if Hope can hear us?"

"I *wish* she could. I'd like to believe she's here in spirit. I come to talk to her, often, and you know that. So, why would you be surprised to find me here?"

"Because, on her birthday, you always come in the evening, and I always come in the morning. I thought we had an unspoken agreement—so we don't bump into each other."

He shrugged. "I never tried to avoid you. I just like coming in the evenings to watch the sunset with her. But, Brigid's coming home from the hospital today, so I came for the sunrise instead. I wanted to get my birthday visit in before Brigid gets discharged, and I don't want to leave her alone tonight."

Of course. It was all about Brigid. "Sure. I get it."

"Thanks, by the way."

"For what?"

"For being so kind to Brigid. She told me you called her and offered to take her to all her doctor appointments."

"And she refused my help. Said she didn't need it."

"She has me. I can easily arrange my schedule to accommodate anything that comes up. But it was thoughtful of you to offer, and we're both grateful."

"You know me—I like to help out where I can, and, after all, she is my best friend."

Jackson's brow rose, and he grunted.

"Hey, since we're both here, and since we're not bickering,

do you want to see what I've planned for today?" Like prior years, she'd brought a tote bag filled with all she needed to celebrate Hope's birthday. She dropped the bag on the ground and pulled out a blanket, spread it on the ground in front of their daughter's grave.

"Sure. I think Hope would like that—us remembering her birthday together."

She sat down cross-legged on the blanket and patted the spot next to her.

After Jackson joined her, she began unpacking the contents of the tote: a thermos of coffee, a birthday candle, a lighter, napkins, and half a dozen maple donuts—Hope's favorite.

"You brought a lot of donuts. Did you plan to eat all of those?" Jackson grinned at her.

"One donut does not a party make." She laughed and passed him a napkin with two donuts. "Here. Stick a candle in one of those please."

"Yes, ma'am." He lit the candle. "Are we going to sing?"

"We are. And then we can both blow out the candle and make a wish."

"I don't need a wish," he said. "You go ahead."

"Whatever you say." She made her voice all the more chipper, because of how much those words stung. The razor blade gouged deeper into her wrist.

He doesn't need a wish.

Brigid had made him happy when Charity could not. After Hope's accident he'd turned so far inward she hadn't been able to reach him. And he'd been little comfort to her. Any time she tried to have fun, to forget her loss for even one moment, he seemed to be judging her.

How can you go shopping at a time like this?

No, we can't go out with friends.

Forgive me if I don't feel like partying when I've just lost my only child.

What's wrong with you?

Why aren't you sad?

When she'd answered back: *I don't do sad.* That had been the beginning of the end.

Jackson had never actually said the words *you're a bad mother*, but she knew that's what he'd thought. All because she hadn't curled up in a corner and sobbed herself silly.

But now, Jackson was happy again—because of Brigid.

"Happy Birthday to you!" They finished singing, and Charity blew out the candle and made her wish.

An hour later, they were still lounging on the blanket, reminiscing about the time Hope had demanded a raise from the tooth fairy, the time she'd found a stray cat and hidden it in her room for three days, and then suddenly, Jackson bolted upright. "Brigid. I almost forgot. She'll be waking up about now."

"Sure. But you brought your guitar. I heard you singing the song you wrote for Hope earlier, but don't you usually play a few more of her favorites?" She knew she was giving herself away, that she'd watched him on his birthday visits to their daughter's grave before, but it seemed like this would be as good a time as any to let him in on that little secret. She liked sharing secrets with him.

He frowned. "You've been spying on me."

"Watching, not spying. That first year after we separated, I came in the morning and back in the evening, too, but I didn't want to interrupt your time with Hope. And, yes, every year since, I've come back, thinking I'd join you, but I haven't been able to work up the nerve until now. I like to keep an eye on the people I care about. And Jackson, I do care for you. I'd hate to see anything or *anyone* hurt you."

One beat of her heart passed, then another.

"One more song then. I think I have time." He pulled his guitar to him, and began tuning it. "But then I've really got to go. I don't want to keep Brigid waiting."

"I went to visit Brigid in the hospital." Charity reached out and touched his knee.

"What? She said you two spoke on the phone."

"That's right. I went to the hospital, but when I was just outside her room, I overheard a conversation between her and Nash, and then I turned around and left without going inside."

He stopped tuning his guitar. "Why did you do that?"

"I think we have a problem, Jackson, and we need to do something about it."

SEVEN

Nearly a week after her return home from the hospital, Brigid still didn't feel *right*, and Jackson had commented several times that she didn't seem herself.

If only he knew.

She wished she could simply unburden herself to him, but the problem was complicated. She didn't understand it herself, and she didn't want to discuss the matter with him until she got a better handle on her feelings. Luckily, there was someone she could talk to, someone she could trust with her deepest secrets.

The familiar click of the gate, as Brigid entered Dr. Mika Tanaka's backyard, triggered a chorus of howling that lifted her spirits. She wanted to race down the path to find her old friend, Kuma, but, instead, she patiently picked her way across the slate stepping stones, taking care not to crush the ice plant blanketing the yard in brilliant purple flowers. By the time she arrived at a white stucco casita nestled behind the much grander, turreted main house, her pulse was jumping in anticipation. She'd missed Dr. Tanaka and, just as much, the doctor's golden toy poodle, Kuma—a small but mighty dog who loved and *licked* with every ounce of his being.

Before Brigid could knock, the petite psychiatrist, dressed in throwback bell-bottom jeans with embroidered blue scrolls running up the legs and a silky emerald blouse with short, puffy sleeves, flung open the door and motioned her inside the casita.

"Shush! Calm down!" Though her voice was stern, a wide smile crinkled Dr. Tanaka's eyes and made her cheeks round, even while she struggled to keep a squirming, yelping, Kuma safely contained in her arms. "Shall I banish him to the big house or can the monster stay?"

"Kuma!" Brigid held out her arms, and the furry brown bundle leaped into them. "Definitely stay. He can be your co-therapist—he's already made me feel more myself than I have since the accident." She then maneuvered him to arm's length, staring him down. "Be a good little bear, though."

"You look well. Your color's surprisingly good to have been through such an ordeal."

Probably the extra blush she'd applied over her pallid complexion this morning. "Thanks. I feel great... physically." Brigid pulled Kuma in for one last hug, then lowered him to the floor and watched him retrieve a rubber bone from a basket she knew to be filled with dog toys. This room was familiar—too familiar. Under a barrage of memories, her earlier relief quickly dissipated. Despite the restful beige and white color scheme, the comfy couch, the casual wicker chair pulled up beside it, Dr. Tanaka's home office was far from soothing to her. She couldn't help but recall all those futile hours spent here with Nash, trying to get him to open up, trying to save their marriage.

And now, here she was again, this time with a different marriage in jeopardy.

Without awaiting direction, she sank onto the couch near the end closest to Dr. Tanaka's high-back wicker chair, *the throne*, Nash called it.

"Can I get you a water? It's hot out."

"I'm good."

"Hmm." Dr. Tanaka took her place. "And yet you're here."

And then, the miserable intuition that everything was wrong, and that she might never be able to put it right again, descended heavily. Brigid's throat closed. Her mouth went dry. She wished she'd accepted that offer of water. At least, on the phone, she'd filled Dr. Tanaka in on the details of her injuries, so she wouldn't have to rehash all that, thank goodness.

"Take your time."

It had been more than a year since she'd sat on this couch, but her connection with her psychiatrist was solid. They weren't friends, of course, but there was that same feeling of knowing someone so well, trusting them in a way that allowed you to pick up where you left off in the relationship without preliminary.

In this case, it meant Brigid didn't have to cover up her nerves. Glancing down at her hands she saw them opening and closing over and over, as if the answers she needed were floating around, and if she grabbed enough air, she might capture them in the palm of her hand.

"You seem anxious. Did your surgeon give you something to help you sleep, because I can write you a prescription if you need one," Dr. Tanaka said.

"Thanks, but the last thing I want right now is to numb myself up—more than I already am, that is."

Dr. Tanaka arched an eyebrow. "You'll let me know if you change your mind."

"Will do." Brigid clucked her tongue repeatedly and Kuma appeared at her side. She lifted him onto her lap and stroked his soft fur. It was a medicine of sorts and one without side effects. "I'd love to get a dog."

"I highly recommend them."

"I worry it wouldn't be fair with my present schedule. I'm still working full time at the museum, but if I ever cut back my hours, visiting a shelter and finding a canine companion will be first on my to-do list. It seems to me the only people you can really count on are your psychiatrist and your dog."

"You're anthropomorphizing, but all animal lovers do, and I'm glad you feel you can count on me." Dr. Tanaka drummed her fingers on the side of her chair. "It sounds like you're saying you've lost trust in someone. After what happened to you, that wouldn't surprise me."

"Maybe. I'm confused about my life at the moment, which is why I called you. Hard to believe that just one week ago my life seemed perfectly fine."

"Perfectly fine. Okay."

"No, really. I had moved past the pain of my divorce—I thought. I'd found a wonderful new husband. Things have been difficult with Tish ever since I left her father, but we were making progress. Nash and Charity and Jackson and I were all getting along. We seemed to be navigating Supper Club and our overlapping social circles without a hitch. But now, it's hard to explain, but since the accident, all those problems I thought I had handled cropped up again." She sighed, and Kuma nuzzled his nose against her chest.

"Perhaps all of you weren't getting along as well as you thought. Is it possible you were putting on an act for your friends' sake and for Tish's? Are you sure you weren't just wearing your game face, trying to keep the peace? I believe I told you I suspected as much before you quit therapy."

"I do remember your saying I'm a peacekeeper."

"What I said was that you play that *role*—there's a difference, you know."

Brigid shrugged. "I'm not sure I understand the distinction, but my point is that before the accident, I was feeling good, or at least okay, about my life, and now I don't feel much of anything —certainly nothing good."

"Did something happen to you besides your injuries?"

"Not anything earth-shattering. One strange thing, though,

is that when I woke up in the hospital, Nash was there, at my bedside and, initially, I didn't realize we weren't married anymore."

Dr. Tanaka's eyes narrowed. "But he told you."

"No. That's just it; he didn't. I suppose he thought I knew. Only I didn't. *I did not know* he was no longer my husband. And then he said something that made me..." She should tell Dr. Tanaka everything, she understood that. But his behavior had been so off, she felt protective of him. "I thought Nash and I were going to go home together."

"And how did you feel about that?"

"I was ready to get out of the hospital. I wanted things to get back to normal. So, I said I wished I could go home with him right away."

"And *then* he told you that you two had divorced and married other people?"

"No. He said he wished for the same thing, but that it wasn't possible. I thought he meant that it wasn't possible to leave the hospital *at that very moment*, not that it wasn't possible to go home *together*."

Dr. Tanaka tilted her head. "Say again?"

"He implied he wanted me to come home with him, too."

"And what else? You were going to tell me something earlier, but then you stopped yourself, which makes me think it's important."

It was true she'd stopped herself—for fear of Dr. Tanaka's reaction. "When I first woke up, Nash grabbed my hand, looked into my eyes and told me that I was the love of his life."

Seconds, maybe a full minute, ticked by.

"And how did you respond?"

"I said something to the effect of *me too*."

"Let me make sure I've got this right. You and Nash had a conversation where you declared your love for one another, but, at the time, you didn't know that the two of you had divorced and had both married other people, and Nash did not set you straight."

"I'm assuming he didn't know that I didn't know."

"Big assumption."

"It's possible."

"Well, it's not *impossible*. So how did you find out? Did someone else tell you? Did you remember on your own? Do you have any more holes in your memory?"

"No more holes. As soon as Jackson walked in, I just understood the truth. One moment I was the old Brigid, and the next I was the up-to-date version. The information about my past was all there, my memories were in their rightful slots. Only I don't *feel* like *up-to-date Brigid*. I still felt... I still *feel* like *old Brigid*, like Nash is my husband, even though I *know* he's not."

"Doesn't help, I'm sure, that he told you he loves you. You've been through a terrible trauma and you're very vulnerable. Does it seem to you like he may be taking advantage of that? Because it does to me."

"I don't think he was deliberately taking advantage. I think he was feeling vulnerable, too, and he felt a need to express himself."

Dr. Tanaka leaned in. "Be honest with yourself. Do you wish you were still married to Nash?"

"I don't *want* to be his wife. The last year of our marriage I was completely miserable. I was so lonely. I was convinced Nash didn't love me. But what if I was wrong about that? What if I'm wrong, now, in assuming he and Charity had an affair? They both, still, deny it. Maybe I should have stayed longer, tried harder. Am I the one in the wrong—like Tish thinks?"

"Setting aside the question of his past infidelity—since only he and Charity know the truth about that, let's focus on what happened more recently. It seems to me that someone who was looking out for your best interests wouldn't dump his feelings on you the minute you regained consciousness after a freak accident. He'd make sure you were lucid and emotionally stable before saying something that could disrupt everyone's life."

"I agree with you on that point."

"But?"

"I'm confused. I understand that Nash was wrong to say those things to me in that moment. He's married to Charity. And I remember how much he hurt me. How I vowed to never let him hurt me again. But..."

"Go ahead. You don't have to stop yourself. This is a safe space."

"But..." She took a deep breath and shook out her hands. "I still feel married to Nash. I don't *wish* it. If I wish anything, it's for that feeling to go away. I *understand* Jackson is my husband, now. I remember marrying him. I remember *wanting* to marry him. I did want to, didn't I?"

"You were head over heels for Jackson. I can vouch for that."

Relief washed over her. "I'm so grateful to have someone who knows how I felt before, because I simply don't know what to feel now."

"I'm happy to help, but maybe you shouldn't focus on what you *should* be feeling so much as what you *are* feeling."

"The truth is no matter how hard I try, I can't really experience the things I *remember* feeling before the accident. Not the most recent things, anyway. My world's topsy-turvy. I remember walking down the aisle and Jackson waiting for me, and being happy, only it's like I'm watching a movie. Like it's all happening to someone else. Is that crazy?"

"Let's jettison the concept of 'crazy', okay?"

"Sorry. I know better. But what's *wrong* with me? Have you ever heard of anything like this before? Where someone can access memories from their recent past but not feelings?"

"I have, but, it's unusual, and in fact, I've never treated anyone with this condition before, so it may be best for me to refer you to a different doctor—although it's so rare, I'm not so sure we can find a local psychiatrist who's worked with this type of problem."

"Please, you know me. I trust you. I can't even trust myself but I do trust you... and Kuma."

Kuma let out a yelp and wrapped his paws around one of her arms.

"It *is* an advantage that I know your history so well. And I suppose I could consult with my colleagues if needed. I'll make you a deal. We can start down the road, and see how far we get, but if we run into issues where either you or I think you'd be better served with someone else, you can transfer to another doctor."

"Absolutely. Thank you."

"It's a deal, then." Dr. Tanaka moved from her place beside the couch to her desk and began typing on her computer. Brigid must have looked as curious as she felt because Dr. Tanaka said, "I'm pulling up your MRI and the rest of your hospital records."

"You can do that?"

"Yes. My hospital privileges include remote access." Dr. Tanaka studied the screen, continued typing on the keyboard. "On the MRI, I see no sign of structural damage to the brain. The radiology report confirms that assessment, but I'm looking at your doctor's progress notes and according to those, you suffered anoxia due to blood loss."

"I don't know what that means."

"It means your brain was deprived of oxygen. That might have had an impact on your hippocampus or your amygdala— the parts of your brain that work together to regulate emotional memory."

"But I told you my memory's fine."

"Not really, though. Your memories lack their accompanying emotions. I've got that right, haven't I?"

She wasn't sure she wanted to know the answer to the question she was about to pose. "So, do you know what's wrong with me?"

"With your permission, I'll discuss your case with a neurologist and another psychiatrist I respect, but, if I'm right, then yes, I think I understand what's going on. It appears you have a rare form of a dissociative disorder that's preventing you from accessing *some* of your past feelings. In other words, you're experiencing what I would characterize as *emotional amnesia.*" Dr. Tanaka seemed to be keeping her words deliberately steady and calm.

"Amnesia? That can't be. I'm telling you I remember who I am and what I've done. I simply don't *feel* like I'm the same person who did those things."

"Like I said, it's a form of a dissociative disorder. We'll call it *emotional* amnesia—since it's the *feelings*, rather than the facts, associated with selective events in your recent past that are missing."

"Can we fix it?"

"I hope so, Brigid. And I'll do everything I can to help." She turned from the computer and rested her chin in her hand. "You know what else is odd? When this does occur, often there have been more typical dissociative events in the past. Are you certain you're not missing any chunks of time—nothing remotely like this has ever happened to you before?"

EIGHT

Located in The Village Square—the beating heart of the small town of Cielo Hermoso, California—Café Francois served the best *Italian* food in northern San Diego county. Here, the spaghetti carbonara was to die for and, after you did, a plate of cannoli welcomed you to heaven. Francois' Italian mama had taught her son of a Frenchman the delights of Sicilian cooking from the time he was knee high and now, Francois earned a small fortune serving up Mama's secret recipes to folks who often drove upwards of fifty miles for a plate of his pasta.

Luckily, Jackson and Brigid's new home was the perfect distance for a leisurely walk to The Village Square with its touristy shops and cutesy eateries. If you were looking for over-priced goods, eclectic dining, or backstairs gossip, the square was the place to go; but Brigid loved it more for its hidden parks. Up ahead, she spied her favorite people-watching spot: a painted red bench nestled in a grove of waxy green bushes perfumed with creamy gardenias.

It would be so easy to stop there, sit, enjoy the sunshine.

Forget about her meeting with Roman and Farrah Benedetti at Café Francois.

It hadn't surprised her when the couple invited her to lunch. Naturally, they'd want to talk—to apologize. What she hadn't expected was her own reaction to the idea of seeing them: the rush of heat to her face, the ache in her jaw, the pounding pulse in her temples.

It was an accident.

Yes, but one that needn't have happened at all. Because of Roman, she'd almost died, left her husband a widower and her daughter without a mother. Because of Roman, her recently sorted life was a complete mess again. Because of Roman, she'd gone from escaping a marriage where she didn't receive love, to finding herself in one where she wasn't sure she could give love. The irony wasn't lost on her, and she was well aware of the potential damage to Jackson's heart. It was Roman who had put her in this position, and part of her wanted to shake him by the shoulders.

But then there was her heart.

It hurt for Roman, for anyone, who'd given up, who'd lost faith that tomorrow would bring change, and if not tomorrow, then another day. Moreover, she wanted to hear his side of the story—see things from his point of view—not because she wanted to play peacemaker, but because she needed the whole truth if she was ever going to be able to put it all behind her. She needed to hear, from Roman himself, what the hell he'd been thinking when he'd brought a gun to their dinner party.

And now, here she stood in front of the café.

Shaking.

Jackson had wanted to be with her today to support her.

He hadn't understood her reluctance to let him come along, and she hadn't been able to find the words to explain why his presence would only make things more complicated. Sooner, rather than later, she was going to have to come clean to him about her emotional amnesia, but first, she had to get through lunch.

Deep breath.

A bell tinkled charmingly as Brigid entered her favorite restaurant, and it had a surprisingly soothing effect. Funny how a small thing can make a big difference in your day. Maybe it was conditioning, but in any case, her pulse stopped jumping and her legs steadied.

Next, at the sight of checkered tablecloths and the smell of baking bread, Brigid's stomach rumbled. She'd barely eaten since her accident, but it looked like Francois' cooking might bring back her appetite.

"Brigid!" Farrah Benedetti, decked out in a red Gucci dress and heels that put her close to six feet, rose from her table, signaling Brigid with a delicate hand. The rock on her ring finger flashed, noticeable even from the distance between the doorway and the table. An Hermès bag sat, like an honored guest, on a chair drawn close to her side and positioned directly across the table from her husband, Roman Benedetti.

Roman scrambled to his feet.

Common as it might be in this affluent community—one of the richest in the nation—to come across a distinguished older gentleman in the company of a vibrant younger woman, and notwithstanding the fact that Brigid had known this couple for years, on this particular day, the contrast between Roman and his wife, Farrah, made Brigid's heart clutch.

Farrah, as expected, was dressed to impress, her long blonde hair extensions styled stick straight, her "natural" makeup perfectly applied, her entire look undoubtedly put together by her personal stylist.

Roman, on the other hand, looked a decade older than usual. His shoulders were hunched, his back rounded to the point he could've been dribbling a basketball. His hair, normally the polished silver hue of a news anchor, hung in a lifeless gray mop atop his head. His clouded eyeballs hunkered down in their sockets, barely seen beneath an overhang of sagging lids.

Come to think of it, he hadn't looked all that well the night of the party, either—but Brigid had been so preoccupied with the changes Charity had made to the house Brigid had once shared with Nash that she hadn't given Roman more than a passing thought.

Perhaps if she had paid him some attention that night, she might not, now, be dropping into the chair he'd scraped out for her, with a bright-green scarf wound around her neck to hide a still angry scar.

No.

That wasn't right. She could've been less self-absorbed, no doubt, but she'd had every right to be annoyed with Charity, and she wasn't to blame for Roman's bad judgment. She was beginning to understand what Dr. Tanaka meant about her playing *the role* of peacekeeper.

It might be who she thought she ought to be, but did it reflect her true feelings?

"Thank you, Roman. Farrah, you look fabulous as always. Is that Gucci?" Brigid offered her warmest smile, intending to convey a *no-hard-feelings* message from the get-go.

Old habits are hard to break.

"You know it is." Farrah's pillowy lips puckered, pleased, as she extended her hand, weighted down by that obscene diamond. "Who are you wearing?"

That was rude, given the fact that Brigid's denim jeans and button-down cotton-blend top screamed off-the-rack. "Levi Strauss," she shot back, and then cocked her head at the server, who'd just brought over a round of waters with lime floaters. "No straw for me, Cynthia, thank you."

"Because of the sea turtles. I remember."

Tish, with her big heart, had begged Brigid to *just say no* to straws, and it seemed to her that was a small price to pay if it helped the planet and made her daughter happy.

Cynthia, her waist visibly blooming with child, reached into her apron and, bypassing Brigid, set out two plastic straws, one for Roman and one for Farrah. "I'll give you folks some time with the menus."

"Hang on, please." Farrah squeezed her lime into her water, gingerly removed it with a spoon, then wrapped it in a paper napkin and handed the dripping lot off to Cynthia. "I don't like the carcass in... it's okay if you forgot."

At the moment, the only difference Brigid could discern between Farrah and a Beverly Hills Housewife was location.

"Sorry." Cynthia's smirk belied her neutral tone as she flipped her long red hair, turned her back to them and headed away, dangling the soggy napkin away from her body like a dirty diaper.

"Farrah, my love, you can't expect Cynthia to remember every customer's eccentricities," Roman said gently.

"But I'm not 'every customer'. This is a small town, and we're regulars. Plus, she remembered Brigid doesn't use straws—or at least she claimed she did—and was I not perfectly polite? If that girl got her nose out of joint it's on her."

"Maybe if you hadn't handed her a dripping napkin, but, you have a point. You spoke to her nicely, and she gave you attitude."

A long pause ensued, tempting Brigid to intervene, but she had nothing to add that wouldn't sound snarky. She could change the subject to what was really on her mind, but since Roman and Farrah had invited her, she thought she'd let them broach the matter first. She didn't want to rush them, or direct the conversation.

This had to be awkward for them.

After all, how do you apologize for nearly killing someone?

Roman cleared his throat.

Farrah tapped her French manicure on the tabletop, then touched the screen of her phone and inched it closer to Brigid.

"I'm so happy you've made a full recovery. I see you're perfectly well today."

Brigid squinted at the phone screen. "Are you recording this conversation?"

"On the advice of counsel. You don't mind, do you?" Farrah fired a challenging gaze at her.

"I guess not. But why?"

"Why do you think?"

"I don't know." She cast a glance at Roman slumping in his chair, his face pale. "Oh! No. Surely you don't think I'm going to sue you. We're friends!"

At least she'd thought so. It had never occurred to her until this moment that Roman and Farrah might have a self-interested motive for asking her to lunch.

"That doesn't stop some people from seizing an opportunity to be litigious." Farrah straightened her back. "But of course there's no grounds, considering the incident at Supper Club was a terrible accident—one caused entirely by your husband and your ex-husband's assault on poor Roman."

"Excuse me?" Brigid stiffened. "My understanding is that, I'm sorry, Roman... but the way I heard it—"

"You heard wrong." Farrah picked up her phone and spoke directly into it. "On the night of the fifteenth of August, at a gathering of friends, Jackson Templeton and Nash Clarence attacked Roman Benedetti, while he held a revolver, which was legal and properly registered. As a direct result of Jackson Templeton and Nash Clarence's violently jerking the gun from Roman's hand, it fired, causing a chandelier to crash, endangering everyone at the party, including Brigid Templeton, who was wounded in the neck by flying glass. Thanks to the quick actions of Roman Benedetti, she survived her wounds. Were it not for Roman Benedetti's quick thinking—" Farrah took a breath and raised her eyes once more to Brigid's " —*you* might well be dead."

"Have you decided on your orders?" Cynthia returned at the most awkward moment possible.

"More time." Roman waved her off, red climbing his face. Once she was out of earshot he said, "Farrah, turn that thing off."

"But—"

"And then take your leave... please."

"Darling, you heard what the lawyers said."

He snatched her phone from her hand, shut it down and fished a black credit card from his wallet. "I believe there's a pair of diamond earrings you've had your eye on at that shop around the corner. Go ahead and treat yourself."

"Fine. I can take a hint." She snatched her phone back along with the card. "I mean no offense, Brigid. Please understand that I'm only looking out for my husband. And on the advice of counsel—"

"Do you want those earrings or not?" Roman's tone turned stern.

"I'll see you back at the house?"

"I'll come straight home after lunch. Now go. Enjoy your shopping spree. Get whatever you like."

Farrah glanced at the card. "This one is good?"

"What do you think?" He waited until the bell chimed as she exited the restaurant. "I am deeply and truly sorry, Brigid. I didn't invite you to lunch so that I could record you or try to convince you to absolve me from blame. I asked you here, today, to apologize. I want to make amends for my behavior, but I don't know how I possibly can. I would apologize for Farrah, but I'll leave that to her, later, when she's not so distraught. Please understand she's frightened, and she's trying to protect me. Misguided though her behavior is, she means well."

Under the table, Brigid's knee stopped bouncing. She took a few shallow breaths and blinked away the tears that were threatening. Farrah's words, casting the blame on Jackson and

Nash, had stunned her, all the more so because there was a grain of truth in what she said. "I do owe you a debt of gratitude for holding pressure on the wound."

"That was nothing. Anyone else would've done the same, only I happened to get to you first. The only credit I deserve is for being an asshole. I've never been happier than when Jackson reported you were being discharged from the hospital in such good shape. I'm asking sincerely, now, not for any official record... are you fully recovered?"

Except for not remembering how to love my husband.

Brigid nodded. "I am. But how are you? You don't have to tell me if you don't want to, but I'm trying to understand what happened that night. I'm worried about you, Roman. Nash says, and Jackson, too, that they heard you mutter something about being worth more dead than alive. They said that you put the gun to your temple. That's why they lunged at you and wrestled it away."

Preemptively, Brigid shot a warning look in Cynthia's direction, who mouthed back, *okay*, before hurrying off into the kitchen.

Roman wiped his eyes with the back of his hand.

He hadn't denied it. "Then it's true. Is there anything I can do to help?"

He dropped his gaze, and she reached for his hand, but he shrank away from her. "I don't know whether or not I put the gun to my head—if so, it wasn't with intent. Maybe I was raising my hand... anyway, I'm a proud man. I'll own that. A rich man in a rich town with a wife... a wife I love dearly. But I don't kid myself. Farrah does care for me. She likes me. I believe, in her own way, she even loves me. But I also know she married me because I can give her the things she craves. The things she deserves."

"Look, it's none of my business but if you two are having marital problems, I can recommend my therapist. Even if she couldn't fix the issues between Nash and me, she's insightful, and she might be able to help you and Farrah."

He shook his head. "It *is* your business, because I hurt you. I never planned to, but it happened. So I'm going to tell it to you straight. I'm having financial problems. Big ones. Someone like me, who handles other people's wealth, ought to have had better safeguards in place, but I didn't. Now, I've lost my job at the brokerage firm, because, with my money woes, they think I'm high risk."

"High risk for what?"

"Embezzlement."

"But I know you, Roman, you're a man of integrity—you'd never steal. Surely, you can make them understand that much, so that you can keep your job and dig yourself out."

"Thank you for your vote of confidence. It's good advice and, actually, I've already set up a meeting with the board of directors. My attorney has some ideas about assurances we can offer to protect the firm. I'm a founding member, and he feels we have a good shot at convincing them. After all, I have a squeaky-clean record and have made millions for them. I've never been caught with my hand in the jar because I've never gone anywhere near a cookie. It's only my own personal finances that have suffered—when I first found out, I did feel desperate."

"You worried you'd lose Farrah."

He cleared his throat, took a sip of water. "I love her. I don't want to let her down, and, for half a minute I had this crazy idea —but that's no excuse. I put you and all of our friends in danger when I took out that revolver. My Lord, I'm surprised it was capable of firing it's so old. Anyway, it was a crazy, one-time lapse in judgment. A terrible impulse. But I wasn't trying to kill myself, even though I know it looks that way."

She reached for his hand once more, and, this time, he threaded his gnarled fingers through her slender ones. "I don't understand. I'm glad, terribly glad, you weren't going to hurt yourself, but if not, then what were you planning?"

"I am so sorry." He released her hand. "I want to tell you everything, but I need to be one hundred percent sure before I say anything else. I don't want to do any more harm to innocent people. Will you, for now, just accept my apology?"

"Of course—" she squared her gaze with his "—on one condition."

"Name it."

"Let Jackson loan you some money to help you get back on your feet." Her new husband was well off, and he hadn't suffered the same losses a lot of people had in this economy because his income wasn't derived from traditional sources. He was a generous man, and she felt confident he'd be ready to help their friend. On the other hand... she made her voice light: "Only what you really need. We're not going to pay for Farrah's earrings."

For the first time since she'd sat down, a hint of mirth lit Roman's eyes. "Neither am I. That card I gave Farrah—it's no good. Shut down with the rest of my credit. I'll catch hell for that later, but I thought it best to speak with you alone, and I knew she'd never pass up jewelry."

Brigid leaned back and unwrapped the scarf that had been concealing her scar. "See, my wound has already healed, and I'm fine. So what about a loan?"

"It won't be necessary. My brother's helping me. Turns out there are many roads out of this mess. It's too bad I didn't realize that sooner. I surely appreciate your generous offer, but the truth is, all I really need, now, is to know that you're okay and that you forgive me."

Maybe he had some other reason for digging out that gun, but he hadn't yet told her what it was, and she had no reason to doubt Nash and Jackson. Of course, they hadn't been all that certain of what they'd heard. "Do I have your word you won't try to hurt yourself? That if you feel like doing something drastic, you'll call me?"

"I promise. And when I give my word, I don't break it."

"Then I forgive you." And she did, but something didn't add up. The stock market had been volatile. She was well aware because some of the other group members, including Nash, had suffered losses to their retirement portfolios. But how did a man like Roman get himself in such dire financial straits?

He raised one finger in the air and looked around. "Where'd Cynthia go? Now that everything's out in the open, I want to buy you lunch. I think I can still afford a plate of spaghetti at Café Francois."

"Only if I can leave the gratuity. Cynthia's got a little one on the way and your reputation as a lousy tipper precedes you." She winked.

At that he tossed back his head and gave a full-on laugh. "A penny saved, my dear. How do you think I got to be filthy rich in the first place?"

NINE

San Diego, California

Brigid would be glad when today was in the rearview mirror. This was the day she'd reserved for those difficult conversations she'd been finding excuses not to have.

One down; one to go.

As uncomfortable as she'd been before today's luncheon with Roman, that was nothing compared to the edgy anticipation she felt now. But she'd driven thirty-five miles from Cielo Hermoso to downtown San Diego to talk to Jackson, and she was determined not to lose her nerve. After pulling in and out and in and out, until her Audi lined up perfectly between the white lines of the parking space, she summoned the courage to get out of the car.

She had to let Jackson in on her secret problem.

If anyone understood how much it hurt to be shut out of your spouse's heart and mind, it was Brigid. And maybe getting her malady out in the open would turn out to be the cure.

Sure, that might be a little optimistic, but her step quickened at the idea, and soon she found herself blinking up at the
letters spelling out *Jackson R. Templeton Community Center*,
stamped in bold gold, onto a sprawling red-brick building.

Most people believed the center, located near an inner-city
high school just south of Interstate 8, was named for Brigid's
husband. A natural assumption given that Jackson was a former
teen idol who'd risen to fame on a television sitcom about a
family band called *The Songbirds*. But, while her husband had,
indeed, founded the community center, he'd named it in honor
of his deceased father, Jackson *Ramses* Templeton.

The clue was the middle initial, R.

Her Jackson Templeton's middle name was Clyde.

As inconsequential as that thought might seem, it was
important to Brigid because it confirmed her factual memory to
be on solid ground—and yet, that made the psychological aber-
ration that Dr. Tanaka had dubbed *emotional amnesia* even
more baffling.

How could Brigid remember such fine detail about her
husband, and yet still feel so disconnected from him. The last
thing she'd wanted when she'd fled a marriage where she didn't
feel loved was to turn around and inflict the same sort of pain on
another person.

Jackson was her husband—she owed him her whole heart.

She also owed him the truth.

The little day-to-day lies Nash had told when they were
together had eroded her trust and contributed to the death of
their marriage.

She would not do that to Jackson.

Even though she knew it would be painful for Jackson to
hear the truth, she believed revealing it was the only way to
preserve their relationship. A marriage cannot be sustained on
lies, no matter how well-intentioned.

After creeping into the community center's auditorium

where Jackson spent five days a week volunteering, coaching kids on how to land an audition, write a killer college entrance essay, or just get through a job interview at the local pancake house, she settled into the back row.

A spotlight, waiting to be filled by a budding star, illuminated an empty center stage. Downstage left, a group of teenagers sat in a semicircle facing Jackson. His back was to the house, in other words, to Brigid.

She held her breath, waiting for him to speak in a way she knew would command the stage and electrify onlookers. That rich voice was partly why viewers had tuned in to *The Songbirds* season after season. In some ways, she understood Charity's disappointment that he hadn't stuck with either acting or singing. It was obvious he could still be a star—but that wasn't what he wanted.

Instead, he wanted *this*.

To hang out with the kids, give them a leg up on the ladder of life, pay it forward. Jackson's substantial but not stupefying income came from television residuals, as well as from royalties from his one hit single. Deeming this "more than enough money", he didn't chase riches or the lifestyle of the famous (or formerly famous), and that had driven Charity mad with frustration.

Brigid, on the other hand, admired him for the choices he'd made.

She heard the woosh of papers shuffling, then Jackson cleared his throat. The whispered conversations of teens abruptly stopped as he boomed instructions. "Now that you know what improv is all about, let's try it. Here's the set-up: You're going to pitch a Disney movie to a big-time producer. Which movie? Suggestions?"

"How about *The Lion King*?" A soft voice, drifted across the stage, followed by a series of groans.

"So, you've all seen the movie. Great! Nita, since this was

your idea, please take the part of Simba. Manuel, you'll be Mufasa; Sammy, you can play Rafiki... and Shakir, you can be the producer."

"But, Teach, those are mostly animals," someone complained.

"Man, I can't sneak anything past you guys. Oh and, Shakir, did I mention the producer is an elephant? Well, he is. Now remember, no questions. Just use your imaginations. This is your show. Ready, places everyone! And... action!"

Brigid's hand flew to her chest. Seeing him in his element, doing what he loved best, made her heart rattle to life.

It shouldn't be hard to love a man like Jackson.

She'd done it before, and she could do it again—all she had to do was excavate the love that had been buried in the rubble of her brain when it came crashing down.

That love was still in there... somewhere.

It *had* to be.

She relaxed back into her seat and focused on the man on the stage. The first time she'd met Jackson in person was in a school auditorium similar to this one. She pictured the walls covered in flyers, the turquoise pantsuit she'd chosen for the PTA meeting, the way her pointy pumps were killing her toes. She tried hard to relive, rather than merely recall, the moment, and was soon rewarded with a spark of genuine emotion—she could *physically* feel those old sensations bubbling up from deep inside, as her body responded to the images flashing across her mind.

Back then, when Jackson Templeton, the heartthrob from the posters plastering the walls of her teenaged-self's bedroom, stepped into the school auditorium—a living, breathing, *gorgeous* man—it was like a hummingbird had gotten trapped in her stomach. Now, for a split second, those wings fluttered again.

Wanting to drag that feeling back, she closed her eyes.

Dressed in beat-up jeans and a white T-shirt that strained against his biceps, sun-kissed hair falling over the corner of one devastating deep-brown eye, Jackson Templeton had strolled into the parent-teacher meeting looking like he'd just leaped off the stage of a Songbirds' concert.

The thrill that had shot through her had brought guilty heat to her cheeks—she was married at the time, and she wasn't the only one. A beaming Charity had clung to Jackson's arm. She'd been dressed in a hot-pink silk minidress that moved when she did, breathed when she did... and sneakers with chunky acrylic high heels (where did she even get those? An Andy Warhol exhibit?). Around her neck had hung a long gold chain with a diamond-encrusted whistle.

If the Parent Teacher Association ever rolled out a red carpet, Charity was properly attired to walk it.

She'd just invented middle school haute couture.

And the look on Jackson's face hadn't been just proud, it had been the look of a man who wanted for nothing and knew how to revel in the moment. As he'd nodded a greeting to each person he passed, it had seemed, to Brigid, there was no place on earth he'd rather be than at the Cielo Hermoso Middle School's PTA meeting.

Wasn't that something?

She heard herself sigh, and then the smile that had been stretching her cheeks faded away.

The PTA meeting.

Brigid had gone to the meeting because Tish attended Cielo Hermoso Middle School—Jackson had been there because his daughter, Hope, did too.

Hope.

Brigid's fingers tensed; her hands clamped into fists.

How could she have forgotten about Hope's birthday?

Her injuries were no excuse. She'd been so focused on her

own problems—she'd forgotten, until this very moment, that Hope would have turned twenty last week.

"Brigid, sweetheart."

She looked up, blinking back tears, to find Jackson striding toward her.

"Hey there, beautiful."

"Oh, ha. I'm sure I look an absolute mess." The car had seemed stuffy, and she'd kept the window down most of the ride.

"I love it when your hair is all windblown, and your skin is all dewy."

"You mean sweaty." She laughed.

He bent to kiss her lips.

Without thinking, she turned her cheek.

The light in his eyes flickered. "What are you doing here?"

"That's a fine welcome."

"Sorry. You know I'm glad to see you. But you also know you shouldn't be driving."

"According to whom? For your information, Dr. Banner gave me the all-clear to resume any activity I feel up to."

"And you feel up to driving thirty plus miles each way? I don't care what your doctor said. If you ask me—"

"Ah, but I didn't." She made her voice jokey and then patted the seat beside her.

Jackson lowered himself, stretching out his long legs as far as possible, then twisted his torso and stuck one foot in the aisle. "So, then, I take it you're feeling better?"

"Mm hm." She took his hand. "But how about you?"

He waved a "go again" motion toward the stage, and one group of students plopped down onto the floorboards, while another group rose to take their turn.

"How are *you* feeling, Jackson?" Inexcusable not to have asked him sooner.

His gaze went to the floor. He didn't bother pretending not to understand what she meant, but he said nothing. His mouth worked as if he wanted to respond, but was fighting for composure.

"I'm so sorry I forgot about Hope's birthday last week," she said.

A good five seconds passed before he brought her hand to his lips. "Don't apologize."

"But—"

"But nothing. You've been doing exactly what you should—resting and focusing on getting healthy. Her birthday—the day of her car crash—was hard. I won't deny it, but I got through it. Your being discharged from the hospital that same day made it a million times better. I haven't brought up the anniversary of her death because I didn't want you to worry about taking care of me. Not with all you've been going through."

"Thank you. But I am better now, so maybe when you finish here we could go visit Hope's grave. We can stop and get flowers on the way. I know a place."

He lifted his eyes to hers. "That's kind of you."

"You say that like I'm some casual acquaintance. I miss her, too, you know." Hope and Tish had been best friends. Much closer to one another than Brigid and Charity had ever been. Over the years, Hope had become a "regular" at Brigid and Nash's dinner table, just as Tish had been a fixture in Charity and Jackson's home. "I want to go together this year. It's her first birthday since we've been married. Unless... maybe you don't want me to go with you. Maybe you want to visit her alone." Another thought occurred. Even though he'd been with her all day, that day, a week had passed since then. "Did you go already... without me?"

He shook his head. "Of course not. I've been waiting for you to get better. I'll just remind the kids of their assignment for next week and then we'll go—*together*." He shifted in his seat, as if to rise.

She reached out to place a hand on his arm. She'd come here with a purpose, and she didn't want to leave until she'd taken care of business. She wet her lips, searching for the right words.

I know I'm in love with you but I'm just not feeling it at the moment.

What an absolutely abominable thing to say to your husband.

And even worse to be living secretly in that twilight zone.

Jackson put his hand atop hers and squeezed. "Speaking of our daughters... I heard from Tish. She called me on Hope's birthday."

"How is she?" It stung, more than a little, that her daughter had called Jackson, when she and Brigid hadn't talked on the phone in over a month.

"Sweet as ever, bending my ear with stories about Hope, including one I'd never heard about the time they snuck Charity's Range Rover out of the garage and got pulled over by the cops. Hope called her uncle Christian. He met them at the station and convinced the police to let him take them home."

"You're kidding."

"You never heard that one either, eh? Seems you and I are the only ones in the dark. According to Tish, Christian reported back to Nash and Charity, who promised to keep mum about it to us in exchange for the girls volunteering in a soup kitchen for a month."

"And all this time I thought they were such little angels for wanting to help the hungry. You think they saw us as the bad guys?"

"I think they saw us as the *parents*. Nash and Charity called dibs on being their BFFs a long time ago. Anyway, Tish grilled me for details about your condition before hanging up. I'm sure that was as big a reason for her call as wanting to talk about Hope."

Brigid felt her throat close. Tish hadn't wanted to talk about Hope with *her*. Tish had sent a couple of *feel better* texts with flower emojis and x's and o's, but she hadn't called or responded to the voicemails Brigid had left her. "Please tell me you told her I'm perfectly fine."

"I said you're feeling well. But she is worried, hon. And she's coming home this weekend."

"I take it when you say 'home' you mean to her father's house?" Nash was still *darling Daddy* and Brigid was the traitor who'd abandoned him. Nash had never owned up to cheating on Brigid, and Tish took it for granted that every word out of his mouth was solid-gold truth.

More than once, Brigid had been tempted to tell her what had really gone down, but bottom line: Tish's happiness was more important than Brigid proving herself right and Nash wrong. The divorce was still new, and in time, Tish would adapt to the new reality. She'd forgive Brigid for leaving Nash, even if she never understood the reason why. Brigid just needed to give her space and a chance to heal.

"Nothing wrong with Tish staying with Nash and Charity. She's a daddy's girl. Don't be mad about that."

Hard to miss the crack in Jackson's voice, and the reason for it was no mystery—Hope had been a daddy's girl, too. "Do you think Tish will really make time for us when she's in town?"

"That's why she's coming."

"*If* that's true, it's only because I got hurt. She's spent two of the three weekends since the semester started at Nash's, but she hasn't even had coffee with me, her own mother."

"Well, she's making plans now. She wants to see, with her own two eyes, that you're safe. Don't turn that into a negative."

"I'm not. It's only that she's nixed every invitation I've extended."

"This is her sophomore year in college, honey. She's nine-teen—you can't expect her to be DM-ing you, right? But you'll be glad to know I tentatively extended an invitation for all of them—Nash, Charity, Tish... and Christian—to come over for a backyard barbeque at our place on Saturday. I made it clear it depends on how you're feeling. We can always have it catered, or we can go out somewhere else instead if you like. I'll spring for a fancy restaurant."

"No. Cooking might be good therapy. And if we're barbequing that means—"

"The men will pitch in for a change."

She nodded. "Let everyone know it's a go. I suppose we must have Christian, too." She sighed, realizing that came out a bit whiny. But it was disappointing enough to have to share Tish with Nash and Charity without tossing Charity's "baby brother" into the mix.

Brigid didn't love the effect Christian had on Tish. Whenever he was around, Tish's personality changed—she tended to get mouthy and rebellious, like that might impress him somehow and, at times, they even seemed to be in cahoots against her. It should have come as no surprise to learn that when Tish and Hope had gotten on the wrong side of trouble they'd called Christian. Hope's uncle was twenty-five. Old enough to count as a supervising adult who could keep them in line, but young enough not to want to.

"Christian and Tish are awfully good friends. And I know you've grown close to him over the years. Naturally, he's welcome in our home."

Jackson's lips jerked like they tended to when he was hiding something from her.

"Did I miss something? What are you not telling me?"

He checked his phone. "Storm alert. We should probably save visiting Hope's gravesite for a different day. One when we won't have to worry about high winds and lightning strikes."

"That's a shame." They should get on the road for home, too, before the weather hit. But it was a convenient pivot, and his changing the subject hardly made her less suspicious. Still, who was she to judge when she hadn't yet done what she'd come here to do? Whatever little thing he might be concealing couldn't possibly be as big as what she was hiding. "Jackson..." She hesitated, hoping he'd jump in, buy her more time, but he didn't let her off the hook. Instead, he leveled his gaze, letting her know she had his full attention. For once, she wished he weren't such a good listener. Staring at her nails, she realized she'd been picking them. She was going to have to remove the chipped polish when she got home.

"I can tell there's something on your mind," he said, at last. "Whatever it is, you can tell me."

No more stalling.

She nodded. "You're right. I'm not one hundred percent recovered. I lost a lot of blood that night at Supper Club, and it had an impact, not just on my body, but on my brain." The only way to say it was to say it. "I have a problem... sort of a type of... amnesia—"

"What?" He tilted his head. "Is that even a real thing or just something in the movies?"

"It's real, I'm afraid, but—"

"You didn't get knocked over the head, although I guess you might have hit it when you fell. And besides forgetting about Hope's birthday, which you remember now, you seem like you know what's up with everything. You do remember *us*?"

"I *do*. My memory for facts is intact. But my brain was deprived of oxygen for a little while, and Dr. Tanaka thinks it affected, possibly, parts of my brain called the hippocampus and the amygdala. And now I don't... I'm *so* sorry, Jackson."

He got a worried look in his eyes. "Whatever this is that's happening to you, it's not your fault. You have *nothing* to be sorry for. If you've lost pieces of time—"

"Just hear me out, please. What I'm trying to say is that I'm not missing time. I'm missing *emotion*. Some of my feelings just aren't there. Or at least I can't find them. It's like I've mislaid them, but I'm sure they'll turn up again. Eventually. Feelings don't just disappear. I remember loving you. I know I still do."

"Your feelings for *me* are missing?" He dropped his face into his hands.

She nodded, and a tear slipped down her cheek. "I believe that I love you, Jackson. I need you to believe it too. But if I'm being honest, I feel disconnected from that love. I feel disconnected from our marriage. I wish, with all my heart, that I didn't."

"Me too." He lifted his head and turned to her. Wiped away the tears on her cheeks with his thumb.

At least the house lights were low, and the kids wouldn't be able to see them well enough to know she was crying. Jackson wrapped an arm around her and she let her head fall on his chest.

"What can I do to help? Shall I move into another bedroom?"

"I think so. I want to be close to you, but I'm not ready for sex. And frankly—" she stopped and gazed up at him "—I've got a schoolgirl crush on you. I might not be able to resist the temptation."

"A crush? That's a good start."

She straightened and dug in her purse for a tissue. "I feel lucky in one way. Most men wouldn't understand." But Jackson seemed to grasp a very complicated situation. She was attracted to him, she liked him, it was only that deep, deep connection— that *forever* love that had made her truly his—that seemed to be dangling just out of her grasp.

"I'm not sure I understand fully, but I want to." He frowned. "Should we go together and talk to Dr. Tanaka?"

"I think maybe it's best if I keep going on my own, at least for now. But at some point, soon, yes, I think we should see her as a couple." She dabbed her nose with a tissue. "What? I can't believe you're smiling right now."

"Yeah. Me either. But I just had an idea. A brilliant one, even if I say so myself. What if we do some improv?"

She blinked, looking from him to the kids on the stage, and then back to him, again. "You mean like the kind of team-building exercise you have the kids do."

"Yeah. I'll play the role of myself." He put his finger on her lips. "And you'll take the part of a woman who's madly in love with me."

She kissed his finger, and then grasped it in her palm. "Okay. What should I do?"

"Whatever you want. You make the rules. But I'll help you with a prompt. If you loved me, and you were really feeling that love, how would that play out, in concrete terms?"

"I'd want to be there for you on the tough days—like Hope's birthday."

"We can't turn back time. But we can visit Hope together someday soon. What else? If you loved me deeply, madly and truly, what would you do?"

"I'd ask you to go away for a weekend, because I'd want to be alone with you. Not this weekend, of course, because Tish is coming, but how about the weekend after that?"

"Separate rooms, though. Until you're one hundred percent ready."

"Thank you." Her shoulders loosened. Her entire body felt lighter. At some point in the last few minutes, the anchor on her chest, the one that had been weighing her down all week, had lifted. Even if he didn't show it, she knew Jackson had to be hurt by what she'd told him. And still, he didn't blame her, didn't give up on her. "Where shall we go?"

His brow drew down in concentration. "You should choose... but I do have a thought. What about Lake Tahoe? We haven't been there in years."

TEN

Cielo Hermoso
North San Diego County, California

Today's lunch with Brigid had gone better than Roman expected—better than he deserved. He wished he'd told her everything, but how could he?

Why didn't you?

He circled his palms across his bare chest and grimaced. The towel tucked around his hips was made from 100 percent organic cotton farmed and woven in Denizli, Turkey. Its cost, about $250, had once seemed a bargain. After dropping the towel, he flexed in front of a silver-framed fused-glass full-length mirror designed especially for him by Italian Villa Custom Creations for a price of $3,939. His marble wastebasket, crafted by the same Italian artisans, had set him back a mere $800. Shrugging, he chucked the remnants from his box of $6 *Just For Gents* hair dye into the basket, and then studied his reflection.

Good enough.

He should've bought the boxed color sooner—there was no shame in it. And no offense to his hairdresser or his personal trainer but it seemed unlikely anyone would guess he could no longer afford either of them. He looked damn good. Post *Just For Gents*, his silver strands positively glimmered in the bedroom light, and the appetite-killing stress of financial ruin had worked wonders on his middle-age paunch.

Except if this was his middle age that meant he'd have to live to be one hundred and twenty.

And he definitely wouldn't if things didn't change around here, which reminded him: Farrah would be home any minute, probably het-up and hammered after handing the jeweler a credit card that turned out to be cancelled.

What was taking her so long?

He'd expected her to head for home as soon as she realized the plug had been pulled on her fun money. It was rotten to trick her like that, but the way she'd tried to dupe Brigid had galled him—even though he knew she was standing up for him the only way she knew how to: with both fists in the air.

His Farrah was a fighter—and he loved that about her.

Too bad he couldn't get her those earrings.

He sucked in his gut and let his gaze travel down to his ample package. In his younger days, he hadn't needed a small fortune to please a woman, and though his stamina in the sack might be flagging, there was an easy fix for that. His heart was willing, his fingers skilled, and a bottle of little blue pills would take care of the rest.

Even without a fat wallet, he had a lot to offer his wife, and he planned on staging a comeback in both the bedroom and the boardroom. He was the first to acknowledge he'd gotten lazy in both arenas, delegating the heavy lifting to his underlings at the company and to Farrah in the lovemaking department. Fifteen years ago, after he'd lost his beloved Kathy to cancer, he'd buried his grief in the pursuit of wealth and younger women. And somewhere along that twisted path, he'd bought into the lie that blow jobs and Beluga make a man happy, make him forget what it's like to love and to be loved in return.

That was his mistake.

And the burden was on him, not Farrah, to correct it.

You can't expect a rose barely bloomed, plucked from behind a department store fragrance counter, to be anything more than a trophy wife. Not unless you show her that you're not just a sugar daddy—that she means everything to you, and you intend to become the man, the husband, she deserves. He'd begin by giving her more and asking less for himself between the sheets. That wasn't enough, of course, to build an authentic relationship with his beautiful young wife, but it was a start, a baby step.

What else?

He pulled on his yellow silk boxers.

Listen to her. Let her know how much you respect her.

After twisting the cap off a bottle of Perrier from the bedroom bar, he downed a blue pill, then startled at the sound of heavy breathing—not his own.

Farrah elbowed through the bedroom door and headed straight for the bar.

"When did you get home?" He hadn't heard the car pull in or the front door open or even her footsteps on the stairs.

"An hour ago."

She must've arrived while he was in the shower.

"What'd you do to your hair?" She plopped a cube of ice into a tumbler, thunked it onto the bar and poured herself two fingers of Crown Royal. "Screw that." She lifted her arm high and flexed her wrist, tilting the neck of the crystal decanter until amber liquid flowed like a waterfall, filling the tumbler and then splashing over the rim.

"I tinted it."

"Yourself? Never mind. That's apparent."

He shrugged, his chest deflating at the remark. "I think it looks good."

"Well, it doesn't. I'll make you an appointment with my hairdresser tomorrow. He's an angel, and you could use a miracle about now."

"Please don't bother."

"It's no trouble."

"Farrah, I think we should talk."

"About what?" With two hands she precariously brought her whiskey to her lips, then slurped a few sips before knocking it back, allowing a goodly amount of $1,500 a bottle liquor to dribble down her front and ruin her Gucci dress in the process —not that she would have wanted to wear it again anyway.

"Money."

The empty tumbler spun across the counter when she slammed it down.

He had her attention. "It's about our finances. As you know, I've gotten in over my head this past year."

"How would I? This is the first time you've chosen to share that tidbit with me."

"Don't feign surprise. You've eavesdropped on my end of plenty of desperate phone calls. And I did drop you a hint when I asked you to put your plastic in the safe and switch to cash-only transactions. Just because I didn't want to burden you with the sordid details until I had a solution doesn't mean..." his voice trailed off as the lights above the bar twinkled and the sparkle of emeralds dripping around her neck caught his gaze. "What the hell is that?"

"This little doodad?" She dropped her chin to gaze at her finery. "It's the necklace you just bought me. You like?"

"But, how did you... the card I gave you—"

"That card was no good. I knew that, hon, I'm not stupid."

"I never said—"

"Stop treating me like a dumb bimbo."

"Maybe I'll have one, too." He poured himself a whiskey, but stuck to two fingers. He needed his wits to keep up with his wife. But Farrah made a good point. In the guise of protecting her from an unpleasant truth, he'd actually been discounting her, failing to trust her about matters that very much affected her well-being. Time to own up to that. "I was embarrassed. I didn't want to lose face in front of you. I'm sorry for sending you out with a card I knew would be declined. I've been thinking a lot, about us, and I know I haven't shown you enough respect. You're a strong woman, Farrah. Tough."

"And clever."

"Very. Which is why I want to sit down with you now."

"Better late than never."

"I want you to know everything, the good and the bad, about our money situation. How we got here. How I plan to get us out of this mess. I'm going to need your love and your support."

"And I'm going to need another drink."

"Please don't shut me out with booze. I want us to build a true marriage. It doesn't matter to me if I lose everything I own, but I can't lose you. I love you, Farrah."

"When did you decide all this? Before or after you sent me to the jeweler's to humiliate myself?"

"After. While I was slathering my hair with *Just for Gents*. I had an epiphany. I want to do right by you. Be a better man. I promise I'll get us back to where we were financially over time, but that's not all."

She wandered over to their bed and lay down, her fingers toying with the hem of her dress. "Aren't you going to ask me how I got the necklace?"

It had been all he could do to let the subject drop. But unless it was a gift from a lover...

Please don't let it be that. "Only if you want to tell me."

"I never tried to use the card. I put it on the line of personal credit we opened at Charles's Jewelers six months ago."

"But I never..."

"Sure, you did. Charlie never bothered to check our credit. He didn't bat an eye when I asked for a signature line. I brought the papers home and you signed them, remember? I've been waiting for the perfect moment to call it in to service, and I believe I found it. I bought several items today, by the way."

He gaped at her. "Farrah."

"You told me to get whatever I wanted, and so I did. You must think you're dealing with a nitwit." Farrah lounged on the bed, blonde hair mussed around her deceptively angelic face, her cheeks flushed from drink.

Shouldn't he be angry with her?

But he was the one who'd left her out of the decision-making process. Whose fault was it, really, that she'd resorted to deception? In a way, he was proud of her for not rolling over. "I should never have patronized you or tried to trick you with that cancelled credit card."

"Damn straight. And you shouldn't have shooed me away from lunch with Brigid. You hurt my feelings."

"Look, it's no excuse, but here's why I did that. I've been crazy with guilt over what happened to Brigid, and I was desperate to talk with her alone so I could apologize. I understand you're worried she'll sue, or press charges, but we had a heart-to-heart, and she's not going to do anything to hurt us. She's not that kind of person, and neither is Jackson. And don't worry about the jewelry. I'm not mad, but I'm going to have to take it all back to the store tomorrow. I'll simply tell Charlie you've changed your mind."

"But why?"

"Haven't you been listening to anything I've said? We can't afford it."

"But we're debt-free now. I overheard you talking to your brother."

"We still have to be very careful—especially now that we have a clean slate. Be fair."

"What about what's fair to me? Is it fair for you to keep all your worries bottled up and then try to blow your brains out in front of me and all of our friends at Supper Club? Do you honestly believe that wouldn't have ripped my heart straight out of my chest?"

"Like I told you that night, and every night since, I did not plan to hurt myself. That is a misinterpretation of events. An understandable one, but you said you believed me and I thought you really did." Because she certainly hadn't acted worried before now.

"You never told me why you took the gun to dinner."

He lay down on the bed facing her. "It was the wrong thing to do. Before the party, I was thinking about my life, and my father, specifically. I remembered he had this revolver, and I was looking at it, and I just stuck it in my jacket because, I thought, possibly—it was an impulse."

She rolled toward him, her whiskey breath sweetening the air between them. "But you must've had a reason for taking it."

"I'd just been fired earlier that week. I didn't have any actual plan, but I thought it might be good to have it on me. I know I owe you the whole truth, so I'll try to explain exactly what went through my head as best—"

"Shut up." She pressed a finger to his lips. "I don't care why you brought the gun to the party as long as you weren't going to kill yourself or threaten anyone else."

"I wasn't."

"Swear to me."

He rolled onto his back, and she stretched out beside him and took his hand. "I swear. I wasn't and I *won't* ever intentionally abandon you. I'm going to take care of you, Farrah. I want to give you all that you deserve, and I'm not just talking about the things that money can buy."

"I don't know what I'd do if anything happened to you."

"You'd find another man, I hope."

"Don't be maudlin."

"And you wouldn't need to worry about money. We need to be smart now—no more emeralds for a while—we're starting over. I had to sell off most of our assets to pay our debts, but we still have this house, and the money from my brother was a gift —not a loan. Because I've avoided bankruptcy and paid off my creditors, there's no increased risk for me to try to defraud anyone, so I'm almost certain to get my job back. Then we'll have an income again. We can rebuild."

"But if anything happens to you in the meantime—"

"I've got multiple life insurance policies. If I die before I make my second fortune, you'll have a nice sum from those. I don't want you to worry, Farrah. I've made sure you'll be well taken care of no matter what."

"Thank you, darling, but you're going to live forever."

"Fingers crossed." He laughed.

She pecked him on the lips and put her hand on his beating heart. "What if... Oh, never mind... you did promise you would never."

"What is it? Now's the time to get your worries out in the open."

"If the gun had... if it had been you who got hurt when the gun went off at Supper Club instead of Brigid, it would've looked like suicide, even though I understand you didn't mean... I'm wondering if the life insurance would have still paid out. Isn't there a suicide clause or something?"

"It still would've paid out. Suicide is only an issue in the beginning, when you first take out a policy, and I've had these for years. So, you see, you have nothing to worry about. Less than nothing because I promise I will never voluntarily leave your side. You're stuck with me, Farrah; for better or for worse, you have my word of honor."

ELEVEN

And then there were six.

Where there should have been seven.

If only Hope were alive, Brigid thought, she'd be overjoyed to be hosting this family barbeque in the new home she and Jackson had recently moved into. It wouldn't matter that Nash and Charity had started up before the divorce and then lied about it, or that Tish blamed *Brigid* for the failure of her parents' marriage, or that Charity's prodigal brother had been added to the guest list.

If only Hope were here.

Brigid often wondered how different all of their lives would've been if she hadn't been working late at the museum the night of Hope's seventeenth birthday; if she had driven the girls to the party. Instead, Hope had picked Tish up on the way to her birthday bash at Rollicking Roller Coasters, and, less than a block from the amusement park, a drunk driver had crashed into the car.

Hope had died at the scene.

Tish had suffered minor injuries.

Enough.

Brigid couldn't allow herself to travel too far down the *what if* road, because no good could come of it, and it set a bad example for Tish who had wondered aloud, on more than one occasion, why her best friend had died and she'd survived.

Let's focus on the task at hand.

Brigid splattered Worcestershire sauce into a giant stoneware mixing bowl filled with ground beef. She churned it with a big wooden spoon so hard her elbow buzzed from the effort, and the blood-red meat turned to brown mush. After massaging her stinging elbow, she spread wax paper over the quartz countertop, telling herself to concentrate on the good stuff before she gave herself a cooking injury.

She loved the kitchen in the house she and Jackson had bought. Its clean, modern design, white cabinets and upscale stainless appliances, bright pendants and hardwood floors were all the rage, and frankly ubiquitous in this exclusive little town of theirs. But Jackson had helped her to make it her own with simple touches. Her favorite? He'd replaced some of the cabinets with open shelving in order to display her mother's collection of jelly jar glasses. And after she'd told him about her emotional amnesia, he'd had photos of the two of them—some taken during their courtship, some from their wedding day—custom mounted onto glass and strategically placed on the kitchen walls.

Gazing at one now, it took her back to that day, to the minutes before they stopped mountain biking for a selfie break. Something stirred inside when she imagined the whip of the wind against her cheeks, the burning in her calves as they pedaled up the dusty mountain path.

Sighing, she washed her hands and patted them dry with a clean towel, then slapped the meat between her palms, shaping and flattening the burgers for the grill. Tish waffled between vegetarian and pescatarian, and sadly, Brigid didn't know her current status. So she'd purchased several swordfish fillets, and she'd make a point of bringing a hibachi out of storage, so the fish could be prepared on a separate grill from the beef.

It was important to Brigid to always be prepared.

Probably because she hadn't been for most of the important events in her life. She hadn't been ready for her mother's stroke and steady decline after, or for her father's "broken heart" attack that took him so quickly after her mother finally passed. Not for Hope's death or the spiral of sadness that had overtaken Tish. Not for the failure of her first marriage. Not for the way Tish had distanced herself from Brigid when she'd filed for divorce—and certainly not for this disquieting disconnect between her head and her heart that made her feel like she didn't belong in her own home with her own husband.

Maybe you don't.

She slapped a burger into final form and dug into the bowl for the next handful of meat.

Crudité and chips and dip and a cooler of craft beers were already set up in the backyard.

Hope's favorite ice cream cake was in the freezer for later.

Brigid regretted that she and Jackson hadn't yet made it to the cemetery. The weather had kept them from going after the improv session at the community center, and since then, it seemed Jackson had been too busy. The least she could do was to make sure they celebrated Hope's memory this evening.

She exhaled a long breath.

She'd done everything she could to make sure the evening would go well for more reasons than one. This was the first time Tish had visited their home since she'd started her sophomore year at USC, the first time Nash and Charity and Jackson and Brigid had spent an evening together without a bunch of other friends there to serve as a guard rail, and the first time this weird, blended family had all been together: Nash, Charity, Christian, Tish, Jackson and Brigid.

Christian hadn't attended Jackson and Brigid's wedding,

despite how much Jackson had wanted him to be there. And that bothered Brigid because it had hurt Jackson, who'd grown very close to him over the years.

In all fairness, she didn't know Christian well enough to claim an accurate read on him. But there was something about his knife-sharp stare, the dangerous edge in his voice, that made her uncomfortable.

By now, Brigid had arranged her handiwork on a large platter, and, using her shoulders, she pushed through the kitchen door into the backyard. Nash appeared, spatula in hand, and unceremoniously spirited the platter from her hands as if he were the host, this was his home, and she was his wife. The gesture seemed presumptuous, but then again, it was such a small thing, she wasn't going to let it bother her. She was probably reading too much into it—it didn't seem to perturb Jackson.

"Man's work," Jackson said, and clapped Nash on the back.

Brigid enjoyed cooking outdoors, but not as much as the husbands, so she decided to let Nash and Jackson enjoy their fantasy—that only men could properly work a barbeque.

They headed off, and suddenly standing there empty-handed, she got that out-of-place feeling again.

Jackson and Nash were gesticulating over the burgers—the fish would come out later for the hibachi. Near the pool, Charity, Christian and Tish were seated on two recliners (Christian and Tish were sharing) poring over a photo album, which no doubt was filled with memories of the girls in high school. She saw, from her stance across the yard, Tish reach out to Charity, wipe something from her cheek and then lean in to give her a hug.

An ugly impulse to rush over and snatch Tish from Charity's arms gave way to reason.

Brigid walked, slowly, deliberately and calmly to the group. "May I join you?"

"Of course!" Charity smiled and released Tish. "I should've

been in the kitchen making the burgers. I guess I just got lost in the memories."

"Not at all. You're my guest tonight."

"Well, at least let me set the places. I don't want you to get tired."

Brigid waved a hand. "I'm fine."

"Are you?" Tish asked, not making eye contact.

"I promise. But I'd love to sit down and look through—"

Tish slammed the album shut. "Thanks for this, Charity. I'm going to put it away in the house, now. Christian, don't let me forget to take it home."

"I'll go," he said, rose and took the album from her hand. "You stay and talk to your mom. I'll put it next to your purse so you don't forget. Where'd you put it—your purse?"

"It's on the bed in the upstairs guest room. Do you know the way?"

"I'll find it," Christian said. "Be right back."

Turning to Brigid, Charity smiled. "I decided this year, on Hope's birthday, to make a scrapbook of Tish and Hope. And then I thought, I have so many photos and mementos, that maybe Tish would like to keep the scrapbook."

Tish hugged Charity again. "You are the best bonus mom ever."

"I'm trying," Charity chimed brightly.

Brigid sank onto the nearest chair, several feet away from Charity and Tish, and covered her quivering chin with her palm. Then swatted the air, as if chasing away a mosquito, waiting patiently to catch her breath and for this feeling that Charity had stolen something far more valuable than her marriage to pass. Then she looked for the right moment to enter the conversation, but it seemed Charity and Tish had a lot to say on subjects Brigid wasn't familiar with—like Tish's friends and the parties she'd gone to at school.

Brigid made a mental to note to arrange a trip to L.A. to visit her daughter at USC. Just her and Tish. If Tish was willing, it would give them a chance to catch up on mother-daughter stuff —and she could probably conduct some museum business at the same time since Brigid had a connection with one of the film professors at USC. That would justify her going up during the work week.

Brigid shifted and checked her watch.

Christian had been gone so long she worried he was snooping through her home. But, she reminded herself, he was family, in a way, and she was being unfair. When, at last, he returned and plopped down next to Tish—too close for Brigid's comfort, an itchy sense of distrust snaked over her skin. She checked her watch.

Fifteen minutes.

It had taken Christian fifteen minutes to locate the guest room and put the photo album with Tish's purse.

Brigid bit back the desire to ask if he'd found whatever it was he'd been looking for. After all, she'd resolved to be a good host. "You look well, Christian. Your hair's different, isn't it?"

"I dyed it."

Pitch black.

But it was a look, and she didn't mind a person carving out their own niche. She was all for self-expression, creativity, living life on your own terms. She hoped she was able to spread that message, about believing in your own truth, and following your heart through her work. Unlike Jackson, Brigid couldn't claim any special talents, but she had a fierce desire to encourage those who did, and as director of public programing at a local museum, she was able to help various artists by introducing them to her community.

"The color suits you." Now that she'd gotten past the initial shock of how different Christian looked, she realized it was true. He had an intense, mournful face to begin with, and now, the black hair contrasting with his electric blue eyes made it all the more unforgettable.

His face flushed, and he looked away.

"Christian has a hard time accepting compliments," Tish said, and then picked up his hand. "I think it makes you look like a swashbuckler."

Brigid blinked hard, staring at her daughter, struggling to translate what was happening.

"What's a swashbuckler?" He looked up at Tish adoringly.

"Someone brave. Daring. Romantic." Tish brushed her lips against his.

Then the kiss between them deepened, and Brigid's stomach flipped in dismay. Things were complicated enough in this family without her daughter dating Charity's brother.

Charity swept an arm around her. "Surprise! Isn't this wonderful?"

"Burgers up!" Jackson yelled.

Brigid shot him a look.

So this was why he'd looked so sheepish when she'd mentioned Christian and Tish being friends. He'd *known* about the two of them but he hadn't told her.

Which begged the question: what else was Jackson hiding?

It had been a hard but sweet evening. Although this "family dinner" was the result of Tish coming home from USC to check on Brigid, because it fell so close to what would have been Hope's twentieth birthday, it had turned into an impromptu celebration of her life. And because Brigid purchased Hope's favorite ice-cream cake, they'd been sharing stories of the summer Hope had worked at The Ice Cream Store and flown up the ranks. She'd been so proud when she got promoted from scooper to cake decorator she'd decided, much to everyone's horror, that she didn't plan to return to high school because she wanted to focus on her career in ice cream.

But by the time fall rolled around, Tish had declared her intention to apply to USC, and Hope had suddenly realized she didn't want to miss out on college after all. So the two young women had buckled down and studied together. They'd both aced their entrance exams and even got their acceptance letters to USC on the same day.

One story led to another, and after dinner, they circled the lounge chairs under the stars. Then Charity begged Jackson to bring out his guitar so everyone could sing along to Hope's favorite songs. As much as Brigid wanted to be part of the celebration, she felt like something of an interloper between Jackson and Charity tonight—whether because of their shared loss, or because of residual issues from Brigid's accident, she wasn't sure.

After a few minutes, she wandered back into the kitchen, leaving the door to the backyard open—the screen would keep insects on their designated side of the universe, and the sound of her family's voices, tangling together, lifted her heart, giving her hope that she could find her way back into the fold soon.

Pulling in a bittersweet breath, she dusted her hands on her apron—the one that said *Kiss the Curator*. Nash had given it to her many years ago, and, when she'd protested that her job at the museum wasn't that of curator, although there was some overlap, he'd told her to relax—that he knew her job title, but *Kiss the Director of Public Programs* didn't have the same ring. She was still smiling at the memory when the sound of the screen door opening and closing, along with the rising strains of laughter and guitar coming from the patio, interrupted her thoughts.

"You've still got the misnomer apron, I see." Nash was behind her.

Without turning, she nodded.

He put one hand on her shoulder, and she softened under his touch, but kept working, rinsing the plates and then loading them into the dishwasher.

"Want some help? I can rinse and load, or I can put away the leftovers, or if you like I can bag up the trash."

She turned off the faucet, and, finally, looked at him. His face told her he was experiencing a mix of happy memories and deep loss, much like she was. "I think Jackson can handle the trash."

He held up both hands. "Not trying to take over as man of the house."

Wasn't he? "I didn't mean to suggest you were."

"I did want to get you alone though... to talk. That's all."

"About?"

"To say thank you for tonight."

"You're welcome. It was my pleasure."

He reached out his hand, as if to touch her hair, but quickly drew it back. "So formal. But you don't need to remind me to behave. That's one of the things I want to tell you. I know we need to talk about what happened at the hospital. But first, I wanted to say it means a lot to me, the way you've put this evening together. Charity doesn't like to let on, but I promise you, she's hurting. You making tonight about Hope, instead of about yourself, even though it was meant to be more of a *hooray Brigid's okay* dinner than a birthday party for—"

"You really don't need to thank me for that. I know Jackson is feeling the loss, too, and I'm really fine. One of the worst things about my accident is that on Hope's actual birthday I was sleeping all day. I wasn't there for Jackson."

"Maybe it was better that way. I think it was good that Charity ran into him at the cemetery, and they took the morning to grieve together."

She whirled back toward the sink and turned on the faucet, trying to let her brain catch up with her ears. She'd asked

Jackson directly if he'd been to the cemetery, and he'd said *no*. She couldn't think of a single reason for him to lie about it.

And he'd encountered Charity there.

Again, she couldn't think why he'd hide that from her.

"How about you leave the dishes?" Nash asked. "I'd like to talk to you face to face."

She shut off the faucet, dried her hand on a dish towel, and motioned to the kitchen table.

Nash eased her chair out before taking the seat across from her. In all the time they'd been married, he'd never stopped opening doors and pulling out chairs for her. She touched her heart, but then quickly dropped her hand to her lap.

Fidelity would have meant a lot more to her than chivalry.

Nash rubbed the scruff on his chin and pursed his lips in a gesture as familiar to her as her own face. In appearance he couldn't have been more different than Jackson. Both men were handsome and a few years older than she and Charity—nearly forty-five, but Jackson had a boyishly young look, whereas Nash sported a more distinguished man-about-town air.

Brigid noticed a little drop of icing had found its way onto Nash's sleeve.

He would hate it if he knew, and it would be so easy to reach out and brush it away.

She steeled her spine, resisting the pull of old habits.

"What did you want to talk about?" This was a good chance to clear the air. Even though they could be interrupted at any moment, at least they wouldn't have to arrange a meeting and then explain that to their spouses.

"It's about what I said after your accident."

They'd *both* said things.

She'd been woozy, sedated on painkillers.

What was his excuse?

"I shouldn't have told you that I still love you."

"But you did."

"And I meant it." He swallowed. "You *are* the love of my life, and if we'd lost you that day... I honestly would have given anything to trade places with you, to take your pain away and put it on me. But I had no right to unburden myself just because I was frightened. You're married to Jackson."

It had certainly made things harder for her. Who knew how much Nash's words, and his deception, had contributed to that unwelcome feeling that she was still somehow *his*.

"And you are married to Charity."

"I am. I'm grateful you understand."

"But I don't understand, Nash. Regardless of anything else, why didn't you tell me, right away, that we were divorced?"

"At first, I didn't realize what was going on—that you thought we were still married."

"When did you figure it out?"

"When you asked if we could go home."

"Yet even then you said nothing."

"I didn't know what to do. You seemed like you *wanted* us to still be together. And honestly, I felt... I feel the same way. The difference is I knew I was in the wrong. That I didn't... that I don't deserve you."

She gripped the edge of the table. This was probably as close as he would ever get to owning the affair he'd obviously had with Charity.

"If that's an apology, I accept."

"You owe me no explanations, but if you don't mind me asking, when did *you* realize our, er, change of circumstance?" he asked.

"About ten seconds after you said Jackson's name."

He touched his fingers to his lips, thinking.

"What is it? You can ask me. I'm fine talking this through. We need to get everything out in the open—at least between the two of us," she said.

"Did you mean what *you* said?"

"Going along seemed like the appropriate thing when I thought you were my husband. My feelings were jumbled up—and they still are. I remember everything we've been through, but my heart seems to be disconnected from my head."

"So?"

"So I want to be crystal clear with you. I am one hundred percent committed to my marriage to Jackson. Have you spoken to Charity about what happened between us in the hospital?"

"No. I don't want to hurt her. And no matter how I feel about you, I know I can't turn back time. I recognize, no matter how much it hurts, that I've lost you forever. Have you told Jackson?"

"I don't want to keep secrets, Nash. I'm going to tell Jackson everything. In fact, I've told him most of it already. My advice is for you to talk to Charity as well. I don't see how we're all going to move forward in this situation otherwise."

"If you tell Jackson, then I will have to tell Charity—I can't risk him being the one to fill her in. But in spite of how you feel about secrets, I'd like you to reconsider. We both love our spouses and we want to make our marriages work. Jackson and Charity have suffered more than most people ever will, because of losing Hope. I think we should spare them this extra hurt, but I'll go along with whatever you decide."

Outside, Charity's laughter pealed.

Nash was probably right. Nothing had happened between them, and it never would. There was no good reason to hurt Charity and Jackson over a conversation that took place when Nash was traumatized and Brigid sedated.

"As long as we're clear on where we stand, I suppose we can keep it between us—but if Jackson or Charity ask me, I'm not going to lie."

"Understood."

She started to get up from the table, but then changed her mind. "One more thing."

"Just one?"

"I'm worried about Tish. I don't think it's a spectacular idea for her to date Christian. Do you know how long this has been going on?"

"It was news to me, too."

"Not that I have anything against him. I don't really know him."

Nash grimaced.

"But you do, and the look on your face is not reassuring."

"I would never say this to Charity, but between us, the kid's got problems. Ever since they lost their parents she's been super protective of him. In her eyes, he can do no wrong. He was picked up by the cops for public intoxication about six months ago, but then released with no charges, and she completely took his side. He convinced her the other guy was looking for trouble and egged him on to drink too much and then started a fight. As far as Charity is concerned, if Christian's in trouble, then it's someone else's fault. The crowd he's hanging around with, the boss who doesn't like him. He's always the victim. When he got fired, I promised to give him a job, and I did. I hope all he needs is a firm hand and a dose of reality. I think he just needs someone to give him real feedback, to call him on his bullshit."

"He's dating our daughter, and Charity seems thrilled and—"

"I'm not happy about it either. But Tish has a good head on her shoulders."

"Does she know the things you've told me? Because I don't see how dating a man like that shows good judgment."

"I'm no psychiatrist, but I don't think Tish has gotten over losing her best friend. She met Christian through Hope. He used to drive them around town… and don't freak out, buy them smokes and beer."

"So what are we going to do?"

"Nothing. Wait it out. If she knows we disapprove it will only make her more determined to date him."

"The Romeo and Juliet effect. I see your point. But not telling her how we feel seems risky, too. And I'm sick and tired of going along to get along. Dr. Tanaka says I'm a peacekeeper. That's the role I play in everyone's life, and I just don't think I can do it anymore."

"I've got all the respect in the world for Dr. Tanaka, Brigid. But I'm not sure this is the right time for you to change your way of navigating the world. If you bring down the hammer on Tish about Christian, you should be prepared for the blowback."

TWELVE

Charity clicked on the link, then settled into her recliner, her laptop resting comfortably on her thighs. A pleasant, spicy aroma wafted off a cup of cinnamon apple tea that sat within easy reach on a small marble table next to her chair. Brigid had declined Charity's offer to drive her to Los Angeles to visit Tish at USC, which seemed more than a little selfish to Charity.

If Hope had lived, she and Tish would've been roommates, and Brigid and Charity would've run up to see the girls, together, at the drop of a hat. But those happy, dreamt of days of visiting her daughter at college had been ripped from Charity in a single moment.

And Brigid damn well knew it.

So when she told Charity she preferred to make this trip alone, it wasn't a slap in the face. It was taking a butcher knife to her chest, slicing straight through sinew and bone, and then carving her heart into tiny pieces.

Fine.

Charity had no intention of bleeding to death—she'd leave that to Brigid.

Earlier today, on the phone, Tish had told Charity she

planned to rendezvous with Brigid for tea around noon. They were meeting, first, in front of Tommy Trojan—a life-size bronze statue of a Trojan warrior—and one of the most famous landmarks on the University of Southern California campus.

The time, now, was 11:50 a.m.

Slipping on her reading glasses, Charity leaned in to study the image on her screen—a feed from the Tommy Cam. A voyeur's dream come true, anyone with internet could tune in for a live glimpse of what was happening in the campus courtyard. She selected full screen mode to better view the students strolling, skateboarding and biking down the courtyard paths.

Behind the Trojan statue, an ornate, renaissance-style red-brick building, complete with tower, stood guard. In the upper corner of her screen, was Alumni Park and, bottom left, Child's Way. The day was bright, and she could see some of the student's shirts were damp from the sun beating down on their backs—the feed was that good.

Then two slender young women, one with bright-blonde curls, the other with long dark braids, jaunted across her field of vision, heads together, shoulders vibrating with laughter, and Charity's hand flew to her throat.

Not because she'd thought she'd seen Hope and Tish on the Tommy Cam, but because she knew she never would.

Shake it off.

Why hasn't Christian checked in?

She glanced at her phone to see if she'd missed a message from her little brother, but there were no notifications lighting up the screen. She took a sip of tea and found the hot cinnamon scalding her tongue a welcome distraction.

Although Tish had said she wished Charity could be there, she hadn't exactly begged her to accompany Brigid, and Charity knew she could have persuaded her mother if she'd really wanted to. But although it was downright mean of Brigid to exclude Charity, Tish was blameless.

All children are, really.

You can't hold the young to account when they've had so little time to learn life's ropes.

This was all Brigid's fault.

But no matter.

Let them have their little mother-daughter tête-à-tête.

Charity had her own tea… and her own plans.

* * *

*University of Southern California
Park Campus, Los Angeles, California*

Even with dark glasses on, the glare stung Brigid's eyes, or maybe, if she was being honest, it wasn't the sun making them water. Up ahead, in front of Tommy Trojan, both arms stiff at her side, stood her Tish, wearing that same *brave-soldier* look she'd debuted at Hope's funeral.

Brigid lifted one arm, signaling to Tish, and was rewarded with a surprisingly enthusiastic wave in return. She quickened her step, and when she, at last, reached her daughter, she didn't stop to ask herself how Tish would react if she hugged her before grabbing her and squeezing the breath out of her.

Miraculously, Tish did not shrink away.

"I missed you!" Brigid forced herself to let go.

"It hasn't been that long, Mom."

In truth, it'd only been a few days since the family barbeque, but Brigid wanted to seize the opportunity to rebuild their relationship while Tish was receptive to the idea. "I guess it only *seems* like forever. You look beautiful by the way!"

Tish tugged the bottom of her cropped pink blouse closer to

the top of her low-slung jeans in a futile attempt to hide her
jutting hip bones. "Everyone says I look just like you."

Brigid opened her mouth to make a self-deprecating remark
and thought better of it. She wanted her daughter to be proud of
herself, and that included embracing her appearance—through
thick and thin, so to speak, and she felt she ought to set an example. Currently, they were both veering into bag-of-bones terri-
tory, which only served to exacerbate the fine lines around
Brigid's mouth and eyes. She considered Tish far more beautiful than her own middle-aged self, but she had to admit there
was a strong mother-daughter resemblance. They both had the
same round blue eyes, the same up-turned nose and tall forehead, the same shock of short blonde curls neither bothered to
straighten. "A compliment to us both, then!"

Tish grinned and the sun seemed suddenly brighter.

It had been a while since she'd favored Brigid with a smile
like that one—the joyful kind a toddler gives her mother when
she wakes from her nap.

Ridiculously, she suddenly wanted to coo at Tish, but
luckily she wasn't so foolish as to actually do that, or say something stupid about her still being her baby girl. "Where're we
off to?"

"Literatea is nearby. Does that work for you?"

"Of course. I'd love a boba tea." Brigid hooked her elbow
through Tish's as they rambled down Trousdale Parkway, chattering away like best girlfriends with the wind and sun swirling
around them, the birds chirping brightly in the trees.

In a movie, Brigid thought, this would be the mother-
daughter montage.

If it took getting impaled by flying glass, coming within
millimeters of death, and waking up with emotional amnesia to
bring her daughter back to her, it was well worth it.

Then she blinked and caught her toe on an uneven brick as
regret dripped down onto her happiness. As much as she was

relishing this moment with Tish, she couldn't help feeling guilty about leaving Charity behind. She didn't care to think about what it would be like to be in Charity's shoes. Even if every conversation Brigid had with Tish, from here on out, turned into an argument, at least she knew she was safe. But Charity had to wake up every morning knowing she couldn't, ever again, hear her daughter's voice, or see her beautiful smile. "I should have asked Charity to come along."

"I'm glad you didn't. We need some us time."

Brigid tripped again, barely managing to stop herself from falling.

"Careful, Mom."

"No worries! We're here. But, gosh, I'd forgotten how cool this place is."

The red-brick courtyard, surrounded by swaying palms and greenery-filled planters, abutted the Doheny library, a marvel of carved Romanesque architecture. Sturdy brown umbrellas cooled the wrought-iron furniture so guests wouldn't scorch themselves when they sat down or rested an elbow on the table. The atmosphere screamed *casual erudite* and Brigid told herself the brooding young woman seated alone near the fountain was penning a "dark academia" novel. And that quickly, she found herself lost in a *what-could-have-been* moment—if only she hadn't dropped out of her senior year in high school.

"Over here!" Christian's voice broke the spell and she choked on a breath of hot air.

What on earth was Christian doing in Los Angeles, and moreover why was he waiting under an umbrella in the Literatea courtyard when she and Tish were supposed to be having a mother-daughter day?

"Christian!" Tish seemed as surprised as Brigid, but far more pleased.

Then he was on his feet, pulling out chairs for them at the

table he'd apparently been saving for all of them, since a plate full of scones and three steaming cups sat waiting.

"I got everyone boba teas. But I'll grab something else if you prefer. I hope this wasn't too presumptuous of me."

"Not at all. But how did you know we'd be here?" Tish pecked him on the lips, before taking her seat. "And these are nice and hot. How did you manage the timing?"

"Just lucky, except I have to confess that when you said you were having tea with your mom, I assumed you'd choose her favorite spot—Literatea. And it is noon, right on the nose. I was, and I am fully prepared to change this fare for something else, but I thought it would be fun to surprise you. I wanted you to be able to sit right down and dig in."

"That's really thoughtful, thank you," Brigid said. Though part of her wanted to kick him in the shins for horning in on their special day. "I didn't realize you were going to be in L.A. today."

He dipped his spoon in his tea and slurped from it. "This boba stuff is wild, but good. I have to admit I've never had it before even though Tish is always raving about it. What are these little balls?"

"Tapioca, I think." Tish smiled.

She looks happy. "So, Christian, why did you say you were in L.A.? Something work related?"

Tish and Christian exchanged a glance.

"More like Tish related."

Brigid stirred her tea, her fingers gripping the spoon, knuckles turning white, while she awaited a more elucidating explanation.

One beat passed and then another.

"I'm so proud of you, Mom," Tish said, finally breaking the silence. "Christian, did you know that later today she has a meeting with the head of the cinema program? She's putting together a film festival for the museum and including indie productions directed by students from USC."

"I did not know that. Nice going, Brigid."

"Thank you, Christian, I—"

"And she doesn't even have a high school diploma. Mom dropped out last semester of her senior year."

Brigid dribbled a little tea.

"Don't be mad. That's a compliment. I'm bragging about what you've accomplished without a degree." Tish reached for Brigid's hand. "I know USC film school was your dream, Mom."

Brigid felt her face warm. Since childhood, movies had been an escape for her, and, yes, she had dreamed of going to film school, of becoming a director. But her work at the Cielo Hermoso Art Museum, CHAM, was gratifying, and she was proud of the way she'd worked her way up from the bottom as a ticket seller to her current position as director of public programs. They'd made a big exception, allowing her to take on that role without a college degree, much less a high school diploma, and she was grateful. Not only that, she understood how lucky she was to work at a job she loved. "Film school isn't *my* dream anymore. All I want, now, is for *you* to have the finest education your father and I can give you. I have everything I've ever wanted already."

"Tish told me you actually got accepted into the cinema program here—on scholarship—but then your mother got sick and you went to work to help pay the bills."

It seemed Tish had told Christian a lot more than Brigid was comfortable with. She didn't like anyone, except family, to know so much about her personal life. Certainly not that she'd had to drop out of school and get a job to help pay the bills. After all, she'd had loving parents, and they'd instilled in her the confidence she'd needed to make her own way in the world. Not only was she living a wonderful life now, in truth, she'd always been fortunate. She didn't want, or merit, anyone's sympathy. "Life happens, though, so what can you do?"

"Tish!" A young woman in a bright-green sundress approached them and interrupted what was turning into an uncomfortable conversation. "I'm glad I bumped into you."

"Hey, Carol." Tish looked up and shaded her eyes. "We've got room if you want to join us."

Carol shook her head. "No time. But here's the deal: Gigi's in town this weekend, and I'm having a bunch of people over tonight. Can you come? It starts at seven or whenever."

"Sorry," Christian said. "We can't make it."

Brigid kept her face neutral.

"But—" the young woman looked pointedly at Tish, not Christian "—it's Gigi. And she's going back to Costa Rica on Monday."

"I—" Tish started.

"We'd love to, really. But Tish's mom is in town," Christian interrupted.

"Oh, no. I'm not staying the night. No need to miss the party on my account." Brigid didn't like the way Christian was speaking for her daughter. It was a small thing, but still, she didn't appreciate the implication that everything was settled without Tish's input.

Tish looked at Christian, then back to her friend. "Sorry, but I'm afraid tonight's not a good night. Please give Gigi our apologies. In fact, maybe you and Gigi and I can have breakfast tomorrow. You wouldn't mind, would you, Christian?"

"Of course not."

"I'll run it by her and give you a call. Unless you change your mind, in which case I'll see you... and Christian... tonight," Carol said. "Kisses." She blew one over her shoulder and trotted away like a woman with places to be.

"Hey—that's my cue." Christian climbed to his feet. "I think you lovely ladies deserve some mother-daughter time. I'm off to take care of business."

So he was here on something work related after all? Brigid sincerely hoped that was the case. Though she knew Christian and Tish had been on a date or two, she hadn't thought it was a steady or, heaven forbid, serious thing.

"I don't mind at all. Lovely to see you, Christian."

He saluted, awkwardly enough, and then turned his back.

Tish dropped her napkin and seemed to be taking an inordinate amount of time to retrieve it. Perhaps she was feeling the same pressure Brigid did at suddenly finding themselves alone. Which was strange, because Brigid had desperately wanted to spend time with her daughter. It was only that she hadn't had an agenda when she'd arranged the visit, and now, unfortunately, Christian had given her one.

Tish's face popped back up above the table. "Christian's great, don't you think?"

"What matters is what you think."

Oh boy.

The look on Tish's face...

"Wow, Mom. Way to ruin the day. And things were going so well between us for a change."

"They *are* going so well. Let's not let Christian ruin it."

"OMG. Christian's not ruining anything. The only thing Christian has done is be nice to you. He went to a lot of trouble today."

Ordering for them? Barging in on their tea? "I think it was sweet of him to show up and surprise you, only it might have been better to ask. Don't you think so, too?"

"No."

"You don't?"

Tish crossed her arms over her chest, like she used to as a

child. Brigid half-expected her to stomp her foot and yell *you're not the boss of me*. And she should've heeded the alarm bells going off in her head, but she couldn't seem to stop herself from wading in deeper. "Well, I do think he should've asked, and I don't like the way he turned down the invitation to Carol's tonight before getting your input."

"He didn't need to check with me, Mom, because he knows we have plans."

"You do?" What if Brigid had wanted to hang around tonight and drive home tomorrow? Apparently that wouldn't have been an option.

"Yes. We're going apartment hunting online, and then we're going to dinner. Maybe catch a movie."

Brigid curled her fingers in her lap and took several breaths before responding. "What do you mean apartment hunting? You don't like your current place?"

"We... need something... bigger."

"We?" She feigned confusion, but she'd gotten it the first time. Christian and Tish were planning to move in together. Her heart sank to her stomach.

"We're in love."

"I thought Christian was working in Cielo Hermoso for your father. If he moves up here, he won't have a job. He'd be living off of your dime. Really, your father's and mine. I understand the appeal for him, but I don't think it's such a good deal for you."

Tish threw her napkin down. "No, Mom, you don't understand. Just because you married Jackson after you screwed up with Dad, doesn't mean you've learned anything. Please do not even try to give me relationship advice."

"Tish, honey, can we both take a breath? I don't understand what's going on."

"What's going on is you don't like Christian."

"I never said that."

"Sure you did. I said *isn't he great* and you said it didn't matter what you thought which is *exactly* the same as saying he isn't great at all. Then you flat out told me he only wants to live with me because he's a freeloader. You have no idea what you're talking about, but you, obviously, have a very low opinion of the man I love."

"I don't know him well enough to have an opinion that counts."

"Ha. You are such a phony. I can't stand it."

Brigid's heart was beating too fast. They'd gotten into a loop of misunderstanding and she wanted to find a way out. "I'm sorry."

"Sorry for what?"

"For whatever I did to make you so mad. I don't want to fight."

"That's the problem! That's what I'm talking about. You're so *fake*. You don't like Christian but you thanked him and told him it was lovely to see him, when what you really meant was you can't stand him and you wish he weren't here at all."

"I was being polite. It's not the same thing as being fake."

"Okay, well, even if I grant you that much, how about pretending to be Charity's best friend when, in reality, you want to pull her hair and scratch her eyes out? I suppose that's not fake?"

"You're exaggerating." A little. "I have never pretended to be her best friend. Not even..."

"When Hope was alive, you did. Have you ever liked Charity? Did you even like Hope?"

"I loved Hope." Brigid blinked away the moisture filling her eyes. "And I love you, Tish. But the fact is, Charity and I are so different. She and I never had much in common. We're nice to each other because we don't want to make people around us uncomfortable, and I don't see anything wrong with that. It's not like I'm being dishonest with her. She *knows* we're not best friends."

"She totally thinks you're her bestie. And nothing in common? Her parents died when she was in high school—your mom had a stroke and needed full-time care. They had no money, and she worked two jobs to support herself and Christian. You had to give up your dream of being a filmmaker. She had to give up her dream of being a journalist. She even met Jackson selling tickets at the movies like you met Dad selling tickets at the museum. And you have the same taste in men —clearly."

"I'm not saying there are no parallels between my life and Charity's. What I mean is that our personalities are different. She's an extrovert, always the life of the party, whereas I'm quieter."

"And you're jealous of her, because she's fun to be around and you're not."

"Thanks for that."

"So you admit it."

"I'm *not* jealous of her. And it's not true that I 'can't stand' her. But if you want me to be honest, not fake, then I will admit that I don't particularly like her. I'm surprised you don't understand why." It was natural, in some ways, for Tish to take her father's side against Brigid, she'd always been a daddy's girl, but to take Charity's side over her own mother's?

"You have no right to be angry with either Charity or Dad. *You're* the one who wanted the divorce."

Of course the argument would end there, where it always did, because there was no way in hell Brigid was going to out Nash to Tish by explaining that he and Charity had an affair. It would do irrevocable harm to Tish's relationship with Nash and she didn't want to hurt her like that. "I'm sorry, honey."

"Once again, you're not sorry for anything. You just want to end the argument."

"I *am* sorry that the divorce hurt you so deeply."

Tish's fists were clenched, her mascara smudged from the way she was rubbing her eyes. Brigid felt like her insides had been scooped out. She wished she had the magic words to erase her daughter's pain, but all she could say was... "I'm sorry. Sorry. Sorry."

Suddenly, Tish buried her face in her hands. "I know about the affair."

Stunned, Brigid made a futile attempt to reach across the table and take Tish's hand. She'd had no idea Tish knew about her father's infidelity.

"But I love you. And I don't want to keep fighting forever. If you're truly sorry, and since Dad seems to have forgiven you, then I guess I do too."

"Dad has forgiven me for what?"

"Oh, Mom, please. Will the pretending ever end? You have to be honest if we're going to move past this. I just told you that I know you had an affair with Jackson while you were still married to Dad. Christian told me everything."

THIRTEEN

Cielo Hermoso
North San Diego County, California

Here's to a better day.

Because yesterday had been miserable. If she let herself dwell on the terrible argument she'd had with her daughter, the awful lie Christian had fed Tish, it would affect her work—and at the moment, work was the one thing in her world still on track.

Better than on track.

Brigid could hardly believe that she'd been able to secure American Music—one of the most sought-after traveling exhibits in the country—for a stint at the Cielo Hermoso Art Museum. CHAM had been competing with the big boys in San Diego for the honor, but in the end, Brigid's concert tie-in sealed the deal in her favor. An entire section of the exhibit was devoted to television-generated pop music featuring groups like The Monkees, The Partridge Family, and... The Songbirds.

She'd figured if she could talk Jackson into giving an intimate concert at the museum, it would be a tie-in the exhibit
promoters couldn't resist.

But Jackson hadn't performed publicly in years.

After Hope died, he'd retreated into the small community
of Cielo Hermoso, rarely venturing into the broader world. She
wouldn't call him a recluse—he still enjoyed gatherings of close
friends and working with the kids at the community center—
but the idea of attending, much less performing at, a gala or a
premiere was something that no longer interested him. That
had been a sore point between him and Charity, and so Brigid
had resolved not to press him if he balked at the idea of a
concert. But, realizing right away this was a chance to raise
awareness for both his beloved community center and for her
museum, he'd, surprisingly, agreed.

Now, flushing with pride, she punched in the code that
unlocked the door to the exhibit gallery, and then ushered in
her friends: Jamal, Darya, Aiden and Rollin. This morning,
Darya had called and invited Brigid to lunch because the
couples had "something important" to run by her—and Brigid
had had the brilliant idea of giving them a preview of the
exhibit.

Sure, she was showing off, but why not? It was a feather in
her cap, and also a tribute to Jackson.

Besides, the curator had just completed the setup, and
though Brigid had previewed slides, read detailed reports,
prepared the necessary contracts, etc. she hadn't yet seen the
exhibit live and...

Wow.

She spun, arms outstretched. "I'm experiencing this for the
first time along with you all. So, everyone, take your time, soak it
up, and at the end of the hall, after you walk through to the
volunteer room, you'll find a table with sandwiches and drinks.
We can talk there. Meanwhile, I'm dying to know what this

'something important' is about. Does anyone want to give me a hint?"

Decked out in a malachite-green kaftan tied with a wide, Tyrian purple belt, and finished with gold stilettos, Darya was an exhibit unto herself. Her sweeping lashes fluttered, and then her lips, so shapely they had Cupid un-quivering his arrow, curved into a smile. "Patience, darling."

"All in good time," Jamal added. In contrast to his wife's exquisite attire, Jamal's outfit looked like he'd been washing his car in the driveway and remembered *lunch at the museum* a little too late. He sported worn sneakers, brown Bermuda shorts and a faded Jimi Hendrix Experience T-shirt with a hole near the hem. But he wasn't fooling anyone. His coiffed dark curls, the Rolex he'd slipped on over manicured nails, and the ultra-masculine scent of his thousand dollar "Verdict" cologne, belied his   *don't-mind-me-I'm-not-actually-a-hotshot-corporate-lawyer* vibe.

That T-shirt, no doubt carefully chosen, earned him a high-five from Brigid.

There was one just like it—minus the hole—on display in the Rock and Roll room.

"Seriously? You're going to make me wait, even after I came through with a sneak peek for the hottest ticket in town?"

"It's a museum exhibit, not Woodstock, sweetie." Rollin's fingers traveled across his bald dome, and he winked, the gesture magnified by his thick lenses. "Not that we're not thrilled."

"Because we are." Aiden grabbed his husband by the hand. "He's just playing it cool. You know how he hates to show his nerdy side, but he's been talking about this nonstop. In fact, he wanted to fly to Seattle to catch the exhibit. When he found out American Music was coming to Cielo Hermoso, and that you were giving us an exclusive preview, he screamed louder than that time he won backstage passes to Taylor Swift."

"You don't have to spill all my secrets," Rollin said, blushing, "but Aiden's right. I'm only teasing. I'm so proud of you, Brigid. And please don't worry, I'm sure everything is going to be perfectly fine."

She frowned. "Things are fine already. I'm absolutely recovered." Except that she wasn't. Not *absolutely*. Did he mean her emotional amnesia?

No way.

Jackson would never have told their friends, or anyone else, without getting her permission. But maybe, somehow, they'd figured it out. Aiden did have a well-deserved reputation as a near clairvoyant—he'd missed the lottery by one number on three separate occasions.

"What do you mean things will be perfectly fine?"

Darya shot Rollin a look that was even more inscrutable than her smile.

Brigid shrugged her resignation. Apparently, she wasn't going to get any more out of them until they were good and ready to make their case, or whatever it was they'd come for... besides the coolest museum exhibit ever. "Oh! I've got brochures!" She'd almost forgotten she had a table of contents of sorts for the American Music exhibit.

She passed pamphlets around. Then they all started in the "synthesizers" room, but, with her permission, they worked their way through the displays at their own pace, each person taking their time, lingering at the spots that interested them most.

For her part, Brigid got stuck in the television pop room, watching a loop of eighteen-year-old Jackson being interviewed on a morning show. At the end of the clip, he sang a verse of the first song he'd written, his big hit, "Lovin' You Groovy Girl". The way his eyes mesmerized the camera made her skin zing with electricity. Again and again, she watched, hoping those sparks would ignite into flames.

"Hey." Darya tapped her shoulder. "Can you tear yourself away? We really do have stuff to talk about."

Brigid had called everyone ahead of time to get their preferences on food—that *be prepared* thing she had going on. Even though she was serving a simple, cold lunch, she wanted to be sure everyone had something they truly enjoyed. She'd learned from her daughter, and from hosting Supper Club over the years, that you never know when someone is going to go on a slim-down diet, or a bulk-up regimen, or a save-your-heart-plant-only kick. As it turned out, Jamal had recently watched a documentary on the meat-packing industry and had been vegan for nine days. Brigid certainly didn't want the blame for breaking a streak like that, so she'd relocated heaven and earth to secure a mixed-greens faux cobb salad with coconut bacon for him.

After ensuring that everyone had their correct order, she took her place at the head of a picnic-style table in the bare-bones volunteers' break room. She unwrapped her ham and Swiss on rye, brought it to her mouth, but then set it down without tasting it.

Living up to his psychic reputation, Aiden said, "You won't eat until we tell you what's up, will you?"

She crossed her arms over her chest and telegraphed, *No, I will not.*

"Go ahead, Rollin." Darya was apparently a mind reader, too.

"Why me?" He pushed his wire-rim glasses up.

"Because you're the most articulate."

"Jamal is a lawyer. He should do the talking."

They needed a lawyer to explain? That suggested some legal matter... but then again, Rollin probably only meant Jamal could "articulate" with the best of them, and from the squeamish look on Rollin's face, he didn't want to be the messenger.

Aiden, on the other hand, wore an equanimous expression —he had the best poker face in all of Supper Club because he'd Botoxed his brow into submission and had an uncanny ability to go long periods without blinking.

"If you make me wait any longer, no one gets brownies," Brigid said.

Aiden held up his hand. "I'll do the honors. There's something we have say to you, but first, we have a question."

"Where did you get this coconut bacon?" Jamal grinned.

Darya elbowed him in the side. "Sorry, Brigid—he's being silly. I believe the question is whether or not you want us to go through with 'Yacht Day'?"

The special event was coming up tomorrow, and Brigid knew a short-notice cancellation meant Darya and Jamal would not be able to recoup all of their expenses. Of course, Jackson, and others, would offer to offset any lost deposits, but Jamal and Darya were unlikely to accept. They'd been chartering a yacht, as summer's last hurrah, for years, and they took pride in offering this premium experience to their friends—much like she took pride in showing off her museum exhibits. There was no *medical* reason to postpone on her account, and she didn't want her personal issues to impact the group. "Of course. Thank you for the consideration, but I'm looking forward to it, as I'm sure everyone else is."

"You can be honest." Darya's tone was low and sincere. "I won't take offense if you tell us to call the whole thing off. The truth is, after what happened at Charity's dinner, I wasn't sure I wanted to go through with any more Supper Club events at all. At first, I didn't feel safe around Roman. But then I talked it through with Jamal and the rest of the group and, now, I realize I'm okay being around Roman. The way he rushed to care for you after the gun went off—"

"Convinced us he never meant to hurt you, or any of us," Rollin interrupted. "He's called each of us to apologize, and we all believe him when he says he will never bring a weapon around us again. But—"

"The most important thing is that *you* feel safe," Jamal added.

"Around Roman? We had lunch, and he explained some things to me, and frankly, at this point the thing that worries me most is how *he* is doing. So again, I thank you for your thoughtfulness, but I want us to move forward. I would hate for what happened to get in the way of our friendships and our traditions."

"We all want you to know that we have your back. But if you're good, I think the rest of us agree we want to get back to normal, too. And we want Roman to feel like his friends are still his friends—seems like he needs that more than ever." Aiden cleared his throat, took a sip of his bottled water, looked at Rollin and then back to her. "Anyway, if we're all agreed I guess we can move to the next topic."

A long pause.

Clearly, they had more on their minds than "Yacht Day". And they were having a hard time putting it out there. "So, I'll see you all again tomorrow, sailors." She took a breath and forced her shoulders to relax. "Now then, what else did you want to discuss?"

Aiden leaned forward. "We want you to know we're sorry for not telling you about Charity and Nash... a long time ago. We should've said something as soon as we suspected."

A small gasp escaped her mouth.

No one had ever mentioned a word to her about Nash and Charity fooling around. She'd just assumed they hadn't been aware. "You mean...? Are you saying you knew about their affair at the time?"

"We love all four of you. Charity and Nash and you and

Jackson. You mean the world to us, and we were trying to be Switzerland. But we've realized we shouldn't keep other people's secrets. You have every right to be mad at us."

"Thanks. I'm not mad, but I don't know why you're choosing to tell me *now*. After all, it's in the past, and we've moved on. I appreciate it though." Especially since her own daughter had, so recently, accused *her* of cheating. "I'm just so grateful someone is finally telling the truth—not to suggest you were lying before."

"But we did lie—by omission. And we want to own that... so anyway..." Aiden trailed off.

"There's more?"

"Yes. The thing is... I'll take it from here, Aiden. Thanks for being the one to start." Darya straightened her shoulders and met Brigid's eyes. "The real reason we're telling you *now* is that we think it *might* be happening again. And after what you've been through with your accident, we don't want to let you down this time."

"I don't understand. I'm married to Jackson. Charity and Nash are together."

"We're not talking about Charity and Nash."

Initially, her vocal cords froze, but after a moment, she managed to whisper, "Who?"

"We're not *sure* it's an affair. We don't know for a fact, but, Jackson asked Rollin and Aiden—" Darya started.

"And Darya and me," Jamal finished her sentence. "He asked the four of us to lie for him. To tell you, if you asked, that he was having dinner with us. More than once. Twice, to be exact. He didn't say what he was doing or who he was doing it with, so, make of it what you will, but we don't want to keep you in the dark. Sometimes you have to choose a side to do the right thing. Do you understand what we're saying?"

"I think so." She stuck up her chin. "But you're talking about Jackson—there has to be an innocent explanation."

FOURTEEN

San Diego, California

Two limos dropped the members of Supper Club at the pier. Brigid hoped the shimmering blue-sky morning, along with the seasick pills she'd swallowed, might be just the antidote for her nerves. She hadn't yet confronted Jackson about his lack of transparency, and she wasn't ready to accuse him of anything more than that without hearing his side. Since they'd previously arranged for him to come with her to her next therapy session, Brigid had resolved to put it out of her mind until Dr. Tanaka was on hand to keep them from careening down the wrong path.

She wasn't keen on hanging around with Charity, after what Christian had told Tish, but, nevertheless, she wasn't going to let that ruin her day.

Unlike Brigid, Roman, apparently, hadn't learned to compartmentalize his troubles. Normally, this was just the kind of indulgence he loved—a shindig on an eighty-foot flybridge yacht with all the trappings of the obscenely rich. But it must be too sharp a reminder of the excess that had led to his financial woes, not to mention he might not be sure of his place in the group. Anyway, he'd declined his invitation, stating he would leave the "frivolities" to his "lovely Farrah".

Farrah didn't seem to mind flying solo, but Brigid wished Roman were here. She worried about his state of mind, and she hated to see him isolate himself from his friends. She wanted him to have a sense of belonging, the feeling his friends were there to comfort him when trouble came his way.

After descending from her limo, Brigid walked sure-footedly toward the yacht. The women in her vehicle, Brigid, Farrah, and Darya, had changed into sneakers and stowed their heels in a duffle, now slung over Jackson's shoulder. In the same duffle, inside a waterproof bag, the members had placed cash, credit cards, electronics—anything they might need to access but didn't want to risk damaging. This wasn't their first rodeo, and certain individuals had learned the hard way that yacht parties, with their free-flowing alcohol, presented a clear and present danger to important personal items that had a habit of sliding around the foredeck, plopping overboard, or disappearing into the Bermuda Triangle aka *too much tequila*. Anything they wanted to keep dry and safe was zipped into the community bag and securely tucked inside a bench on the foredeck.

While Jackson strode up the ramp, and then clambered onto the deck, readying to assist any of the ladies who might need a hand with boarding, Brigid hung back, debating.

In some ways, today was the perfect opportunity to confront Charity about Christian. But was it right to do it now and risk ruining everyone's day by creating drama while they were trapped at sea?

You're such a phony, Mom.

Tish's accusation stung all the more because, at least in part, it was true.

Brigid did occasionally sacrifice authenticity for the sake of keeping the peace—Dr. Tanaka had pointed out the same thing, albeit in a kinder, gentler way.

Charity, who had arrived in a different limo and was up ahead of Brigid, slowed her pace until Brigid had no choice but to catch her.

"Check it out." Charity pointed at the sleek, silver yacht sparkling atop the waves. "We've come a long way, you and me."

It took no small effort for Brigid to force her cheeks into a smile. "Indeed."

You don't see the parallels in your lives?

With Tish's words echoing in her mind, she said, "I have to admit I never imagined I'd be yachting around San Diego. Not in my wildest dreams."

"Oh, I did. Plenty of times. We deserve this." Charity hooked her arm through hers and Brigid stiffened.

To hell with this. "You know, Charity, I've been thinking a lot about us lately, and we don't have to pretend to like each other. We can still be polite. But this faux friendship is starting to wear on me, and I suspect it's a strain for you, too."

Charity didn't miss a step. "What in heaven's name are you talking about? I *adore* you."

"That's just not true."

"Oh, but it is. Have I offended you, somehow? No. Don't tell me right this minute. Let's board, and then we'll kick back with some margaritas and hash it all out. If I've done something wrong I apologize. Whatever is bothering you, I want to know so I can make it right."

"I don't think this is the time or place to talk about our differences."

"What differences? And sure it is. I don't like secrets. It's better to do things out in the open. It'll be fine, you'll see. You just need a good stiff drink to take the edge off."

"I'm not drinking today—I took some seasick pills and with my—"

Charity lifted one shoulder. "I'm not one to push liquor on anyone. Not after... But that's what limo drivers are for."

"I'm not a big drinker these days."

Charity arched a brow. "Don't take this the wrong way, but that's probably for the best."

She'd just said she didn't want to overdo it. "I don't need you to police my drinking, Charity."

"Okay, something must be bothering you because you're not your usual sweet self this morning."

"Is that a problem?"

"Not at all. I like feisty Brigid."

The enclosed decks of the yacht were nothing less than spectacular. All the surfaces that could be, including the built-in lounges and the crystal hutches, were covered in polished golden teak and finished with ocean-blue marble accents. Hundreds of recessed lights turned the saloon into a dazzling showcase, and Brigid half-expected a hidden stage with Pavarotti or Lady Gaga to rise from the floor.

"Oh my word. This is so so so chic!" Charity exclaimed, pulling out her phone and snapping selfies all over the place. "I can't wait to send these to Tish!"

Charity was definitely not one to play it cool, and her unabashed enthusiasm for life was something Brigid, who was far more reserved, used to admire. In the past, before all the deception and drama, they did have fun together. Charity had a way of loosening Brigid up, allowing her to enjoy life more than she otherwise might've. Like the time all the women had gone on a "girls' trip" to see a Broadway musical and by the time they'd arrived at their hotel, starving after a long flight, room service was shut down for the night. Charity had dragged Brigid up and down the halls in their pajamas, scavenging sandwiches and chips for the group from leftover room-service trays waiting for pick up outside the hotel room doors.

Shocked, Darya and Farrah had refused to partake, but Brigid had dined on far worse. She was one hundred percent fine with cutting off the bitten end of a perfectly good sandwich and gobbling it down. But maybe you had to know what it was like to go hungry, really hungry, to understand.

Of course, that was long before Brigid knew Charity had slept with Nash.

Appreciating Charity's uninhibited personality was one thing.

Forgiving her for having an affair with her husband was harder... and allowing her to come between her and Tish —impossible.

Brigid might be a peacekeeper but she drew the line at stealing her daughter's affection.

Scowling at Charity, she sank onto a plush cushion on one of the built-in sofas and waved off the cocktail a crew member offered. "Can I get a virgin greyhound, instead?"

"Just grapefruit juice?"

"Yes, thank you."

Charity cozied up next to her with a margarita. "I'm ready for our chat."

Brigid glanced about the empty cabin. Laughter drifted down from above. The others were all up on the outside decks enjoying the sunshine and sea air. If there was going to be a moment... "Okay."

"Mine's delish." Charity's tongue darted around the salty rim of the glass.

The server returned with Brigid's grapefruit juice, and she took a small sip. "Mine, too. I think it's freshly squeezed."

"See how easy this is. You're my best friend, and you can say anything to me."

Brigid thunked the glass down on the table in front of them. "How dare you?"

"What did I say? What have I done?"

"You call yourself a friend... my *best* friend? After you lied to my daughter?"

Charity stirred her drink, which was still nearly full. "I promise you, I have never fibbed to Tish. I love her, and I wouldn't do anything to hurt her."

"What's going on down here?" Darya popped her head through the doorway and then descended the stairs with Farrah and Aiden following close behind.

"Brigid has a problem with me, and I'm just trying to get to the bottom of it."

Darya took a seat facing Brigid and Charity. Aiden offered a hand to Farrah, who was already wobbling and flush-faced, and then they both settled on the couch next to Darya.

Charity snapped her fingers and a crew member appeared with a tray of margaritas and martinis. "Leave those if you don't mind."

"Of course." He disappeared.

Charity polished off her margarita and reached for another. "Continue, please, Brigid. You were saying how dare I lie to Tish, if I'm remembering correctly."

A sharp gasp from Darya, then, "Sorry. Go ahead."

"Yes. Don't stop on our account. I love drama." Farrah tapped her ample chest with her fist. She'd changed into a tiny silver bikini and the cover-up she wore wasn't living up to its name.

Brigid twisted the stem of her martini glass, which

contained her virgin greyhound, between her fingers. "Never mind. I don't want to ruin the day. I apologize for—"

"Saying sorry is like a magic trick for you. You think you can wave your 'I'm sorry' wand and make everything okay, but you can't," Charity said.

The cabin spun, making Brigid wonder if the seasick pills she'd taken on an empty stomach were to blame. "This is just between us. Let's talk another time."

"That was quite an accusation. It's hardly fair to leave it hanging and let our friends imagine the worst. What lie did I tell?"

On the other hand, witnesses might be useful. "You told Tish that I had an affair with Jackson while Nash and I were still married. But that's a lie. You're the one who slept with *my* husband."

Four hands reached for four drinks.

The men's deep voices carried from above, filling the silent room.

A clock ticked.

Their server tiptoed upstairs and out of the saloon. Whether he was going to get help or simply minding his own business remained to be seen.

Charity reached out and rested a hand on Brigid's knee.

She batted it away.

"Honey, I don't know where you got the idea that I said anything to Tish about you having an affair with Jackson."

She itched to slap Charity, but fortunately, there were those witnesses present, because otherwise she didn't know if she would've had the self-restraint. "Stop this, right now."

"Stop what?"

"You just implied that it's true—that Jackson and I had an affair."

"Is it true?"

"Of course not. *You* had an affair with Nash. *You* stole *my* husband."

"Wow. Your marriage was on the rocks for a long time, and you are the one who filed for divorce. Yet here you are, after all this time, *still* making Nash and me out to be the bad guys. But to ease your mind, I promise you I've never said a word about your indiscretions. I could've given Tish an earful, but I didn't."

"Why am I the one defending myself? Aren't the rest of you going to say anything? I thought you had my back, Darya. Aiden?"

"We do." Darya's eyes drifted to her hands, and she folded them in her lap. "But you're *shouting* at Charity. You're accusing her of saying something *awful* to your daughter, and whatever else Charity's done, I've never seen her be anything but loving to Tish. If Charity really told her something like that, it would be inexcusable, but..."

"I did not say a word to Tish," Charity repeated. "Brigid's making it up."

Brigid climbed to her feet, extending her hands out to steady herself. "I guess Tish didn't actually say you told her."

"See?" Charity smirked.

"She said Christian did. And that's the same thing. Where would he have gotten that idea if not from you?"

"No clue. And if you say you and Jackson didn't do anything before we were separated I believe you. But you owe me the same courtesy," Charity chided in an infuriatingly calm tone.

"I don't owe you *anything*!" Brigid couldn't get away from Charity fast enough. She stumbled upstairs to the upper deck, all too aware of the gang chasing after her.

Jackson.

Where was Jackson?

Oh, thank goodness.

There, kicked back with Rollin and Nash on a white

lounge. She ran toward him, tripped on her own feet, but thankfully landed safely next to him. Tugging her sundress over her knees, she looked up to find Farrah, Aiden, Darya and Charity arranged in a semi-circle in front of her, gaping like she was some kind of mental case.

"It's not her fault," Charity said.

Her matter-of-fact tone enraged Brigid. She was supposed to be the voice of reason, not Charity.

"I think those seasick pills were too strong. They can make you... anyway, I think we should all just take a breath and get on with the day." Charity eased down onto one of the lounges and Aiden and Farrah followed suit.

Nash switched places with Rollin. Now, Brigid was bookended by Jackson on one side and Nash on the other.

"Are you okay, Brigid?" Nash let his hand fall onto her shoulder.

Charity's face turned bright pink. Though she didn't comment on Nash's attentions to Brigid, it seemed obvious she wasn't pleased.

Jackson threw his arm around Brigid, displacing Nash's hand. "I can take care of my own wife, thanks."

Nash lifted one shoulder. "Then do."

"Here." Jackson offered her his margarita.

"I better not," she said. "I'm not feeling so great."

"What the hell?" Nash rose on his haunches. "She's recovering from a serious injury, man—her doctors said... Listen, the last thing Brigid needs is a drink."

"No. The last thing she needs is you telling her what she needs. But..." Jackson let out a long breath. "It might be good to get some food and water into her."

An hour later, the yacht had made its way to an anchorage safe for swimming and snorkeling. Farrah, Jamal, Charity, and

Rollin were splashing in the waves. Below deck, Nash talked to his office on his phone, and Aiden had set up his tripod on the flybridge for a photo binge. After forcing down a bottle of water and a blueberry muffin, and letting Jackson fuss over her for a full hour, Brigid finally convinced him to go for a swim, leaving her in Darya's capable hands.

Her head throbbed as she watched him climb the ladder down into the ocean. "This was a monumental mistake," she said.

"I'm sorry you're not feeling well," Darya said. "Is there anything I can do? Are you sure you don't want to go below deck and have a nap?"

"No. It's not that bad." She laughed. "I shouldn't have taken those pills without eating breakfast, but that muffin helped. I feel a lot better, now. What I meant was that it was a huge mistake to confront Charity in front of the group, or really, to confront her at all."

Darya scoffed. "I'm not so sure about that. You have to speak your truth. I hope it didn't seem like... I don't know what you think, after our conversation at the museum. But I care about you both. I don't want either you or Charity to be treated unfairly."

So the consensus was what? There was no right or wrong. Everyone had their own perception, their own separate truth. Since when did facts become so fluid, so open to interpretation? "Either Tish lied to me, or Charity did, and I believe my daughter."

"I understood you to say, though, that it was *Christian* who told Tish you and Jackson had an affair."

"Yes, but where would Christian get that idea if not from Charity? She's never going to admit what she's done. If she'll lie about having an affair with Nash, she'll lie about spreading rumors about Jackson and me. It was foolish of me to think she'd ever own up to *anything*."

"I don't know. But it's possible Christian just made the whole thing up himself. Maybe he's the one trying to drive a wedge in between you and Tish. Or maybe he just got the wrong idea somehow. Maybe he heard about..."

Laughter and squeals rose from the water. Brigid's head ached and she didn't want to keep going in circles with Darya. She walked over to the rail and leaned across it.

"Brigid?" Darya eased in beside her. "We can drop it, for now. But, if you ever want to talk about anything, I'm here."

A wave crested against the boat, and the deck rolled beneath them. She tried to find a spot on the water and fix her eyes on it, hoping to quell the sick feeling in her stomach... and then she saw it.

An arm flailing above the water.

"They seem to be having a blast," Darya said.

Jackson circled Farrah like a shark in the water. Farrah squealed, and then dunked him.

"You don't have to babysit me. You can swim if you like." Brigid put one hand on her stomach, clinging to the rail with the other.

"And miss this show. No, thanks. I'll stick with my bird's-eye view of the performances." Darya's words sounded like they were bouncing around in an echo chamber.

Jackson blasted out of the water, then grabbed a gleeful Farrah by the shoulders, pushing her beneath the waves, holding her there, before finally lifting his hands in the air.

Brigid held her breath, waiting for Farrah to reappear, counting to ten, then twenty. Her pulse throbbed behind her eyes, her arm trembled from the tight grip she had on the rail.

How long had Farrah been under? Why didn't somebody do something?

"Farrah! Farrah!" Brigid's knees locked. Her heart was racing, her hands and feet had gone numb. Suddenly, she couldn't breathe.

Darya wrapped her arms around Brigid's waist. "I've got you. I've got you."

Brigid punched out a hard breath and that seemed to restart her lungs. Greedily, she gulped in air, as she searched the vast, blue emptiness enveloping the boat. "Darya, where is she? Where is she? I can't see Farrah anymore!"

FIFTEEN

Cielo Hermoso
North San Diego County, California

Including Jackson in one of her therapy sessions had seemed like a good idea when he'd first suggested it, but, now, it was imperative. Between Brigid's wild experience on the yacht the other day, and the things her friends had revealed about Jackson during the preview of American Music, she was more confused about their relationship than ever.

They needed this safe space to iron things out.

Still, it was disconcerting to sit beside him on this particular couch.

Everything about this room reminded her of her failed marriage to Nash: the scent from the lavender cuttings in a vase near the picture window, the white coffee table with its geode coasters, the dog bed in the corner where Kuma lay curled, paws jerking in his sleep, but especially Dr. Tanaka, herself, enthroned in her high-backed wicker chair.

And here Brigid was again, with yet another husband, one she wanted, so badly, to trust.

She clamped her jaw shut and inched closer to the edge of the couch, sitting with shoulders straight, knees forward, avoiding eye contact with both Jackson and Dr. Tanaka. If only Kuma would stop chasing dream kittens and come cuddle in her lap—that always made her feel better—but telepathically summoning him didn't seem to be working.

"It must be hard for you, Jackson, knowing that Brigid hasn't been able to fully recover her emotions from before the accident," Dr. Tanaka said.

Tuning in to those words, Brigid realized she'd been drifting for the past few minutes.

"I'm more worried about her," Jackson said, reaching for Brigid's hand. "But yes, it's hard to hear that she's somehow mislaid her deepest feelings for me—even though we both believe they're still there, waiting to be uncovered."

The firm grip of his hand closing around hers, the way his body canted toward her, made it even harder to speak up—she didn't want to hurt this man, and she knew the truth would.

"Could we get back to the panic attack I had on the yacht? Like Jackson mentioned earlier, Farrah is fine, thank heavens, but I still want to talk about what happened. And about my dream. I have a dream. A nightmare, really." Brigid put space between herself and Jackson.

"That's quite a pivot." Dr. Tanaka picked up her notebook, her pen poised and ready. "Does this mean you prefer not to discuss your emotional amnesia today?"

"I thought we'd ease into it later, if there's time." Brigid squeezed Jackson's hand to reassure him she didn't plan to dodge the issue entirely. "And I have some questions for Jackson, but would it be okay to talk about the dream first?"

"This is your hour," Dr. Tanaka said. "When you say you

have a dream, that seems to imply this is recurring. Am I understanding that correctly?"

"I had it a few times in the past, years ago, and then, since my accident, it started up again."

"How often would you say?"

"I'm not sure."

Jackson released her hand and crossed his arms over his chest. "I've been sleeping in the room next to our bedroom, temporarily, until Brigid feels more comfortable. I can hear her crying through the wall sometimes during the night. Last week it happened three times. I asked her if she'd had a bad dream, but she said she didn't want to discuss it."

"I'm discussing it now." Brigid sighed, wishing she didn't sound so defensive.

"And you think this dream has something to do with the panic attack you had on the yacht," Dr. Tanaka said. "That's why you're juxtaposing the subjects."

"Yes. I think my panic attack happened because Farrah's near-drowning reminded me of my nightmare."

"Except she didn't nearly drown."

Now it was Jackson who sounded defensive.

"Right. I was mistaken. I wasn't having a great day to begin with. I'd had a confrontation with Charity, and I also took two seasick pills on an empty stomach, so those things might have factored into my misperception."

"Do you think there's something happening to her brain?" Jackson said, looking at her, even though he was addressing Dr. Tanaka.

The intensity of his gaze made her want to edge further away from him, but she clenched her hands and stayed put.

"What makes you think that?" Dr. Tanaka asked.

"Because, as I understand it, she experienced a lack of oxygen for a short time after the accident."

"Anoxia," Dr. Tanaka supplied the term.

"Now, she says she feels 'disconnected' from her emotions, and on the yacht, she completely lost it. She thought that our friend, Farrah, was drowning. She thought I *deliberately* tried to drown her."

"Jackson," Dr. Tanaka said. "I hear you, but I'd prefer to allow Brigid to elaborate, and then we can circle back to your concerns."

"Sure. I'm sorry."

"Brigid? You were saying that the incident on the yacht reminded you of your nightmare. Can you tell me more about that?"

"I don't remember all of it—only bits and pieces. But in my dream, it's nighttime, and I'm barefoot, splashing in water—the ocean, perhaps. Then I see a person—I'm not completely sure, in the dream, if it's a man or a woman, but I think of him as a man—and he's forcing a woman under the waves. He turns and looks at me, and he knows I've seen him, and he chases me."

"Does he catch you?"

"I don't know. When I wake up, I feel disoriented. It takes time for me to realize I'm in my own bed, that I'm alone. *Safe.*" Brigid closed her eyes, took a breath, picturing frothing waves, Farrah's arm reaching above the water, and then... Jackson holding her under. Her heart started to pound, her hands to tingle.

"You're safe now, Brigid." Dr. Tanaka's voice soothed her. "Try breathing through it."

Inhaling deeply, Brigid opened her eyes, keeping them aimed straight ahead, not veering away from Dr. Tanaka. "When I saw Jackson dunk Farrah, even though it was playful, it reminded me of the man in my dream. And when she didn't come back up, I thought Jackson had drowned her. For one terrible moment, I thought... *it's him...* that *Jackson* was the man from my nightmare." She reached out and touched his knee.

"I'm sorry. I know that's an awful thing to say, but I have to be honest with you."

His silence told her what she already knew: how much her words, her accusation, hurt him.

"So, what actually happened? Why did Farrah stay under so long?" Dr. Tanaka asked. "We touched on this briefly, at the beginning of the session, but I'd like to get the details clear. This seems quite important."

"That's just it." Jackson found his voice. "Farrah wasn't under long at all. She came up right away, but somehow Brigid didn't see her pop out of the water. Then, Farrah swam around to the other side of the boat—the only one who didn't see her do that was Brigid. That's about the time Brigid collapsed."

"Did she hit her head on the deck?" Dr. Tanaka slipped forward in her chair.

"Luckily, no. Our friend Darya noticed how pale and shaky Brigid was becoming, and she grabbed her, just before she fainted. The crew turned the yacht around right away and called for someone to meet us when we got back to shore. The medics were waiting when we docked, and, after checking her out, they said she'd had a panic attack and recommended she take a tranquilizer—she has a prescription already from her hospitalization, but she doesn't seem to think she needs it."

"Don't be afraid to take one," Dr. Tanaka said. "Tranquilizers aren't a long-term solution but if you need them to get through a brief adjustment period, there's nothing wrong with that. It does sound, to me, like this dream and the panic attack are directly related. I wonder why you haven't brought it up before."

"I hadn't had the dream in so long. And I wanted to focus on my emotional amnesia in our sessions."

"Speaking of which, she's explained it to me to some degree —" Jackson dragged a hand through his hair "—but I'd like to learn more about her condition. I've never heard of it before, and it's why I'm wondering about her brain."

"What she's described to me can be categorized as a disso-ciative reaction—her psyche disconnecting from her experience. I'm using the term 'emotional amnesia' as a shorthand, because I think it conveys the main problem in a way we can all under-stand. But labels aren't important. I prefer to focus on what we can do to help her move forward," Dr. Tanaka said.

"Makes sense." He shifted to face Brigid. "Can you tell me, sweetheart, what I can do to help?"

It was so difficult to find the words. "We talked about going away together, and I want to do that, but, if I'm being one hundred percent honest, I have questions. I need to be able to trust you before—"

"Wow." Jackson shook his head. "Was not expecting that. First, you accuse me of trying to drown Farrah, and now you're saying you don't trust me in general. What the hell have I done to lose your..." His voice trailed off, and he covered his mouth, then let his hands drop into his lap. "I'm sorry. Ask me anything."

"I don't want to hurt you, Jackson. But when I was with Nash, he lied to me about where he was and what he was doing; at least I believe he did. You went through the same thing with Charity, so you should understand. I expect more transparency from you."

"How have I not..." He put his hand up. "Never mind. I'm not going to make you ask me. There are some things I've kept hidden from you, and I realize, now, that was wrong. I was trying to protect you."

Dr. Tanaka cleared her throat.

"And myself. I didn't want to lose you. I *don't* want to lose you, so when you first told me about your emotional amnesia, I was afraid to show you how much that hurt me. How confused and lost I felt. So I called Dr. Tanaka, and she recommended I get my own therapist to help me cope. I went to see a counselor twice, and then she released me, saying I could come back again if needed. I asked some of our friends to cover for me on the evenings I went to therapy—I didn't tell *them* what I was doing because... how could I without revealing your condition? I didn't want you to feel worse about your problem because of how it affected me. But I see, now, I should've been truthful. You're a strong woman, and I should've given you more credit."

"Is there anything else you've neglected to tell your wife?" Dr. Tanaka asked. "Because now would be the time to get everything out in the open."

"Yes. I went to Hope's grave on her birthday, and I spent some time there with Charity. Then I lied about it because it seemed so important to Brigid that she and I go together—and because Charity told me we had a 'problem' that we should do something about. I didn't want to get into that with Brigid because our relationship is obviously on shaky ground at the moment."

"What 'problem'?" Brigid asked.

"At the hospital, Charity overheard a conversation between you and Nash. She thinks the two of you might still have feelings for each other. So you can see how I might be distressed and need to talk to someone, to a professional, about these things."

"I do see that, but don't you think you should ask *me* how I feel about Nash?"

"Okay. How do you feel about Nash?"

She twisted her hands in her lap and looked longingly at Kuma, still chasing his dream kittens.

"This is a safe space for you, Brigid. If you're not ready you don't have to go any further," Dr. Tanaka said.

"I want to be ready," she said. "I just feel so guilty."

"You haven't done anything wrong. I promise, whatever you say, I'm going to be here for you, and I'm going to be okay. I've already lived through the worst thing that anyone can." Jackson didn't drop his gaze, and the look in his eyes broke her heart.

He'd lost his only child, and yet, here he was, ready to be the strong shoulder for her. But no matter how much it hurt her to hurt him, she couldn't lie. "I remember our first kiss. I remember being overjoyed when you proposed. I remember that I love you. But I remember as if those things happened to another person—like it's a book I read about someone else's life."

"You're saying you don't actually feel those things now."

"I want to. I want to believe we can get back to where we were before."

"Me, too. And I'm willing to be patient, to give you all the time and space you need. But frankly, at the moment, it seems like you're afraid to tell me about Nash. You haven't said how you feel about him."

"Are you leaving something out, Brigid?" Dr. Tanaka asked.

She took a deep breath. "At times, I still *feel* married to Nash. When I look at myself in the mirror, it's as if I'm looking at the old Brigid, the one who is still his wife."

"You're in love with him?" Jackson whispered the question.

"No. It's not that. I'm not in love with him. But we were together a long time." She looked to her psychiatrist for help. "Dr. Tanaka can confirm that I had to work through a lot of different emotions before I was able to leave that marriage and fall in love with someone else—with *you*. But now it's as if there are two versions of me, and one of them is that older version, the one who still hasn't worked through all those issues. But I don't want to be stuck in the past, as old Brigid; I want to break free of her and feel fully in love with my husband, with you."

Dr. Tanaka was scribbling furiously.

Jackson claimed a death grip on her hand. "True love doesn't just disappear. Even if you suffered a lack of oxygen. Even if parts of your brain are still recovering. If you ever truly loved me, and I *know* you did, those emotions are still there."

"But what if I can't find them? What if they're buried too deep, or gone completely because of my brain injury."

Dr. Tanaka suddenly stopped writing and looked up. "As I've said, dissociative reactions are uncommon, and the form this one is taking even more so. There are no rules or fully proven therapies that I'm aware of—and I've consulted a number of colleagues."

That didn't sound good to her, but Dr. Tanaka's tone was matter-of-fact. It didn't sound like she thought the situation was hopeless.

"So what do I do?" Brigid asked.

"What do *we* do?" Jackson corrected.

"Here's what I'm thinking. Suppose we come at this from a different angle. So far, we've been talking about how to help Brigid recover her *old* feelings. But let me be as honest with you as you've been with each other. I'm hopeful, but not certain, that Brigid can reconnect her memories to her emotions. Maybe those circuits will repair themselves, and maybe they won't. It's possible, too, there's some past trauma we don't know about, piled on top of the anoxia, that's exacerbating the problem. Making everything worse. But watching you together, I'm quite convinced of your commitment to one another. So here is my recommendation: if you are both determined to make this marriage work, then I suggest you stop worrying about getting Brigid's old feelings back and focus on forging a new bond."

SIXTEEN

As she peered through the window of a Crate and Barrell, Charity did not press her nose against the glass. And the weather today was balmy. So why did she feel like the poor little matchstick girl left out in the cold?

Inside, Tish and Brigid posed next to each other in front of painted white shelves loaded with gleaming kitchen accessories. There was no mistaking the biological relation between them. And not only because they had the same blonde curls and big blue eyes—there was something intangible, but nonetheless striking, about the mother-daughter connection. Their facial expressions, their gestures, even their posture was so similar one had to wonder if such things were genetically coded.

Hope, too, had resembled Charity with her dark hair and eyes fringed with dramatic lashes. Charity blinked, imagining Hope, standing there, next to Tish. Hope would turn, and, through the glass, their eyes would meet. Hope would lift her hand to wave Charity inside.

You're always late, Mother!

Hope invariably called Charity *Mother* in public, but in private it was always *Mom*.

Now, Charity followed a trundling woman, bundled in a double layer of sweaters despite the heat, through the door. Given their altercation on the yacht, it was a small miracle Brigid had not vanquished Charity from this shopping expedition.

Unless, perhaps, Tish had failed to mention to her that Charity would be here?

A welcoming hug from Tish was everything she needed to vanquish her self-pity and lift her spirits. It didn't matter that Brigid shot Tish a look so full of disappointment you'd have thought she'd just informed her she wouldn't be home for Thanksgiving break.

Only that wasn't Tish's news at all.

"Sorry I'm late!" Inwardly, Charity smiled.

* * *

"No need to apologize," Brigid said. "I had no idea you were coming, so how can you be late?"

"Then, surprise!" Charity exclaimed.

Brigid couldn't tell if she was covering up embarrassment or rubbing it in that Tish hadn't mentioned she was coming. Either way, Charity would expect Brigid to pretend she welcomed her presence. And up until recently, she would have done exactly that. But new Brigid had made a resolution.

No more faking it. "It certainly is."

"Mom." Tish shot her a look through narrowed eyes.

Which was unfair, because hadn't Tish admonished her to be more authentic?

Careful what you wish for.

No doubt one motive for ambushing Brigid with Charity was to forestall any conversation they might have been able to have about Christian. "Will anyone else be joining us?"

"No." Tish lifted a stainless-steel pineapple cutter, and twisted it, the blades glinting in the powerful overhead lights.

Good. At least she wouldn't have to deal with Charity's brother. Brigid hadn't yet wrapped her head around the fact that he was moving in with her daughter. He'd just gotten settled into his new job working for Nash, and now he was going to give up that job and transplant himself to L.A. to be with Tish, after they'd only been dating such a short time? It made no sense to Brigid. But the plan was still on, she presumed; otherwise they wouldn't be here.

Tish had announced she was driving down for the weekend, and she needed a full set of dishes, proper cookware, and a new couch. She'd complained she couldn't make do with the college-girl furnishings Brigid and Nash had bought her when she'd started USC.

"That's one of my favorite items." A double-sweatered woman with a name tag that read "Margaret" wandered toward them. "Let me know if I can answer any questions."

"What is this?" Tish asked.

"A pineapple corer. You just cut off the top, push it on like so and twist. Perfectly sliced pineapple every time."

"Christian's allergic to pineapple." Tish frowned and slipped the corer back onto the shelf. "Cool gadget, though. Mom, maybe you and Jackson could get one."

"I think we're set," Brigid said. "Besides, we're here for you today."

"What are you in the market for?" Margaret asked.

"Lots. But I think we'll start with everyday dishes." Charity hooked an arm through Tish's. "Thank you so much for explaining the corer, Margaret. You've got the right idea with those sweaters. As soon as I walked in the store, I thought, 'Where are we? Alaska?'"

"I know. Wouldn't you think the management would want

to save money and turn off that air-conditioning? This is San Diego, for Pete's sake."

"I'm with you." Charity smiled in her super friendly way, and Brigid tried not to let her impatience show.

They were in no hurry, and Brigid used to admire how friendly Charity was with everyone she encountered. Besides, any hope of an intimate conversation with her daughter exited when Charity entered.

Brigid picked up the pineapple corer, considering making the purchase after all, then put it back. Compared to her bubbly counterpart, Charity, Brigid felt like a drip—but she wasn't going to pay $60 for this gizmo in order to prove she wasn't.

"Let me show you the stoneware. We've got some fun new patterns," Margaret said, leading the way to the far corner of the store.

An hour later, Brigid was on the verge of collapse from the twin trials of making small talk, while simultaneously assisting her daughter's preparations for what could easily turn out to be the biggest mistake of her life.

At the register, Margaret painstakingly wound bubble wrap around each dish before loading them into a giant shopping bag. Then Tish proudly paid with her very own credit card—her first. Tish's enthusiasm was almost enough to win Brigid over to team Christian—she hadn't seen her daughter smile this much since before Hope died.

If only she believed Tish could count on Christian.

She understood that her daughter, like every other woman with a beating heart, was going to get hurt, sooner or later. But there are heart aches, and then there are broken hearts.

Broken hearts—the kind that go along with a certain kind of man—sometimes never fully mend.

Brigid had already made it clear she thought moving in with Christian was a mistake, though, and if she kept harping on it, she would only drive Tish further away. "Where to next, Tish?"

"I need a bigger bed."
Lovely.

After dropping the dishes in the car, Brigid, Charity and Tish trudged to Furniture Palace.

Brigid smirked openly when Charity headed straight for the most expensive beds on the floor, their frames constructed of double layer fir, their headboards made to order from your choice of Tuscan, Etrusco or an assortment of other fine leathers.

If there was one thing Brigid knew about her daughter, it was that she wasn't going to choose an animal product if she had any other choice—and here, there were so very many choices.

"Doesn't it come in vegan leather?" Charity frowned at the selection list.

"Hey, this might work," Brigid called them over to her side of the aisle.

And, when Tish squealed at the classic, tufted fabric head-boards, Brigid played it cool, though she secretly wanted to high-five herself. "It's within budget, too."

"What budget?" Charity sounded positively astonished.

Even Tish's eyebrows rose at Charity's comment. "I have an allowance for my living expenses, and I'm supposed to budget my money to learn how to become fiscally responsible. You didn't know?"

"Oh, right, of course. Your budget. But, since this is for both you and Christian, I assumed I would, I mean *Christian* would chip in. I don't think we need to be concerned with the price of the bed."

"Well, it doesn't matter, because it's within budget, and it's *perfect.* I love it."

As they were walking toward the register, Charity lagged behind, and Brigid felt her tug the back of her blouse.

"What?"

"Listen, I think you should chill out," Charity said in a stage whisper.

"Seriously?" Did she not just help pick out a bed for her daughter and her boyfriend?

"I mean later... in case Tish has news or anything."

Brigid took a breath. "I'm not playing this game, or any game, with you anymore. Apparently, you know something I don't. But if that's the case, you should allow my daughter to tell me in her own time. And in private."

"I understand, Brigid. I'm honestly not trying to upset you. But I think Tish might have invited me to tag along for a reason. Again, no offense intended but I'm sure she doesn't want a scene."

They'd caught up to Tish at checkout. Brigid's throat burned from the acid flushing her throat, but she swallowed it down. She wasn't sure if Charity was trying to give her sincere advice or stirring the pot—but if this were Vegas, she'd put money on the latter.

"I'm sorry, ma'am. I need a different card. This one did not go through," the clerk said.

"Oh, could you try again please?" Tish asked.

Brigid stepped closer to Tish. "It's okay, honey. If you're over your limit I can pay and then we can take it out of your allowance."

"But I'm not over my limit. I'm sure it'll go—"

Charity reached out and snatched the card from the clerk, then handed him a different one. "I'm buying."

Tish and Brigid both shook their heads.

"I insist," Charity said. "It's my housewarming gift to you and Christian."

A tense silence descended as the clerk completed the transaction. Brigid was torn. On the one hand, she appreciated Charity's generosity with Tish. On the other, her interference was galling. Brigid and Nash were trying to teach Tish how to handle her finances for her own benefit, not because they didn't want to spend money on her. Moreover, in the highly probable event this relationship with Christian didn't last forever, Brigid didn't want there to be any question who got to keep the furniture.

"Don't overreact," Charity whispered again, this time loudly enough that both Tish and the salesperson likely heard.

"I got it the first time," Brigid said, keeping her tone as even as her growing frustration allowed.

"This will be ready for delivery on Tuesday next week." The clerk handed Charity back her card.

"From your L.A. warehouse?" Brigid had let Charity distract her, and she hadn't heard the whole discussion between Tish and the clerk. She wanted to be sure Tish had told him this was an out-of-town order.

"No. This is a local address. Cielo Hermoso."

Good thing she'd asked. Tish must've given either Brigid or Nash's address, which was silly. There was no need to load up a U-Haul and drive the bed up to her when the store had a warehouse in L.A.

"You have the correct address," Tish said. "Charity, would you wait for the receipt and the delivery details? I want to talk to Mom outside."

"Why?" Brigid's feet rooted to the ground.

Don't overreact.

Charity had warned her.

"Our new place, Christian's and mine—it's here in town. But don't worry, he's paying full rent. And I've already found someone to sublet my apartment in L.A. I'm staying on budget until I find work, and then you and Dad are off the hook completely."

"I don't care about the damn money." She could barely get

the words out, her heart was pounding so fast. "I care about school."

Tish rolled her shoulders back. "I do, too. But I'm taking a leave of absence until I can decide what I really want to do with my life. USC is allowing me to take a year, and then I can either go back, or if I'm not ready, I can reapply in the future."

"But you worked so hard for your acceptance. You *wanted* to go to USC. You said it was your dream. I-I don't understand."

"It was my dream. And maybe it still is. But freshman year was hard, and this semester hasn't been any better..." Tish cast a glance at Charity.

"It's okay, you can say it, hon."

"Since Hope died, I don't know anything anymore—except that life is short, and I plan to live mine to the fullest."

SEVENTEEN

Like most Cielo Hermoso evenings, this one was perfect—not too hot, not too cold, air so fresh you could taste its tangy flavor on your tongue; a gentle breeze caressing your skin, bringing you the sweet perfume of summer flowers. Hand in hand, Jackson and Brigid strolled through the park, past the red bench surrounded by gardenia bushes, to The Village Square. The sun had set and, up ahead, the street lamp in front of Café Francois flickered to life. The lights were meant to flare on all at once, but by a quirk of fate and flawed technology, they burst on one by one, in sequence, like an invisible lamplighter was trotting around the town square with his wick and pole.

At the end of the sidewalk, the street lamp in front of Clues in Your Coffee came on just as Brigid and Jackson arrived. Charity had called a meeting at Aiden and Rollin's mystery bookshop to discuss the state of Supper Club. It was so last minute you might suppose the members would've declined, but Charity had such confidence in her own ideas, such a flair for painting every plan as not only irresistible but imperative, that it was hard to say "no" to her.

People rarely did.

In fact, that was how they'd all gotten to be friends in the first place.

Charity had devised a brilliant scheme that had pulled a group of strangers, who happened to live in the same town and frequent the same bookshop, together to execute it. Of course, Brigid and Nash had met Jackson and Charity through their daughters and school functions, but they weren't actually friends until the night the lights went out in the bookshop.

Back then, it had been called Cielo Hermoso Mystery Books, and had looked quite different: a plainly furnished room with tomes shelved in orderly fashion, a register, and two hard-back chairs behind a desk where Rollin and Aiden sat reading, patiently waiting for customers to materialize.

Now, its giant picture windows tempted passers-by to peer in, and, if you loved books, the shop's character pulled you through the front door. Inside, dark, distressed hardwood floors, softened by plush oriental rugs in rich reds and golds, played host to oversize roll-arm couches upholstered in forest-green leather with deep, buttoned-down tufting. Books, books, books, filled the floor-to-ceiling mahogany shelves in the main room, which adjoined two spaces—one oversized and one undersized.

The larger adjoining area housed a coffee café with brick walls, a barista counter and glass cases filled with pastries and sandwiches; a cash register disguised as a replica antique type-writer, and long community tables.

The other was a windowless space, about the size of a child's bedroom, where first editions and other fragile books stood on baked enamel shelves with just enough space between them to protect the bindings without allowing them to topple. The overhead light was a plain bulb in a simple fixture, to be switched on only when the room was occupied. A thermo hygrometer was employed to keep the room a chilly sixty-five degrees and approximately fifty-five percent relative humidity. Polyester blackout curtains hung inside the entry to prevent sunlight from reaching the fragile books whenever someone opened the door to the sunny main room.

Brigid and Jackson stepped into the shop just in time to see Rollin shimmy through the blackout curtains from the rare books room with a copy of a distinctively bound, red leather volume in hand, and then quickly close the door behind him. Though, from where she stood, she could not make out the title, Brigid knew it must be the first edition of *The Hound of the Baskervilles* by Sir Arthur Conan Doyle—and that Aiden would be reading from it tonight.

It was so like Charity to think of recreating the event that had first bonded the friends together. Whatever resentments Brigid held toward Charity, she had to give her credit where it was due.

"Looks like we're on time." Jackson gave Brigid's hand a squeeze before pulling her toward a grouping of green sofas where everyone had taken seats—save Roman who was notably absent. In his place, Farrah lolled in a stunning, black silk minidress and knee-topping boots, her skirt riding high above tanned thighs.

"Roman's not coming?" Brigid asked.

"Migraine." Farrah crossed and uncrossed her long legs revealing, intentionally or not, a glimpse of red lace panties, at the exact moment she sent Jackson a coy smile.

"Please let Roman know we miss him," Brigid replied.

"We?" Farrah challenged. "No one's been knocking down our door asking how he's doing."

"I've texted him a number of times, inquiring after his well-being," Darya huffed, and scooted to the edge of the sofa, "but I speak for myself and Jamal when I say we *do* miss him and want to welcome him back anytime—providing, of course, he leaves his gun at home."

"The gun went off by accident."

"And we're all agreed on that point." Charity straightened

her back. "But you have to admit Supper Club hasn't gone as smoothly as one would hope lately. My beautiful chandelier was completely destroyed."

Nash put his hand on Charity's arm. "Honey, the chandelier doesn't matter."

"Maybe not to you, but it was one-of-a-kind. I've ordered another, obviously a different piece, from the same artist, and Brigid is fully recovered, and Roman... anyway, everyone's okay and that's what counts." She coughed. "Now then, I asked everyone here tonight because I don't want to see people separating into cliques or taking sides. I want us to refresh our friendships by recreating the event that brought us together and, unlike some people, I invited *everyone*."

Darya cast a glance at Jamal who grimaced. Rollin's ears turned pink, and Aiden's knee began to bounce.

"We were just previewing the American Music exhibit," Darya said. "It was last minute, and we didn't mean to hurt anyone's feelings by leaving them out. We wanted to talk to Brigid to make sure she felt safe."

"And I do." Brigid's face heated. "Everyone, please, there is no need to coddle me. I had a panic attack on the yacht. I'm a little shook up, by recent events, but I'm getting professional help, and you all mean so much to me. I would hate to be the cause of the group splintering or disbanding."

"No one wants to disband. Do they?" Charity arched an eyebrow. "We're a team, aren't we?"

A soft murmur went around the group.

"Exactly. We've always been there for each other, and I hope we always will be. And that's what tonight is about. I want everyone to close your eyes, just for a moment, and remember the night we all came together for the first time."

"Well, I'd love to, but since I wasn't part of the group back then, I really can't." Farrah did the panty-peek leg-cross thing again.

"Sorry, Farrah. I'll fill you in." Rollin pushed up his glasses. "The bookshop was failing, and Aiden and I came up with a last-ditch promotion to bring customers in: a reading from *The Hound of the Baskervilles* where we raffled off a first edition of the book. Only I hadn't paid the electric bill, and in the middle of the reading, the lights went out. I thought it was going to be a disaster, that it spelled the end of the road for our business, but when the customers made a beeline for the door, Charity got up on the podium and yelled out—"

"Hold it right there!" Charity shouted commandingly.

Jamal chortled. "We all stopped in our tracks like a bunch of naughty children."

"And then everyone turned on their phone lights. Rollin dug out some battery-operated emergency lanterns from the storage area so that I could finish my reading," Aiden said. "Afterwards, when we explained what dire straits the shop was in, we all went out to dinner to brainstorm a way to keep the shop open—and that was our very first Supper Club. I'm sure, Farrah, if you had been with Roman back then, you would've been a big help, too."

Apparently both mollified and curious, Farrah rested her elbows on her knees and her chin in her palms. "So how did you do it? Turn things around for the shop?"

"Charity came up with the idea of adding a coffee bar." Nash sent Charity a wink, and her face opened up into a wide smile.

"Then Nash said he had the inside track on the space next door through his real estate dealings. He knew it was about to be leased, but thought he could convince the owners to let Rollin and Aiden have it for the coffee area instead."

"But how could they afford a lease if they were broke?" Farrah asked.

"Because *Roman* loaned us money," Rollin said.

"If it wasn't for Roman, for all of you," Aiden continued,

"we would've lost our life savings. Every single person played an integral part in saving the shop. Brigid came up with the idea of renaming the place Clues in Your Coffee, and then, she worked on branding and community awareness with Darya. Darya and Charity redecorated, and Jamal handled all the legal red tape gratis."

"So you see, Farah, we owe Roman, and we aren't going to turn our backs on him," Rollin said. "I'm not going to lie. I was shocked by what he did, but we *all* want to bring him back into the fold."

"And the way he took charge when Brigid was injured proves how much he cares. He's our friend and we love him." Darya pressed a hand against her heart.

"I know that, between the accident and the panic attack and the misunderstanding with Christian, things have been dicey lately," Charity said, "but I just want the group to remember how much we care for each other, and that, together, we can get through anything."

"Okay, honey, we get it." Nash grabbed Charity's hand. "Who wants to hear Aiden read about a hound?"

Aiden, ever so carefully, closed the book and surveyed his audience. "And, so, Sherlock Holmes and Dr. Watson embark on the case. Will they be able to protect Sir Henry Baskerville from a terrible fate?"

After the clapping died out, Farrah changed couches, squeezing in between one arm of the sofa and Jackson.

"How does it end?" Brigid heard Farrah drawl near her husband's ear. Farrah had drunk more than a few flutes of champagne during the short reading and, no surprise, her words were fuzzy, her eyes glazed.

"I won't spoil it for you." Jackson tipped his head close to Farrah's and whispered, "But trust me, you'll enjoy it. Shall I loan you my copy? It was me who won the first edition that evening."

"Oh, please!" Farrah oozed enthusiasm.

Huh. Brigid really hadn't pegged Farrah for a reader. Some wives might be irritated by Farrah's flirtatious behavior, but Brigid knew how kind Jackson was. He understood, as did Brigid, that Farrah, as the youngest member, and a relative newcomer to their group, was something of an outsider. Anything he could do to make her feel at ease, he would.

It was nothing.

And certainly not to do with the nights he'd asked some of the others for a cover story.

He'd explained that perfectly in Dr. Tanaka's office. Brigid shifted forward on the couch and was about to reach for one of the finger sandwiches that Charity had set out on a silver serving tray when Nash caught her eye and mouthed something that looked like *can we talk?*

She shrugged.

He stood, and then he walked away from the chattering group in the direction of the rare books room.

She hesitated.

There was nothing wrong with speaking with Nash alone, and in truth, she wondered what he thought of Tish's announcement that she was taking a leave of absence from school. Jackson was happily engaged in his private side conversation with Farrah, and Charity was gesticulating wildly to an enthralled audience—Jamal, Darya, Aiden and Rollin.

From across the room, Nash motioned impatiently to Brigid.

She didn't want Charity to get the wrong idea, but Nash clearly had something on his mind, and that something, most likely, was Tish. Charity never had any qualms about pulling Jackson aside, or anyone else for that matter. It was only Brigid who tiptoed around everyone else's feelings. She would've excused herself, politely, but no one was paying attention, so she jumped up and went to join Nash, feeling only slightly sheepish.

"Took you long enough." Nash opened the door to the rare books room, fumbled for the light switch, and then parted the blackout curtains for her as they entered. "I hope you don't mind—this place is on the cold and dark side, but I did want a private word."

Brigid brisked her hands over her arms and looked around for a chair, but didn't find one. "What's up?"

Nash pushed a hand through his hair, widened his stance. "That's my question for you. I know it's not my business anymore, but whether it is or isn't, I do care about you."

She stepped back.

"Please don't worry. I'm not going to try to assert my feelings again. We've talked about things. We've been honest with each other and my intentions haven't changed. I respect your marriage to Jackson and mine to Charity. But..."

"No buts."

"Right. I'm only trying to say that I'm concerned about you. What happened on the yacht that upset you? You were so—"

"I had a panic attack. It happens. I thought you called me over to talk about Tish."

"I want to be sure you're okay. If you ever need to talk about anything, I'm here."

"I want to discuss Tish."

He turned his palms up. "Sure. I know this thing with Christian—"

"We need to present a united front. Things have escalated. It doesn't seem like being supportive and staying quiet is working out that well."

"And you think ordering her to break up with him, to go back to school, will change her mind?"

"No. I just—shouldn't we at least let her know how we feel?"

"I did. I told her I think she's making a mistake, but that it's hers to make. And it is, isn't it?"

"I suppose so." She shivered. "You know what? You're right. It's cold in here, and I feel uncomfortable sneaking off together. I mean, if the shoe were on the other foot and Jackson and Charity—"

Click.

The room went dark.

Completely dark.

There were no windows in this tiny space. Nothing around her but thick, suffocating air. Heart in her throat, she lifted a shaking hand, feeling in front of her for the door. "What's happening?"

"You're okay, Brigid. I'm right here."

Nash's disembodied voice echoed in her ears. She reached out, confused, legs trembling, arms trembling—*heart* trembling.

She couldn't speak, couldn't catch her breath.

Her knees buckled.

Again, she reached out, trying to grab something, anything, for support and suddenly, something cold and thick was filling her mouth, blocking her lungs. She was drowning, flailing, fighting the waves, sinking in cold, black water.

Strong arms came around her. "I've got you. I'm here."

Nash.

"You're okay. I won't let anything happen to you."

Her chest loosened, and after a beat she managed to get in one breath, and then another. "W-what happened?"

Nash tightened his arms around her.

Relaxing against his chest, she heard a metallic sound. The door flung open just as the lights flashed on.

Tangled around her legs, she saw the reason she'd been

drowning—fallen blackout curtains, she must've pulled them down on top of her, and there was something worse.

At the threshold, between the main room of the shop and the rare books room, arms crossed over her chest, face red, eyes blazing, loomed Charity.

EIGHTEEN

Tish and Christian's kitchen sparkled from elbow grease and the kind of love one pours into one's first real home. Charity wanted to crow because she and Nash had beaten out Jackson and Brigid for the honor of being the first dinner guests. To give the kids a break from organizing and cleaning, Charity had insisted on ordering takeout from Christian's favorite Indian restaurant and, now, the "dining room", which was actually a nook attached to the kitchen, smelled like curry and fresh paint.

"How was the team building last night?" Tish laid her fork atop the bit of remaining rice on her plate, and then reached for Christian's hand.

Nash cleared his throat.

Ignoring the uncomfortable look on his face, and inspired by the young lovers, Charity laid her hand atop Nash's. Was she hurt by Nash's behavior at Clues in Your Coffee?

Who wouldn't be?

And in that first, unguarded moment, she hadn't been able to conceal her true reaction to stumbling upon her husband with his arms around Brigid. But, now, she'd had time to compose herself. "It was a lovely evening. A wonderful reminder of how much we all mean to each other."

"Sounds like you haven't spoken to your mother." Nash eased his hand out from under Charity's. "Because it wasn't *lovely* for her. Brigid had another panic attack, and I'm afraid Charity had something to do with that."

"Darling, if anyone should be complaining it's me, not Brigid." It was one thing not to admit he'd hurt her, but quite another to allow him to make her the villain of the piece.

"Brigid's not complaining. *I* am."

"Let's change the subject—"

"Wait a minute, if Mom had another panic attack, I'd like to hear what happened," Tish said.

Charity planted her forearms on the table and, unfortunately, into a dollop of spilled sauce. She dabbed at the yellow-brown mess with her napkin. "It was a simple miscommunication. I was trying to recreate the events that brought the members of our club together—the reading of *The Hound of the Baskervilles*, the lights going out—but my timing was off and the electricity got cut *after* the reading while your father and Brigid were... conferring in the rare books room. There're no windows and so—"

"Brigid was trying to get out and she pulled the blackout curtain down on top of her face. She couldn't breathe." The vein pulsing in Nash's forehead was disconcerting. Charity was the one who should be angry—not Nash.

"Anyway, she's fine. All's well that ends well." Charity threw down her napkin and dusted her hands together. Time to move on.

"I'm glad, she's okay. It doesn't sound too serious, so... why are you two mad at each other?" Tish asked.

"We're not mad. Are we, Nash?" Charity smiled.

Christian let go of Tish's hand and looked at Nash. "Don't be angry at Charity. It was an accident, just like she said. But if anyone's to blame, it's me. Charity told me, specifically, to cut the lights at eight p.m., while Aiden was doing his reading, because that's the same time it happened ten years ago. But I got tied up at the office. One of your junior real estate agents needed a market study ASAP. I should've texted Charity to ask if I should go ahead with the plan, but I didn't think it would be a big deal if I cut the lights at eight-twenty instead of eight. How could I know Brigid would be in a room with no windows?"

"You couldn't," Charity said.

"I never meant to scare anyone, especially not Brigid, after everything she's been through."

"Of course, you didn't," Tish said. "But, Dad, why were you and Mom in there in the first place?"

"We were just talking."

"About *me*?"

"Your name came up. But mostly, I wanted to be sure your mother was recovered from her accident. She's been having a rough go of it, from what I can tell, so I was checking in to let her know I'm still here for her if she needs me. If she needs *us*." He jerked his chin toward Charity.

How nice. Nash was including her as an afterthought.

"It wouldn't be a bad idea, Tish, for you to check in with Brigid, too. It seems like things are thawing between the two of you since her accident, and, in my opinion, that's long overdue."

Brigid. Brigid. Brigid.

Nash was so busy worrying about his ex-wife he couldn't see what Charity was going through. Just because she didn't go around fainting on yachts and pulling down blackout curtains didn't mean she wasn't in pain. If Nash couldn't see through the brave face she put on, she wasn't going to weep and moan about it. But she wasn't going to sit around and watch him fall in love with his ex all over again either—apparently, he was susceptible to damsels in distress.

Charity wasn't willing to play the victim, even for Nash, but she could do what was in her power to make Brigid seem less of one.

There was something Nash had been after her to do.

He'd said if Tish was going to believe them, it had to come from Charity. Well, if he wanted her to be the bigger person, then she'd be the bigger person. "I agree with your father, Tish. You should reach out to your mother. And there's something I've been wanting to clear up—I recently learned—I'm not sure how Christian got the idea that Brigid and Jackson—"

Christian reared back in his chair. "What? Are you going to throw me under the bus after I just took the blame for—"

"No one's throwing anyone under the bus." Charity dipped a piece of naan in yogurt, and then paused with it near her lips. "Naturally, believing that Jackson and Brigid had an affair, you thought you owed it to Tish to tell her about it."

Tish jumped to her feet. "What do you mean, *believing* they had an affair?"

"Just that. Christian told you something he believed to be true. But it's not. At least to my knowledge there was no prior relationship between Jackson and your mother." She bit off the end of the naan, chewed, swallowed, washed it down with a gulp of vino. "Jackson and I split up because it was too painful to be with each other after we lost Hope." Losing first her daughter and then her marriage had been the worst things that had ever happened to her, and it was a relief to admit, for once, that she wasn't made of stone.

Tish turned her back.

"Where are you going, hon?" Christian's voice sounded low and morose.

"To call my mom. I owe her an apology... thanks, so very much, to you."

NINETEEN

Kuma bounded from Brigid's lap, then trotted over to the casita door, barking like mad, as if an unseen danger, known only to him, was just outside, lying in wait.

Dr. Tanaka got him settled down, then placed him in his bed, before taking her seat, once again, in her favorite chair. "Sorry about that. What else is on your mind? We still have time."

They'd covered one topic in depth during the first half of the hour: Brigid's relationship with Tish—including Brigid's concern that her daughter was making a huge mistake taking a leave of absence from school and moving in with Christian, and Brigid's strategy, to lay low, in order not to alienate her daughter. Tish wanted her mother to give Christian a chance, and it was only fair to do so. Sincerely—but with her eyes open. If she saw anything that could hurt her daughter, she'd promised herself to speak up, and Tish had apologized for the "misunderstanding" about an affair between Brigid and Jackson. For once, things were moving in the right direction with her daughter.

What they hadn't covered: Brigid's disconnect from Jackson, her recurring nightmare, and the small matter of yet another panic attack. "Jackson and I have plans to go out of town—to Lake Tahoe."

A sharp line appeared between Dr. Tanaka's eyebrows. "I like the idea of the weekend away—to forge new bonds, I presume—but after your recent panic attack on the yacht, I wonder if a lake is such a great destination."

"Umm, actually, I had a second panic attack the other day. I can't pretend I'm not a little apprehensive, but I don't want to let my problems keep me from enjoying a romantic weekend with my husband."

"Another attack?"

"Yes, I was in a rare books room—the kind with no windows —when the electricity went out."

"That's unfortunate. I think I might've panicked, too. Who wouldn't?"

"No kidding. And then, to top it off, I pulled a set of curtains down onto my face and I couldn't breathe. I felt like I was suffocating—drowning, really—and that somehow merged with my nightmare and the incident on the yacht. I don't know, but Jackson and I plan to stay away from any sort of water-related activities when we visit the lake. I really want to go. I simply can't allow my fears to limit me."

"I'm not against it, then. As long as you take it slow. But if your body starts sending you signals like a racing heart, short-ness of breath, or tingling in your extremities, those can be signs of an impending panic attack. My advice is to heed the warning and remove yourself from the situation before it's too late. But if you're smart about it, exposing yourself to the things you fear can help desensitize you—decrease their potency and their ability to disable you."

"My dad always said you should run toward your fears, not away from them."

"He sounds like a wise man. But remember to watch for those body signals and protect yourself." Dr. Tanaka flipped a page on her notepad. "So how's it going with you and Jackson? Are you feeling more 'real' around him these days?"

"Actually, I am. I've been doing some exercises at home. I was thinking about how you used to give Nash and me homework when we were in couples therapy, and how it helped me, even if it didn't save our marriage. But, anyway, I made up some homework on my own, and it seems to be helping."

"I'm impressed. I love that you came up with your own therapy exercises. Care to share?"

She nodded. "First, I spend time every day looking at our wedding album. I think about that day, and I focus on a specific thing. For example, this morning, I looked at pictures of Jackson and me dancing. Then I closed my eyes and did some deep breathing, and I got a warm, sweet, fluttery feeling in my belly."

The corners of Dr. Tanaka's mouth twitched as if she were trying not to smile. "Go on."

"Next, I go into the bathroom and smell his cologne, and then, this will make you laugh..."

"It's nice to laugh."

"I sit down at the kitchen table, and I pull out a pen and paper and write out my name many times and many ways: Mrs. Jackson Templeton. Brigid Templeton. Mrs. Brigid Templeton. Mr. and Mrs. Jackson and Brigid Templeton. Any way I can think that connects me to him. I know it's silly, like what a schoolgirl would do, but it helps it sink in, on a visceral level, that I'm *Jackson's* wife."

"And how does that make you feel—to be his wife?"

"Great. I'm definitely not in the same place I was when I married him. I can't honestly say I have that deep, deep sense that we belong together—it's more like I'm crushing on him, but one thing has definitely grown: my trust. I have a much greater sense of safety around him than I did even a short time ago, like that day on the yacht when I melted down."

"Have you been intimate?"

"Not yet, but maybe this weekend, if we're both feeling it... I don't want to rush it. I want to be fully present, and I don't see how I can be if I'm still struggling with this disconnect and... speaking of which, there's something you mentioned before that I've been thinking a lot about."

Dr. Tanaka clicked her pen. "Mm hm."

"You asked if I had any holes in my memory. It seems as if you think that might be important."

"But you said you did *not* have any missing time, as I recall."

"I did say that, but, now, I think that I might." Brigid hesitated. "But nothing like what I'm experiencing now."

"If you've ever dissociated before, even if it was different than this lack of *feeling memory*, it might show a pattern."

"How do you mean?"

"If you've lost time in the past, it could mean that your preferred way of protecting yourself from trauma is to separate yourself from it. In one instance, to deny that it ever happened at all—to forget it entirely. Another, like now, would be to remember that it happened, but not allow yourself to feel anything about it—like you watched a movie starring someone else. Those two ways of adapting to trauma aren't all that different. They're both about denial, compartmentalization, *dissociation*."

"I can see that. But is this my psyche or a physical insult to my brain? I thought my emotional amnesia was because of anoxia."

"That likely plays a role. Your brain, your emotions, the psychology of you, is frankly complicated and multifactorial. If any doctor tells you they fully understand the complexity of human behavior and the brain... they're full of it." Dr. Tanaka dropped her pen and pad and leaned forward. "But enough jargon. Are you or aren't you missing a piece of time?"

"Yes, but I'm not sure it counts."

"If you've lost time—it counts."

"Okay, well, I got blackout drunk on my thirty-sixth birthday. I didn't tell you about it earlier because I was embarrassed, but more than that, I thought since it was alcohol related it was completely dissimilar to my current problem."

"Maybe the alcohol played a role then, like the anoxia you experienced after your accident is playing a role, now."

"I don't understand. Not to keep going in circles, but do I have a physical problem or a psychological one?"

"A physical insult, such as too much alcohol or a lack of oxygen, can make your psyche more vulnerable. If you're unable to cope, you may adapt to that vulnerability in unconventional ways."

"You think so?"

Dr. Tanaka shrugged. "Just a theory—but an educated one. Don't forget what I said about doctors not having it all figured out."

"I understand. You're not making an official pronouncement." Brigid noticed the wall clock. "Hey, before we finish, I want to mention something else. My dream has been changing. Does that seem strange?"

"Not at all. Dreams are fluid."

"Well, this one is getting more and more detailed. Now, in my dream, I can hear a duck taking flight, and in the distance, I see an island. It's like I'm finding lost puzzle pieces in the bottom of a junk drawer, but I'm missing the picture on the top of the box, so I don't know what the final image I'm working toward is supposed to look like."

"Interesting..." Dr. Tanaka touched her chin. "Tell you what, since you like therapy homework, I've got an assignment for you. I'd like you to start writing down your dreams. Maybe a dream diary will help you make sense of your nightmare."

TWENTY

Lake Tahoe, California

A knock at the door startled Brigid.

"Room service!" Jackson's voice, muffled by the adjoining door between their hotel rooms, sounded all the more sensuous, rumbling through layers of wood.

"I'm decent," she called back. Having been awakened by her nightmare yet again, she'd been up since 5 a.m., and had long since applied a light coat of nude lipstick, a hint of sheer powder, and donned a purple paisley jumper along with her least prized pair of sneakers.

"Damn shame." The brass handle dipped and Jackson shoved through the door, carrying a wooden tray. He'd dressed for the day in bicycle shorts and a sky-blue T-shirt. The natural highlights in his hair and his tanned complexion completed his *California dream come true* look. Jackson Templeton, Brigid thought, was a walking, talking tourist attraction. She could picture him in a commercial with a voiceover saying: *Book a stay at our fabulous Lake Tahoe resort and wake up to this!*

What red-blooded woman could resist? She raked her hand through her tousled curls, considering whether to ask how long he intended to stay in a separate bedroom—but she already knew how he would respond: *however long you want me to.*

And that was an answer she simply couldn't give him yet.

Part of her, the flesh and blood part, was more than ready, but her feelings for Jackson were still akin to infatuation, and she didn't want to stake her marriage on chemistry and crushes. They'd had a connection that was deep and true, once, and she wanted that back. Jackson deserved a wife who loved him with her whole heart.

Brigid stifled a sigh, crossed the room to open the door to a veranda that overlooked the lake and the surrounding Sierra Nevada peaks. The smell of damp air and pine wafted in—the same scents that made her dream so vivid. She shook out her hands. "Shall we breakfast on the terrace?"

"Where else?" Jackson settled a tray with two covered plates, coffee and juice on the outdoor table and pecked her on the lips. "You slept well, I hope."

She dropped into a wrought-iron chair and waited for him to sit next to her. "This smells delicious."

"Waffles." He winked. "I know what my wife loves."

"Thanks."

"I ordered both orange juice and tomato juice. Coffee, of course." He uncovered the platters to reveal the full fare—waffles, bacon, scrambled eggs and potatoes.

"You don't expect me to eat all of this."

"Up to you, but I've planned a big day. My advice is to carb up."

"What are we doing?"

"You first. I asked if you slept well, and you dodged the question."

She bit into a piece of bacon and decided it was under-cooked, put the remainder of the strip back on her plate and dabbed grease off her fingers with her napkin. "Sorry. I didn't want to spoil the mood, but I know I promised to be honest with you. So, no, I had a tough time falling asleep, and when I did finally doze off, I dreamed the dream."

"Are you keeping that diary like Dr. Tanaka recommended?"

"Yes. As soon as I wake up, I write down everything I remember. And it seems to be working. I'm able to recall more and more details."

He leaned forward and touched her knee. "And this morning? What new details did you remember?"

She let her gaze travel across the lake to the mountains. "The body of water. The ocean where the man drowns the woman—it's not an ocean at all. This whole time, I've been assuming it was the Pacific, but now I realize it's a lake—Lake Tahoe."

"Interesting. Are you certain that's not because we're here, and that's influencing you?"

"I don't think so. In the dream, there's a ring of mountains surrounding a lake, but it's not only that. I'm walking on a beach —that's the first time I've recalled that part—and it has to be Tahoe because I'm reminiscing about my parents; about the summer we spent at Camp Richardson, and I'm thinking about how the camp is just down the road."

"So, in your dream, are you a teenager?"

"No. I'm all grown up, looking back on a long ago summer. And I wade in the water, and then I see a hand dart above the surface, then a struggle, and then the man holding a woman under." She shuddered. "It's awful. I just don't know why I would dream such a terrible thing. I've been reading Freud's book, *The Interpretation of Dreams*, and according to dear old Sigmund, dreams represent unfulfilled wishes."

"I hate to contradict the father of psychoanalysis, but you'll never convince me that you *wish* you could witness a murder."

"That's my point. So what *does* it mean? There's obviously something quite important about it. Otherwise I wouldn't keep having it. If my subconscious has something to tell me, I wish it would just come out and say it, instead of making me decode a damned nightmare."

"You don't have to sort it out today... or maybe ever. Maybe just talking about it and writing down these details is enough. Maybe in time, you'll realize it's only a dream and there's nothing to be afraid of."

"And then it will just go away?"

He wiped his mouth and dropped his napkin. "Let's hope so. Thanks for keeping me looped in. Your trust means everything to me. I think we're making a good start toward rebuilding our marriage."

"I agree. So, I've answered your question. Now it's your turn. What have you got planned?"

"Nothing much. Just a multi-pronged adventure to make you fall head over heels in love with me again—all in one day."

"Sounds ambitious, but I'm in. I'd love to hear the specifics."

"First, we're going to ride bikes up to Emerald State Park, and then, we'll hike down to Vikingsholm Castle. That's my itinerary, anyway. But I'm open to suggestions if you—"

She jumped up and hugged him. "Sounds amazing. Thank you!" Her parents had often recounted the history of Lake Tahoe's hidden castle, but she'd never actually seen it. You could only get there by boat, or by hiking down a steep trail in Emerald Bay State Park. Then, once you got to the castle itself, the tours operated at set times. Her parents hadn't been able to fit a tour in between their off hours, but they'd promised to take her the next time they worked the summer at Camp Richardson.

"You've never been?"

"No," she said, and cut her gaze away. "We were planning to go, but then my mother had her stroke, and we never made it back to Tahoe."

He rose, pulling her up with him, wrapped his arms around her and rested his chin on top of her head. "I'm sorry. If Vikingsholm brings up sad memories, we won't go. We can do anything else you like instead."

"Absolutely not." She sighed against his chest, listening to his heart. "I want to go to Vikingsholm. And I want to go with *you*."

At the bottom of the steep, dusty trail, Brigid caught sight of Vikingsholm, and it made her breath catch. Flanked by towering pines, the castle was even more impressive than she'd imagined. A formidable example of Scandinavian architecture with massive boulders sewn together with mortar, hewn timber, intricate carvings of gargoyles and battling dragons, a thatched roof where, in season, wildflowers bloomed—Vikingsholm was straight out of a fairy tale.

Her gaze froze on carved serpent heads, and, despite the heat, she shuddered, suddenly reminded how wicked some fairy tales can be.

"I'm off to find tickets for the tour," Jackson said, and then abandoned her.

Taking respite on a bench near the entrance, she continued to study the Norse carvings, and an eerie feeling made the back of her neck bristle.

There was something disturbingly familiar here, but she couldn't put her finger on it.

Of course, her parents had described Vikingsholm many times, so maybe that was all this creepy sense of déjà vu amounted to.

There was no monster hiding under the bed—only her childish imaginings. It would be foolish to let such nonsense ruin their plans. This was a perfect opportunity to grow closer to Jackson, the man she'd promised to love and to cherish until death parted them.

And just because her muscles were twitching, and she was short of breath—that didn't mean she was going to have another panic attack. She'd indulged in a big breakfast, then followed that with a long bike ride and a steep hike at an altitude she wasn't acclimated to. Glancing about at all the other panting hikers, it seemed unlikely she was the only one who felt as if their death was imminent.

This was a simple case of misinterpreting her body's physiologic signals as anxiety.

Remove yourself from the situation before it's too late.

That was what Dr. Tanaka had advised, but…

Jackson returned with their tickets. "Tour starts in twenty minutes."

She resisted the urge to run into his protective arms. "I hope the castle is air-conditioned."

"Your face is flushed, but give it a minute and you'll cool down. You're just overheated from the hike." He picked up her wrist. "Or maybe my diabolical plan is working. Your pulse is jumping like a rabbit… or a woman in love."

With so many ways to interpret her body's signals, why not choose the most positive? "I am having a lovely time with you —" her gaze fell on a gargoyle "—but these spooky carvings give me the heebie-jeebies. Everywhere I turn I see snakes, or are they dragons?"

"Don't look at them. Look at me instead." He rested his hands on her shoulders and turned her toward him. "I'm here, and as long as I live, I promise I will never let anyone hurt you. There's nothing to be afraid of, Brigid."

Their eyes locked, and as they gazed at one another, something shifted inside her, like the barriers between them were physically melting away. "Jackson, I feel—"

"Excuse me. Sorry to interrupt. But, aren't you Jackson Templeton—*Stone Songbird*? Can I get an autograph?" A woman, mid-forties, dark, wet hair, braided Princess Leia style, wearing a one-piece yellow bathing suit and sheer cover-up, inserted herself between Brigid and Jackson, breaking the spell.

Brigid stepped back, wanting to hang on to the emotion— that fleeting certainty she'd felt that Jackson was *right* for her and she for him—but it was too late, the moment was lost. Something precious had been within her grasp, and she'd let it slip away.

"I'm afraid I don't have a pen," Jackson said.

The woman handed Jackson her phone.

"Of course. Okay." He politely snapped a selfie of the two of them.

Meanwhile, Brigid planted herself on the bench again, to wait it out, smiling back at Jackson whenever he sent a glance her way.

She knew the drill.

These days, Jackson didn't get recognized that often—many of his fans had aged out, but when one person spotted Stone Songbird, it inevitably turned into a cavalcade. Jackson didn't encourage the attention, but when it found him, he was always generous with the selfies and autographs, taking time to listen to stories of how *The Songbirds* had impacted someone's life. Today, about a dozen people, who'd been waiting for the castle tour, swarmed him.

Brigid sipped water, crossed and uncrossed her legs, checked her watch—it'd been nearly fifteen minutes since the braided-hair lady started the avalanche of autograph seekers, and now, the crowd began, ever so slowly, to disperse, until, finally, only two middle-aged women, remained.

Brigid was shaking the last drop from her water bottle into

her mouth when the women suddenly turned and raced down the hill toward the beach.

Jackson came over and extended his hand. "Sorry about that."

She let him pull her to a stand. "Not your fault. You can't help being you. But what happened? Those two left in a hurry."

"I told them I'd seen Mark Zuckerberg down on the beach."

The social media king was one of many celebrities with homes on Lake Tahoe. "That's kind of genius."

Jackson grinned. "I feel mean, but the tour's about to start, and I did mention, several times, that my wife was waiting for me. They just wouldn't take the hint. Do you think I'm a jerk?"

"I think you're great, and I can't wait to get you back to the hotel." Surprising herself, she tiptoed up and gave him a peck on the lips.

His hand coasted up and down her back and she felt her body softening in all the right places. "Are you sure?"

Lust or love or both?

She wasn't. Not quite, but before she had a chance to respond with an honest *almost*, she heard a bell clang, signaling the start of the tour. "Saved by the bell." Laughing, she tugged him toward the entrance where the guide, an older woman in a park uniform was already speaking.

"If everyone could please stay together and remember—no wandering off on your own." The guide extended one arm, patting the air with a downward palm, leaving no doubt about who was in charge. "I'll be your host for the tour, and it's my pleasure to tell you, as a girl, I stayed here as Mrs. Lora Knight's guest. In nineteen twenty-eight, Mrs. Knight built her magnificent summer home in the Scandinavian style she dearly loved..."

With their guide narrating, the group filed in through the magnificently carved entryway making their way room by room through the public parts of the house. Now a museum, Vikingsholm had been preserved with an eye to its rich history, keeping either the original furnishings or substituting exact replicas throughout. Inside, the serpent motif continued, but here the foreboding sense of doom Brigid had felt outdoors, gave way to enchantment.

In the parlor, the omnipresent ferocious dragons were tempered by yellow tulips carved from wood, a blue writing desk stenciled with pink flowers, an antique typewriter, a piano forte. Brigid could easily imagine Mrs. Knight and her guests gathered round that instrument, singing and recounting stories.

But the kitchen was her favorite room, with its dishcloth hanging over the faucet, the counter strewn with colanders, canisters, serving spoons and whatnot. A painted white ice box, its doors flung open, waited for *Cook* to hurry in with the butter. Brigid envisioned the scene, felt the room come alive. Mrs. Knight and her staff and her summer guests were real people, not some characters in a story, and they'd left their mark—the air was drenched with their humanity.

"Thank you," she whispered to Jackson, as they moved on, entering Mrs. Knight's personal bedroom.

"You're welcome. I take it the place is growing on you."

"It's truly wonderful. Magnificent, in fact." She pointed. "Imagine sitting down at your desk and looking out the window at..."

"That's Fannette Island."

And that quickly, her body's alarm system rang out. She knew, instantly, this was the moment Dr. Tanaka had warned her about. Her fingers tingled, her vision dimmed. Her knees threatened to buckle.

"Fannette Island is the only island on Lake Tahoe," the guide continued her narration as if Brigid's world wasn't spinning out of control.

"I'm going to step away for a minute. I need air," Brigid managed, backing out of the room.

The next thing she knew, she was outside the castle, with no recollection of how she'd gotten there. She didn't remember putting one foot in front of the other, or Jackson following her. But he must have because he was here—by her side.

"What's happening?" Jackson's voice reverberated spookily in her ears.

She faced the beach, her eyes drawn by that island. Pulled by some unseen force, she strode toward the water, and then made a sharp left, heading into a forest of giant pines.

"Brigid! Wait!"

With her heart pounding, she broke into a run.

"Brigid!"

Faster!

He was gaining on her.

Faster!

She stumbled over an exposed root, and Jackson reached out, catching her before she hit the ground, lifted her up, pressed her body against his.

"Let me go!" She drew back, pounding his chest with her fists. "Let me go!"

And then she was running again, caught in a tumbling kaleidoscope of trees and sky; the wind whipping her legs, the birds screaming a frenzied warning in her ears.

"Brigid! Stop! Look out!"

Ahead she spied the edge of a rocky cliff, beside her trees, behind her... *him.*

She was trapped.

Hide!

The enormous pines were her only hope. She ducked behind the broadest trunk in sight, and made herself as small as she could, wished herself invisible.

"Brigid, honey. It's only me. Please come out. Let me help you."

She wrapped her arms tightly around herself hoping, praying, he wouldn't hear her panting.

"Sweetheart." He approached her tree, one arm extended. "Take my hand. Let's get you home."

A sob caught in her throat.

"I won't force you, but you can't hide behind that tree all day. I can see you, so you might as well come out."

"S-stand back," she ordered.

He put his hands in the air and backed away slowly. "Come on, Brigid. I'm not going to hurt you. *No one* is going to harm you. Remember my promise."

As long as I live, I promise I will never let anyone hurt you.

Her racing thoughts circled back to the words he'd spoken earlier, the sound of his heart, beating in her ear when she'd laid her head on his chest.

"How did you know?" she whispered.

"Know what? Tell me, Brigid. Let me help."

"You *know*. Why did you bring me here? To the castle. To *this* place with *that* view of the island."

"I'm sorry. I didn't mean to upset you. I just thought it would be a nice place to spend the day. You've mentioned it before."

"I haven't."

"Yes, Brigid, we talked about this. You said you wanted to come here with your parents, before your mother got sick. I can see, now, it's been too much. It hasn't been that long since your accident. The bike ride, the hike, the nostalgia—"

"No! I'm not sick. I'm not so frail I can't handle a hike. Down there is the beach from my dream. Don't you understand what that means?"

"I wish I did," he said. "Please, my love. Please trust me. Whatever it is, you can tell me."

If only it were that easy. But how could she trust him, or *anyone*, when she couldn't even trust her own thoughts and feelings? She stepped out from behind the tree. "This is it. This is the place."

"Darling, that's only a dream. And dreams, not even nightmares, can hurt you—they're not real."

"But this place *is* real. And that means it's not just a nightmare, Jackson. It's a *memory*... hiding inside a dream."

TWENTY-ONE

Outskirts of Cielo Hermoso
North San Diego County, California

A giant mechanical mouse with long, pointy incisors crashed a pair of cymbals together, crescendoing in an ear-splitting clang. Then, thankfully, the curtains on stage drew shut, shrouding the monster until the next show—which hopefully would not be for a very long while.

Brigid shivered as the corner of her paper napkin curled beneath a blast of cold air from the vent above their booth. The black vinyl upholstery was cracked like marble and the stuffing leaking out of the corner was stained blood red—from pizza sauce, she *hoped*. Outside, a driving rain pelted the window, while the storm howled, wolf-like, against the backdrop of a dark sky, though it was barely 4 p.m.

"I feel like I'm in a horror movie." Brigid half expected Mosely the Mouse to jump out from behind the curtain wielding an axe.

"You used to love this place." Nash planted his elbows on the table and rested his chin in his hands. "My bad. I guess I thought it would fun for old times' sake. Bring back some good memories."

"It's changed." There was no smiling eight-year-old Tish, cuddled beside her, clapping her hands and laughing and making the world seem impossibly bright.

She missed that Tish.

"Order number two seventy-four. Number two seventy-four." A man's macabre voice crackled over a microphone.

"Be right back." Nash dragged one finger across his neck, made a death-like gurgling noise, then grinned. "Isn't that what you always say just before you get your throat cut in one of those slasher flicks?"

"Hilarious."

"Couldn't resist. But seriously, I shall return bearing one delicious mushroom pizza with extra cheese. Meanwhile, you should relax and enjoy the rich sounds and smells of birthdays past."

She forced a smile that disappeared as soon as he turned his back.

Located just off the interstate, around ten miles south of Cielo Hermoso, in what had once been a nice area, Mosley's Cheeseria appeared to have been hit hard by the same recent economic decline that had affected so many businesses. The parking lot was filled with potholes, and the restaurant empty save for a handful of customers, although Brigid hoped that was due to the rain. If this was what business was like on a sunny day, she didn't think Mosley's would last much longer.

And that would make her sad.

Because Nash was right: she used to love this place. Eleven years ago, the pizza had tasted as good as any, and the delight it brought their daughter, the face time with a busy Nash, had elevated Mosley's to the best joint around. Plus, it had been the site of Tish's sixth, seventh, and eighth birthday parties. But then, Tish had prematurely declared herself too grown up for "stupid talking mice"... much like she'd, now, prematurely declared herself ready to drop out of college in order to move in with an older man with questionable judgment.

Not that Brigid didn't believe in second chances.

She did.

And to be fair to Christian, he seemed to have turned his life around. Nash said he was one of his best employees in his real estate firm. Hard working, a fast learner. He was studying for his real estate exam and Nash expected him to pass with flying colors. As soon as he got his license, Nash planned to move Christian up from his assistant to sales. With his good looks—a big plus in any sales industry—and Nash's connections, Christian might well be earning six figures in no time, and that could multiply exponentially in the stock market—Nash was already tutoring him on investment strategies.

But where did all that leave Tish?

A faint scent of burnt crust grew stronger, and the queasy feeling in Brigid's stomach intensified, when Nash set a steaming hot pizza pie onto the table and slid back into the booth across from her.

"Tell me," he said, as he shoveled a slice for her, and then one for himself, onto a serving plate. "What's on your mind?"

She put a hand on her stomach and nudged her plate to the side. "A couple of things, actually. Thanks for meeting me, and I'm sorry if I'm being a wet blanket. This was a fun idea, that just didn't..."

"Pan out?" He turned his palms up. "Man, I crack myself up. But, yeah, Mosley's has gotten older—like us, I guess."

"Flatterer."

"Hey. You're as beautiful as the day I met you. Do you remember that day?" His hand stretched across the table.

"Nash. Please, don't make this more difficult."

He pulled back, and his smile dimmed. "I'm sorry. That was out of line. I don't want to put either of us in a difficult position. I guess I shouldn't have told you how I felt that day in the hospital. I-I just didn't expect it. But when I thought I might lose you..."

"Stop. We agreed—"

"We did. I promise, I'll try not to... No. I *will not* put you in an uncomfortable position. I know you love Jackson, and I do love Charity. We're both committed to our marriages. The past is the past. Right?"

"Right."

"But we have a daughter."

"We do."

"I'm assuming that's why you wanted to see me. It sounded urgent."

"Did I say urgent?"

"It wasn't what you said, it was your tone. I figured it was Tish. Especially since we were interrupted the other night by the lights going out and we didn't get to finish our conversation. I know the situation isn't ideal—"

"It's a disaster."

"Moving in with Christian or dropping out of school?"

"Both. And there's so much more that worries me."

"Such as?"

"I don't know if he's a good guy or not."

"Is there something specific that makes you say that?"

"Oh, I have a list. Starting with the fact that he's older, and Tish is more susceptible to his influence because he's Hope's uncle. Then there's that time at the family barbeque he was upstairs alone in my house for ages—I think he was snooping, or possibly even stealing."

"Are you missing something?" Nash brought a fist to his mouth.

"No, and I suppose that's an unfair assumption on my part.

But I don't like the way he speaks for Tish. When I visited her at USC her friend invited her over and he declined without even consulting her. And the worst, of course, is that he lied about Jackson and me having an affair."

"I'm so sorry about that. I don't know where he got that idea, but Charity cleared it up with both of them. Tish was going to call you."

"She did." Brigid released a long breath. "And she apologized, which was not necessary at all. But, believe it or not, Tish is not the main thing that I want to talk about. I realize, now, that what you said at the barbeque is right. The more we fight her about school and Christian, the more she's going to dig in her heels. The important thing is we're on the road to rebuilding our relationship. Charity setting the record straight for her about Jackson and me was a turning point in my relationship with Tish. I don't want to do anything to risk the progress she and I have made—even though I'm sure she's making a terrible mistake."

Nash scarfed down a triangle of pizza and poured beer from a pitcher into a mug.

"Is that your second beer? The roads are—"

He set the mug down, and it thunked against the wooden tabletop. "Point taken I'll switch to water. You're right about drinking and driving, but have you ever considered that you might be wrong about Tish?"

"Meaning?"

"Meaning she's got a good head on her shoulders. I think we should trust her. Look, I want her to go to a fancy school as much as you do. But—"

"It's not about USC being 'fancy'. It's about her getting the absolute best education she can. I would've given anything to—"

"No. You wouldn't have given anything. I know this because you didn't. You chose to drop out of school to help your family when your mom had her stroke. I know you wish you could have gone to college, but I think, even if you had a time machine, you'd do the same thing all over again."

"I... oh, no. Nash, do you think, because *I* dropped out of high school, that's influencing Tish to think education isn't important?"

He reached out again, but seemed to quickly think better of it, hastily wrapping his hand around his water glass. "No way. It's not that. She's just confused. She lost her best friend. Her parents got divorced. And who knows? Maybe she and Christian are really in love. I don't want to be the one to interfere with true love. Do you?"

"No. I—you're right. We can't live our children's lives for them. Only, I really, really want to."

"Sorry, ma'am. Those are the rules." He slugged his water back and finished another slice. "This pizza tastes better than it smells. Are you gonna have some or what?"

She looked down at burnt mushrooms swimming in orange grease. "You take it home for Charity."

At that, he threw back his head. "You are too generous."

"No, really." She smiled slyly. "I want her to have it."

"Okay. We'll box the rest up for her before we go, if it makes you smile, I'm all for that. But how am I going to explain what I'm doing with a Mosley's Cheeseria box?"

Her shoulders stiffened. "You didn't tell her you were meeting me here."

"I will. But first, I thought I'd find out what it's about. You told Jackson, then?"

"I did."

"And how did he take that?"

"He's fine with it. I don't have any secrets from him."

"Good. Then I won't worry about his reaction. Not that I—"

"Look, it's getting late, so I better get on with it. I need to talk to you about my thirty-sixth birthday. The night I got so drunk I blacked out." Just saying those words aloud made her blush.

"Okay. Do you mind my asking why, all of a sudden, you want to bring that up again? It was a long time ago, and I don't hold it against you. I don't think you should hold it against yourself either. One night of overdoing it isn't anything to—"

"I need to know *exactly* what happened."

"Why?"

"Because I'm asking. Because it's my life, and I have a right to know."

"Yes. And I'm more than willing to give you a blow by blow, but you making a big deal over the past, out of the blue, worries me. I know you, Brigid. I can see something's not right. But if you don't feel like explaining yourself to me, I guess I understand."

She held out her mug. "Half a glass. No more."

He took her mug and tipped it to discourage the beer from frothing as he poured from the pitcher. "Say when."

"When." If she was going to drink even this much beer, she supposed she better choke down some of the pizza, too. She stared at him, staring at her.

"Either you trust me or you don't," he said. "But if you don't, then why're we here?"

Because she needed information.

Because even though her dream might not be a perfectly duplicated memory—she knew enough from reading Freud's *The Interpretation of Dreams* to realize her nightmare wasn't likely to be identical to her actual experience—it had to have been triggered by a real event. And that event happened near Vikingsholm; otherwise Fannette island, an island she'd supposedly never seen, couldn't wind up in her dream.

She'd walked that beach before—of that she was dead certain.

"Brigid?"

Nash didn't need to know about her nightmare, but she ought to share something with him as a gesture of good faith, since she was asking for his help. "I've been having some problems since my accident—I'd rather not go into too much detail, but Dr. Tanaka asked me if, in the past, I've ever lost any pieces of time."

He was silent for seconds, maybe a full minute, and then he said, "When did you start seeing Dr. Tanaka again?"

"I started up right after my release from the hospital."

"Is it helping?"

"I think so. But I'm trying to get to the bottom of something, and I'm hoping with your help I can resurrect some buried memories."

"And you think the night of your blackout—"

"I don't know if what happened that night is relevant or not, but if there's more to it, if I suffered some kind of trauma that I've been repressing... I know it's a stretch, but I want to leave no stone unturned. I need to get back to being myself—not my old self, my new self."

"I don't know what you mean by that."

"It's not important that you do. Can we get back to what happened that night? I worry there are things you never told me. If I've buried a memory..."

He pushed a hand through his hair. "I'm sorry. I always figured that what happened that night was simply the result of too much booze. But maybe I should have been more forthcoming with you. I didn't want you to feel embarrassed or ashamed, so I might have minimized things. If that's hurt you in any way, I feel terrible."

"So you're saying there's more to the story than my getting drunk and passing out."

"Yes," he whispered. "I'm afraid there is."

TWENTY-TWO

Cold beer and pizza grease clashed and curdled in Brigid's gut as she gazed out the window, sheeted with rain. Her instinct was to flee, to run away and spare herself the humiliation of what was to come, but the downpour outside, and her desperation for answers stopped her. She shouldn't have waited so long to face whatever happened that night.

There's no truth so terrible it's worth the consequences of hiding it from *yourself*.

But maybe losing her memory of that night wasn't like her emotional amnesia at all. Other people get blackout drunk and forget what they've done—only Brigid wasn't that kind of a drinker, and it had never happened to her before or since. Dr. Tanaka thought that because she was experiencing a dissociative reaction now, she might have had a dissociative reaction, of some type, in the past, forgetting, not just feelings, but whole memories.

The bad news was Brigid had, indeed, lost a piece of time *before* her accident at Supper Club—the night of her thirty-sixth birthday. The good news was Nash had witnessed the entire debacle. She might have repressed her own memory, but his worked just fine.

"Where do you want to start?" Nash asked, his voice soft, kept low even though there was no one at any of the nearby tables to overhear.

A stick, hurled by the storm, slammed against the window next to the booth, and they both jumped.

"I'll go first," she said. "Starting with everything I remember, and then you can pick up the story where my memory leaves off, or... if your recollection doesn't mesh with mine—"

"I'll jump in."

She downed water to wash away the bitter taste in her mouth. Beer wasn't going to make this any easier. She wasn't much of a drinker, and that was how the trouble had started... "I remember being so happy to be in Tahoe with all of our friends. It made me feel important that you arranged a special Supper Club birthday bash. We all stayed in that nice hotel right on the water—but most of the group was in the main building. You and I rented one of those detached bungalows—on the premises but more secluded. You took me for a romantic birthday dinner at The Lakeview. The chateaubriand was overcooked, and they made it up to us with a free bottle of champagne."

"On top of the wine we'd had with appetizers. And I was driving, so I only had a sip. You, I'm afraid, drank most of it."

"Right... you suggested I take it easy."

"In hindsight, I should've insisted you'd had enough, but I'd hate to think I'm one of those obnoxious, controlling husband types—and it was your birthday. What else do you remember?"

She closed her eyes, clasped her hands together in her lap, concentrated on putting herself back there, in the moment, breathing deeply, in and out, until she could hear the drone of conversation from the other diners at The Lakeview, the strains of soft music in the background, taste those fizzy bubbles with notes of vanilla and almond on her tongue:

"I'm not going to waste a free bottle! Not on my birthday. And anyway, I have you to watch out for me." I'm feeling lonely, even though Nash has planned a perfect night, an entire weekend actually.

Although maybe a weekend alone would've been more romantic than dragging the whole group to the lake with us. Lately, he seems bored when it's just the two of us. Like now, he's checking his phone instead of listening to me. "Can't you put that away for one night?"

"Rollin just texted. The gang's over at the Waterside Bar, and they've scored a table for ten. You still want to meet up with them after dinner?"

"If you do."

"We can't disappoint them. Everyone wants to party with the birthday girl."

My head is already spinning, and if the night goes late, I know I'll fall straight to sleep. Which means no birthday sex. But I'm not sure if I want that with Nash. I wish I wanted it.

After dinner, we drive to the Waterside Bar and everyone is waiting.

There's cake... the cream cheese frosting melts on my tongue. It's sweet; so sweet I wash it down with a sip of wine. The light sparkles on the deep-red liquid swishing in my glass.

Jackson is lounging next to me. He presses my hand. His fingers tighten around my wrist, sending sparks shooting up my arm. "Careful not to spill your wine."

"You wanna dance with me?" The music throbs, and he doesn't seem to hear me. I wobble to my feet, go around behind him and loop my arms around his neck. I whisper in his ear. "You wanna dance?"

He stands. I sense his hands at my waist. I'm slipping, sliding, but he holds me up, helps me find the dance floor. I don't know what happened to my wine. I'm thirsty, and I want more to *drink but then, I stop thinking about the wine, because I'm in Jackson's arms. And I feel... I feel...*

Nash and Charity bump into us on the dance floor.

Charity's face is red, her voice edgy, cutting underneath the music like a knife skinning a fish. "It may be your birthday, hon, but that's my husband you're slobbering all over. We should change partners."

I raise my head off Jackson's chest, and see her dark eyes flash. "I'm sorry."

I'm not sorry. I don't want to change partners. She can have Nash if she wants him.

Brigid opened her eyes and blinked in the dim light of the pizzeria. "Oh, no. I-I just remembered something. Was I flirting—?"

"With Jackson. Yeah," Nash said.

"And Charity—"

"Smoke was coming out her ears."

"And you?"

"I understood. Hell, the guy was a teen heartthrob. You admitted to me when we first got to know Jackson and Charity that you'd had posters of Jackson up in your bedroom when you were in high school. You were drunk that night, and you'd been feeling insecure—at least I thought you'd been doubting yourself."

"Why would you think that?"

"Because you'd been acting more needy than usual. Whenever I had to work late, you'd get suspicious, grill me for details about where I'd been, who I'd been with. Forgive my saying so, but it seemed like you were having a mid-life crisis. Worrying that you weren't as attractive to me as you'd once been—even though it wasn't true. So, that night, I chalked your behavior up to a combination of liquor and you worrying about another candle on your birthday cake."

"You weren't even a little jealous?"

"In hindsight, I wish I had been. Clearly, I missed the big flashing neon sign spelling out how unhappy you were. If I could turn back the clock, I'd sweep you up, out of his arms, take you home and..." He rubbed his forehead. "I wonder, if I'd been more macho back then, if I'd punched him in the nose, right there on the dance floor, would that have proved to you how much I loved you. But that's not me."

"I'm glad it's not you. And it wouldn't have made me happy for you to get into a fight with Jackson. But what happened after that? I'm trying, but I have nothing but a big blank hole in my memory—until the next day, when I woke up in our bungalow—it was late and the others had gone back to Cielo Hermoso. I remember feeling badly that I didn't say goodbye."

"Two o'clock in the afternoon you woke up—or came to. I'm not sure which is the more accurate description. I thought you needed the sleep, so I arranged for a late checkout. And then we went home, and I tried to act like it wasn't a big deal, but it did shake me up. Not flirting with Jackson, but how out-of-it you got and..."

She turned, watching the rain spattering in fits and starts against the pane. "So what happened next? I made a scene at the Waterside Bar, and then what?"

"You wanted another drink, and I stupidly let you have one. If it makes you feel any better, Charity was wasted, too. So, after about half an hour of you two shooting barbs at each other, Jackson hauled her back to the hotel. Then, Jamal and I managed to get you out to the car, and I drove you back to our bungalow. You may want to talk with Jamal or the others about what happened at the nightclub. But there's not much more to tell."

Her cheeks felt hot, her hands were trembling, but at least she was hearing it from Nash and not some stranger. They knew each other as well as anyone can know another person—the good and the bad. And as embarrassing as this was, the only real difference between what happened that night and what she remembered was how badly she'd behaved—flirting with Jackson while he was still married to Charity. "So you took me back to the hotel, and I slept it off."

Outside, the wind whistled hauntingly, rain gushed as the storm picked up momentum again.

"There's more," he said, and his tone compelled her to meet his gaze.

"Okay."

He reached across the table and took her hands, and she didn't resist. "I'm sorry to have kept this from you. Are you sure you want to know?"

She nodded, not because she *wanted* to know, but because she had no choice. She couldn't keep burying the truth in the basement of her mind if she wanted to feel whole again.

"Here goes. You passed out on our bed, or so I thought. I was hot and tired and fed up with you by then, and I took a long, cool shower. I just left you there. I assumed you'd be okay, but when I came out of the bathroom, you were gone, the dress and heels you'd been wearing strewn on the floor. I was beside myself. I threw on some sweats and went out searching for you. I considered calling the cops, but I didn't want to create problems when you were probably just out for a walk, sobering up. Eventually, I went back to the hotel, and I waited for hours. I told myself, if you weren't home by morning, then I'd get the police involved. I was just about to call them when I heard something banging around outside."

"Me?"

"Yes. And I've never seen you like that. You seemed even more drunk than you'd been at the club. You'd changed into a sundress—I recognized it as yours, and I was relieved you hadn't run out naked or anything. But man, you were a mess. Clothes and hair wet—not soaking, more like you'd been swimming in your clothes at some earlier time, and now they were beginning to dry." He cast his gaze back over his shoulder and lowered his voice even more. "You reeked of vomit."

She yanked her hands from his.

"When I asked if you were okay, you managed to tell me you were fine, but you flat out refused to say where you'd been. Then, I got you cleaned up—I checked you, in the shower, for cuts or bruises or any sign that you'd gotten hurt, but didn't find anything—except your feet were pretty banged up. You remember that, the next day, the bruises on your feet?"

"You told me I'd taken my shoes off and walked barefoot from the car over rocks. I-I can't believe you never told me any of this. Why didn't you?"

Bits of napkin littered the table where she'd shredded hers to bits.

He lifted his eyes. "I'm sorry. I shouldn't have lied about your feet or anything else, but I didn't want you to feel ashamed. I see now that I should have told you the whole truth. But the next day, you said you were mortified that you'd gotten drunk—that you didn't know how you could face our friends. You couldn't even look me in the eyes. You seemed so sad, so... fragile, and it took you a long time to get back to being yourself, afterwards. I didn't want to add anything extra to the distress you already felt. I didn't see what good it would do to tell you, and I wanted you to get back to being Brigid."

Her hands found a new napkin to shred, but then, she exhaled a long breath and met Nash's eyes. Anytime she'd wanted answers, he would've provided them. She was the one who'd been running, not him. "It's me who's sorry. You're not responsible for my foolish behavior. I could have asked you, anytime, for details, but I chose not to. Thank you for telling me now—this is on me, not you."

"I'm glad it's finally out in the open. I hope it helps."

"It does." Because now she knew this wasn't a simple case of blackout drinking. Something had *happened* that night when she'd left the bungalow—and her nightmare was her scrambled mind's way of forcing her to face it.

TWENTY-THREE

San Diego, California

There are a few reasons that occur to me for choosing to rendezvous at the Balboa Park Rose Garden. According to my map, the three-acre site is a veritable maze, with over 1,700 plants and 220 varieties. Thus, reason number one, obviously, would be that you love roses... or the scent of roses... or bees... I hear some people are quite fond of bees.

To each his own.

Reason number two—you want to impress a lover of horti-culture—for example, your great-aunt Betsy who's in town for the week.

And finally, reason number three—you don't want to be seen or overheard.

The Balboa Park Rose Garden is the definition of hiding in plain sight.

Good news for me.

They will be comfortable.

I will be invisible.

As long as they haven't changed the meeting location from the concrete bench near the Marmalade Skies display, all will be well.

The brim of my hat is doing double duty today, both concealing my visage and preventing me from showing up later with a suspiciously sunburned face. I've chosen sunglasses that are neither too large or too small—I don't want my accessories to draw undue attention. I'm wearing a unisex gray T-shirt and khaki Bermuda shorts, like the volunteer staff do, and I've slapped on the name tag I managed to snag earlier for good measure.

While awaiting my targets, I've rather enjoyed strolling about the place. Of course I haven't had a chance to see everything, but so far, The Dark Lady roses are my favorite—dusky crimson with a pungent scent, and let's face it, an intriguing moniker.

I turn the map sideways and trace a path with my finger, finishing at a mandala-shaped garden labeled S4. It takes me a bit to walk there from my current position, and I'm glad I had enough foresight to arrive early.

Curled in my hand is a tiny listening device. I take a seat on the bench next to an elderly woman who is loosely holding a leash attached to a harness attached to a boy: a delightful hooligan who looks to be a preschooler.

"How old?" I ask as I smile at the boy who is threatening to trod into the flower bed.

"Four. My grandson." She offers the explanation as if one is needed. "And he's a handful, but also the love of my life."

"I bet that's mutual." I lean forward, like I'm checking out the row of ants between my feet, reach between my legs, and stick the microphone to the bottom of the bench.

I tug my lobe, adjusting my earpiece, and leap to my feet.

"Oh, I hope we didn't frighten you off. He'll settle down if I ask."

"No, no. I just remembered I've forgotten my phone at the front desk. By the way, be sure to make your way over to The Dark Lady display in S3. They're something else."

"Thanks for the tip. There's so much to choose from, and we can't cover the entire area in one day."

"So, The Dark Lady and... I bet your grandson will get a kick out of Yabba Dabba Doo, over in N6. It's a hike from here, but worth it. Let me help you up."

She didn't look all that frail, the way she was marshalling her charge like a steer-roper at the state fair, but I extend my hand anyway, to encourage her to get moving. I need this bench nice and empty in order to tempt Brigid and Roman into stopping and smelling the roses while they confab.

As much fun as it would be to sleuth along behind, as they traipse all over the garden, I'd have to settle for breadcrumbs—the leftover bits and pieces of conversation I'd be lucky enough to overhear—when I'm hungry for a feast. But if I can keep them on this bench, then I can listen in from a safe distance and hear it all.

"I'm Doreen, by the way," she says, ignoring my outstretched hand and rising to her feet without assistance.

"Nice meeting you." I point at my name tag and smile. Then hurry off in the direction of the volunteer desk.

I march a minute or two, and then turn on my heel, preparing to return to the bench to clear the way for Brigid and Roman, in case more interlopers have arrived, when I see I've gotten lucky. Roman's already in front of Marmalade Skies with one knee propped on the bench, waving Brigid over.

"So gorgeous. What a delightful idea, Roman. Can you believe I've never been here?" I hear the words plainly over my earbud, not a whisper of static, though the shuffle of her shorts is painfully magnified by the microphone as she takes her place beside him on the bench.

"Shall we walk and talk?" Roman asks.

I hold my breath.

"In a little bit, yes, but first, let's sit and relax. I got a late start, and I've been rushing around like mad. Besides, I want to give you my full attention. I worry I'll be distracted wandering among these beautiful roses."

He nods, and I exhale a jet of air.

Their backs are to me. I can move closer without drawing attention, so I do.

I stride toward the bench with the confidence of someone who has every right to be in this exact place at this exact time. I mean, if they spotted me and recognized me, all I'd have to do would be to peel off my name tag and pretend to gawk at the roses.

What a coincidence bumping into you two! It's a perfect day to visit the park. No, ha ha ha. I certainly did not spot the meeting on your Google calendar when I was snooping on Roman's phone.

I'm so close now, I can smell his cologne. It irritates me that he wore fragrance to a rose garden. The distinctive scents of each hybrid rose will be confounded with "Aventus by Creed".

I'm irritated, even more, by the awkward silence that's set up shop between those two.

Get on with it please.

At last, Roman clears his throat. "Thanks for meeting me."

Brigid must be, I'm sure, almost as curious as I am. "Thank you. I know this is personal, and I appreciate your willingness to share more detail with me about what's been going on with you. Your state of mind or anything else that led you to bring a gun to Supper Club."

"It's the least I can do. But I need your promise you'll keep this to yourself. You can't even tell Jackson."

I hear a quick sigh.

"He's my husband, Roman."

"I know, but I'm confiding in you because my behavior affected you, personally, and I feel I owe you an explanation. I don't want this getting around because I'm not sure who I can trust. Can I count on you to keep my secret?"

"I promise." Brigid adjusts her position on the bench, sideways, and for an instant I think she's spotted me.

I back up a step, and then drift away from the pair.

"You're making me nervous." Brigid is coming through loud and clear on my earbud. "What's going on?"

I pull the brim of my hat lower, just in case, but she hasn't noticed me—she's too focused on Roman.

"I feel I must warn you," Roman says.

"About what?"

I can hear their unease in the way their voices rise and fall, and I detect a tremor in Roman's. The microphone accentuates nuances I might not catch otherwise.

"I'm in financial trouble," he continues, "mostly because I made some damn poor choices in the stock market. I took risks I shouldn't have with my portfolio, but that isn't the only reason I'm in dire straits."

Do tell.

"My identity was stolen and, unfortunately, I wasn't well prepared for such an event. It's been going on more than a year. In the beginning, I was reluctant to report it, because I thought Farrah was behind most of the credit card charges. I just paid them... at first. Then someone used my personal information to open multiple new accounts, routing the bills to phony addresses. I never saw those bills, and they were never paid at all, and that devastated my credit rating."

There's a long pause before Brigid says, "I don't mean to offend you, but are you sure it wasn't Farrah?"

"I'm not one hundred percent certain, but I don't believe

she's behind this. The scheme is too complicated for someone with her lack of—she's just not cunning enough. You see, more recently, a rather large sum—I won't say how large—was transferred from my bank into an account in the Cayman Islands. I don't think Farrah is capable of setting up offshore accounts and then funding them. Regardless, the combination of credit card fraud, bank fraud and real losses in the stock market has put me in significant financial peril. I only managed to avoid bankruptcy by selling off a number of my assets. And now, certain investigative bodies are involved. They haven't outright accused me of wrongdoing, but they're asking lots of questions. I'm cooperating, of course."

"You mean—"

"The FBI," Roman whispers this.

Good thing they're not walking and talking or I would have missed this critical piece of information.

"The IRS too. So you see why I need you to keep this just between us."

Tick tock.

Just when I think she's been rendered speechless, Brigid says, "I'm even more worried about you now. Hearing all of this —understanding the scope of the problem, I wonder if you were truthful when you said, at Café Francois, that you never intended to harm yourself."

"I give you my word, I did not plan to hurt myself or anyone else. But I wasn't thinking clearly either. Grabbing that gun was irrational. I didn't even check to see if it was loaded. Brigid, I had this idea. I kept asking myself—I *keep* asking myself *who*? Who knows me well enough, who has enough access to my personal information they could hack into my accounts? And I keep coming up with the same answer—Supper Club."

"Is that the reason you skipped our yachting day and the reading at the bookshop?"

"Yes."

"I hate to see you cutting yourself off from your friends at a time like this. You need our support more than ever. I can't believe any of us would do such a thing. Surely, someone at your office, or, again, I'm sorry to say so, but Farrah has more access to your private information than anyone."

"I don't believe it's Farrah, but you could be right about someone at my firm. In any case, you should watch your pocketbook around the gang. And, please don't take offense, but I'm going to skip Jackson's concert at the museum. I know you worked hard on that American Music exhibit, and this concert means a lot to you, so I wanted to tell you in person. I don't know who I can trust in that crowd, and until I do, I won't be joining you at Supper Club or the museum or anywhere my so-called friends are."

A loud thud sounds, and I realize Brigid has knocked her purse off the bench.

She bends to pick it up, but I'm not concerned. She'd have to get on her hands and knees to spot the listening device.

"You're not to worry about hurting my feelings. If you don't feel comfortable coming to the concert tomorrow night, I understand. But I hate the way you're isolating yourself. Before we leave here today, I want you to swear that if you're feeling low, you'll call me."

"I said it before and I'll say it again, I never intended harm to anyone—myself included. My actions were worse than foolish—they were inexcusable—because you wound up getting hurt. I brought the gun on impulse—with no plan at all. And then, once I got there, I started to think that, maybe, if I said 'woe is me, I'm worth more dead than alive,' and showed the group I'd found my father's gun, I might smoke out the devil who did this to me. Make them feel so guilty they'd confess right then and there. But, looking back, I understand why that plan—that impulse—never had a chance of working."

"Because you've come to your senses and realized we're

your friends? That none of us would do anything so despicable?"

"No. I still think it's someone in the club. I mean that trying to make whomever feel sorry for what they've done to me would never work."

"Why not?"

"Because the devil doesn't feel guilt."

And on that count, Roman is right.

TWENTY-FOUR

Cielo Hermoso
North San Diego County, California

Farrah stumbled back to her seat.

"She's drunk," Charity whispered to Christian. "If Roman could see the spectacle his wife makes of herself whenever he's not around, he might think twice before shipping her off to a concert loaded with opportunity like this one."

"How do you mean opportunity?" Christian asked.

"Rich men. This place is loaded with them. And Farrah is having a field day. Probably picking out her next husband since Roman's finances have taken a turn," she rushed to finish her sentence just as the aforementioned cheeky woman dragged her chair closer to Charity.

Brigid had reserved a table upfront for family and friends at Jackson's concert for CHAM. Charity and Christian were on purse-watch, while Darya and Jamal, Nash and Tish mingled with the crowd. Rollin and Aiden were there, too, but those two were so busy canoodling they wouldn't have noticed if a crew pulled a moving van up and started loading the loot.

"Ooh. It's all so pretty," Farrah cooed in her ear.

Charity had to admit, Brigid had done a bang-up job with this event. The museum's outdoor garden was brimming with a mix of Stone Songbird fans, friends of the museum, and supporters of the Jackson R. Templeton Community Center.

Candles dotted the tables in between the fabulous center-pieces—bouquets of miniature guitars, keyboards and drums. Above, flowers hung upside down from canopies attached to ivy-covered poles, while transparent balloons, magically filled with colorful LED lights, floated about the grounds.

"Thanks very much." Jackson, microphone in hand, applauded the crowd, from center stage, after finishing his set. "I appreciate everyone coming out to support CHAM and the community center. If you haven't had a chance to check out the American Music exhibit, I'll just say this: It rocks!" He pumped his fist in the air, to a chorus of whoops and clapping. Once the applause died down, he added, "It's been my honor to play for you tonight, friends. And now, I'd like to suggest you stick around because, after a short break, the Jackson R. Templeton improv troupe is going to perform, and you don't want to miss this talented bunch of kids. It'll be a lot of fun, I promise you that."

"Oh, honey—" Farrah used her teeth to capture the olive off the swizzle stick in her martini "—you must be crazy."

Mildly interested in what Farrah meant, since it involved her, Charity shrugged a shoulder. "How so?"

Farrah leaned in so closely Charity could've failed a field sobriety test just from inhaling the woman's breath. Then Farrah pointed to the stage, where Jackson was busy securing his guitar onto a stand and speaking off mic to a group of teens— the kids from the community center, no doubt. "Stone Song-bird. What kind of cuckoo bird lets a man like that get away?"

"He didn't get away. I left him." Not that she cared what Farrah thought. Not that Farrah could ever understand what it was like to live with a man whose every expression, every gesture, reminded you of the child you'd lost. Still, she didn't want anyone, not even Farrah, to have the impression *she'd* been the one jilted.

"That's even worse. What a dumbass thing to do. Trading in Stone Songbird for Nash Clarence. C'mon, girl."

"Well, I think you might be confusing Jackson for the character he played on TV."

"I'm not confused at all—that is one fine man up on stage, singing his heart out. Jackson Templeton brought Stone Songbird to life. That show would've been nothing without him. People sure weren't tuning in just to watch a single mom raising a boyband... and where are the others now? No one knows or cares."

"Teddy just won CMA entertainer of the year."

"Besides Teddy."

"Genie just won an Oscar for a climate change documentary she directed."

"Genie who?"

"Genie Boston."

"Who's that?"

"The actress who played Lady Songbird."

"Oh, the *mom*." Farrah winked at Christian. "I bet you wish I had another drink."

"My wish is your command." He tipped an imaginary cap and scrambled to his feet. "Anyone else want anything while I'm up?"

And then he was off before Charity could say, "hell yes". She could use something to wash down the bile in her throat because Farrah was right about one thing, Jackson had been the star of that show. He was the real deal. The rest of the actors were good. Each one charismatic in their own way—but Jackson was the heartthrob that all the women, and plenty of the men, dreamed about. And, unlike most of the cast, he had real musical talent. He and Teddy were the only members of *The Songbirds* who actually played an instrument, and Jackson had written the song that made it to number one on the charts.

So, would she rather be married to Stone Songbird than Nash Clarence?

Yes, of course.

If they hadn't lost Hope, would she and Jackson have stayed together?

Probably.

But in truth, they'd never been suited for each other. Jackson was hardly Stone Songbird—he didn't want fame, or the lifestyle that came with it.

Nash, on the other hand, was all for living large. And unlike Jackson, he didn't expect Charity to sit at home, weeping, while he spent all his time hanging out with those lost puppies at the community center. Jackson had always been a do-gooder and a sucker for troubled teens, but it got so much worse after Hope died. He wanted to spend all his time with those kids, and she could hardly bear to look at them.

Too many memories of Hope.

When she was with Jackson, *everything* reminded her of what she'd lost, so, no, even if Jackson had suddenly gotten ambition and turned into Stone Songbird, things wouldn't have worked out between them.

But... she didn't love being replaced by Brigid.

Perfect, sweet Brigid, who could do no wrong in anyone's eyes. Brigid, who didn't appreciate how lucky she was to have a daughter like Tish. A living breathing child who would throw her arms around your neck and tell you she loved you.

Christian returned with two martinis. He handed one off to Farrah, and then Charity snatched the other out of his hand.

"Hey, that was for me," Christian complained.

Charity slurped it down in two gulps.

"I guess you needed it more than I did. Everything okay over here. What did I miss?"

"I don't know what you're talking about." She belched a quiet ladylike burp, then turned and beamed around the table. "Wasn't Jackson wonderful? I'm so proud of him."

Only she would've preferred he'd been half as willing to do her bidding as he was to do Brigid's.

"I didn't think we'd ever see him take the stage again," Rollin said.

"He did it for Brigid," Aiden chimed in. "Romantic, don't you think?"

"He did it for the community center," Charity corrected. "Christian, get me another drink."

* * *

Brigid shut the door to the green room behind her and glanced around, pleased to find Jackson sprawled on the couch with a champagne glass in his hand—she'd been looking for him ever since the improv group took to the stage. She'd expected him to join her at the group table for their performance, but he'd mysteriously disappeared—for over an hour—and hadn't responded to her texts until a minute ago. "Anybody hiding in the bathroom?" Brigid teased. "Or are we alone?"

"At last," Jackson said.

Another glass of champagne stood on the coffee table in front of him. "You're drinking for two, then?"

He laughed. "I poured you a glass of bubbly as soon as you texted you were on your way up. Let's toast your success."

"I already had champagne at the table, but I guess another won't hurt." Her one and only drink had been two hours ago. It'd been a long night and she was tuckered out, and happily surprised to find the green room empty save for Jackson. "Where is everyone?"

"The kids? They're out in the courtyard. Basking in the glow of their newfound fans," he said as he got to his feet and made his way over to her. He ran his hands down her arms, then tipped her chin up with one finger until their eyes met. "Thank you for tonight."

"Thank you. I'm the big hero, now—the miracle worker who got Stone Songbird back on stage. I know how hard that was for you, and it means a lot to me. The museum is getting a lot of attention tonight, and that means more funding when the city council makes their budget allocations next week."

"I'd do anything for you." His voice melted the room.

"Stop. The evening was a big success, thanks to you."

"It was your brilliant idea—the tie in between the American Music exhibit and the Jackson R. Templeton Community Center. We raised a lot of awareness tonight, and I'm sure we'll be getting more donations." He stepped in, dipping his face near hers, brushing her lips with a quick kiss. "I am so damn proud of the kids. I know, from all the applause, they were incredible out there."

"Is that why you snuck up here by yourself? I should've realized when I couldn't find you why you went into hiding. You didn't want the attention on you. You wanted the kids to feel like stars."

"Maybe. Good to know you missed me—"

"I did. And I'm not the only one. I've been looking for you for ages—so many people want to congratulate you. Everyone kept asking where you were, and I didn't know what to say. Why didn't you answer your phone?"

"You know me, I hate the spotlight. When my cousin talked me into auditioning for *The Songbirds*, it was one of the worst 'best things that ever happened to me'. I apologize for ducking out—I guess I just needed some space."

"It's fine. I don't mean to pressure you."

"You're not. And I love watching you in your element. I haven't seen you like this for a long time—you're positively beaming."

"I do love my job. Honestly, when I'm busy running around making sure everyone else is taken care of, it makes me forget my worries." With him so close, the glow of the evening clinging to him, she could feel her breathing speed up, a flush rising to her cheeks, muscles tightening in her abdomen. "Let's improv," she said.

"Okay." He grinned.

"What would you do if you were madly in love with me?"

"That's not improv," he said. "I am madly in love with you." His lips and tongue found hers, lingering, swirling until she was tumbling, falling.

She pulled back. "I think..."

"Don't say anything, Brigid. If you're not ready, that's okay."

"I was going to say, I'm falling in love with you—all over again."

"The old feelings are back?"

"It's hard to say if it's that, or if I'm making new ones."

She heard laughter and footsteps hurrying down the hall. "I need to go check on the volunteers. I want to let them know they can take any of the catering leftovers home. But I'll meet you at the front in, let's say, half an hour, and then we can go back to the house and pick up where we left off."

"Count on it," he said.

Moments later, she paused on the second floor loggia to lean over the banister and survey the courtyard below. Guests were still mingling, enjoying the crisp night air and conversation. She could see a small throng gathered around the kids from the community center and a woman with a mic interviewing them, a cameraman in the background. That was a nice surprise. She'd put out a press release, but she hadn't been sure they'd get television coverage. It was a testament to Jackson's evergreen appeal. Leaning farther forward, to listen in, she got a head rush. Maybe that second glass of champagne hadn't been such a good idea. She still had to see to the volunteers and count and log the ticket proceeds.

"Congratulations." Charity's voice preceded her as she ascended the stairs and took her place near Brigid. She looked stunning in a powder-pink silk gown, her dark hair swept into the kind of updo that took hours but seemed as though she'd simply gathered up her locks and casually clipped them into a designer barrette. "To you and Jackson."

How sweet. Brigid bit back a sarcastic retort. It was hard to hold her tongue when Charity had been making doe eyes at Jackson the whole time he'd been on stage.

"I haven't seen Jackson this happy since... well, I haven't seen him happy in a long time. His performance was magnificent," Charity said.

"It certainly was." So what, now that Jackson had the spotlight again, even for one night, Charity wanted him back?

Over her dead body.

Brigid covered her mouth to stop words she knew she'd regret. Obviously, that champagne had gone to her head—she'd forgotten she hadn't eaten all day. Anyway, Charity was the one who'd scuttled her marriage to Jackson, and she'd never given Brigid a reason to believe she regretted that decision. Charity's words were kind, her tone sincere. Brigid was the one thinking, if not behaving, like a tipsy fool. "He was wonderful. Tonight's success was all him."

"Don't be modest. It's hard enough to throw a party in one's home, much less create a public event like this. Just thinking about it makes my head swim. And how you got my husband... I mean... so sorry, I'm sure you'll forgive the slip."

Brigid's legs felt watery, and she stiffened her back, offered a smile she didn't feel.

"How you got *Jackson* to agree to perform, and even include 'Lovin' You Groovy Girl', is beyond me. Heaven knows I tried to get him to stage a comeback often enough, and he shot me down every time."

"It's hardly a comeback." Charity's plans, as usual, were far afield from Jackson's. "He only wants to raise awareness about the community center and the needs of underserved youth. And he wanted those kids to have a chance to perform and gain confidence. He did it for them."

"Sure. But he did it for you, too. He wouldn't have done it for me."

Brigid squeezed her heavy lids closed, and then opened them again. "What are you doing up here, anyway. This area is off limits to the public."

"I'm hardly 'public'. I wanted to congratulate Jackson. Rumor has it he's in the green room. Where is it?"

There was no point arguing. Brigid refused to ruin a perfectly wonderful evening with a petty disagreement. She extended her arm. "That way. Now, if you'll excuse me, I have the volunteers to see to."

"Congrats again!" Charity blew a kiss and turned away.

It was too warm. Brigid wiped perspiration from her forehead, and took a step, or rather a stumble forward. When she got to the volunteer table, she'd sit down, take a minute to rest.

She reached the top of the long marble staircase.

Looking down it made her dizzy.

She wobbled onto the top step.

Unbelievable.

She was such a lightweight. Two glasses of champagne and she could barely walk. She should go back to the green room, lie down for a few minutes and then let Jackson take her home. He could go down to the volunteer room and count the ticket sales for her...

At the same moment her knees threatened to buckle; she sensed a presence behind her and reached out for help. "Sorry, I can't seem to get my balance."

And then she felt it, not a reassuring, steadying hand held out to save her, but rather a quick, startling shove propelling her down the stairs.

TWENTY-FIVE

"Please, just take me home," Brigid said.

By the end of the night, Farrah was so wasted Brigid and Jackson felt obligated to make sure she got home safely, and so they'd buckled her into their Toyota Highlander, driven her to her house, and waited in the car while she fumbled with the door for several minutes before going inside.

Then, about a mile from Roman and Farrah's place, at a fork in the road, where one prong led home and the other back to highway (and the hospital), Jackson had pulled onto the soft shoulder and killed the engine.

Brigid checked her watch.

Midnight.

That meant they'd been hunkered down in the car with a "difference of opinion" for the past half hour.

"I think we should swing by the emergency room and have you checked out, just to be safe," Jackson said for the umpteenth time.

"I don't want to go to the hospital. I'm perfectly fine. I slid on my bottom down four stairs and got up on my own power. There's absolutely no need."

"You slipped or someone pushed you? Which is it? Because you've changed your story several times, and I don't know if you've dissociated again or—"

"Please listen to me. I'm not changing my story. I sensed someone behind me..." which was why she'd reached out for help, but found the railing instead "... and then I felt a shove. I slid down a few stairs on my bottom. But because I'd already grabbed the railing, I was able to quickly stop myself. I didn't hit my head. I'm not confused. I stood up and looked around, but there was no one there. So, I don't actually know whether or not someone pushed me, but I can't rule it out."

Jackson twisted in the driver's seat to face her and put both his hands on her shoulders. "I'm glad you're not physically hurt. I'm willing to take your word for it since you seem to be walking and talking just fine, but can you hear how crazy... sorry, how strange all of this sounds? On the yacht, you thought you saw Farrah drown—and that I'd drowned her. At Vikingsholm, you accused me of deliberately taking you back to your nightmare beach. Then you told me you believe your nightmare is actually a memory hidden in a dream—which is to say you think you witnessed a murder. And now, you're saying someone might have pushed you down the stairs at the museum."

"So, *you're saying* that even though I fell on my tush, it's my head you want examined."

"I'm worried about your state of mind... a little. Who, exactly, do you think pushed you?"

The intensity of his gaze told her he was not going to let her off the hook. But she knew, in her heart, he wouldn't like the answer. "*Might* have pushed me."

"If you want me to trust you when you say you don't need a doctor, then I need you to trust me, too. Sweetheart, what is going on?"

She shook her head. "When I got up, I didn't see anyone around but... just before I fell or slipped or was pushed or whatever... Charity and I were talking. And then she went to find you in the green room."

His hands tightened on her shoulders and even in the dim light she could see a muscle twitching in his jaw. "I know you don't like her, but Charity thinks the world of you, and she would never hurt you. And even though Charity and I are divorced, you should try to remember that she's Hope's mother."

"And you feel a need to defend her. I get it."

"I'm not defending her. I'm telling you straight up she would never do something like that. And besides, she was with me in the green room so—"

"So Charity didn't push me. Most likely, no one did. Can we go now?" She'd been sure someone had been there—that she'd felt a shove. But now she wasn't certain at all, and she was so tired. She hadn't slept well last night because of her excitement over the concert, and she'd worked on the setup all day, not even stopping to eat. No wonder she couldn't think clearly. "I need to sleep. In my own bed. Please, Jackson. If you're still worried about me in the morning, I promise I'll call Dr. Tanaka. But for now, can we please, please, please, just go home?"

He loosened his grip on her and tucked a curl behind her ear, pressed his forehead to hers. "If you're not in any physical pain—"

"I'm not."

"Okay. I suppose you are already in therapy."

"I am. So—"

Jackson's phone chimed, interrupting her.

He sighed, pinched the bridge of his nose, and then tapped his phone's screen. "Hey, Farrah, I'm here with Brigid, you're on speak—"

"It's Roman," Farrah wailed, and then her words broke into sobs. "Please, Jackson, come back. I-I'm so afraid—"

"Is Roman all right?" Brigid's chest tightened. Her pulse pounded in her throat. "Did you call nine-one-one?"

"N-not yet. I'm unlocking the front door for you, now, Jackson, p-please, hurry! Roman's dead!"

* * *

On shaky legs, Brigid followed Jackson through the Benedettis' front door.

"Farrah!" Jackson called out, waving his hands in front of him like he was finding his way in the dark, despite a huge chandelier lighting up the foyer in all its marbled glory. "Where is Roman?"

"Upstairs," Farrah's plaintive voice sounded nearby.

A few strides more and they spotted Farrah draped across the bottom of the staircase, eyes closed, one arm flung across her forehead, her long blonde hair cascading through ornate, iron balusters. A black silk negligee, with ivory frastaglio embroidery, clung to her hips. The straps fell off her shoulders. The bodice gaped, exposing her breasts.

For one gut-wrenching moment, Brigid thought Farrah was dead, too, then realized she'd only just called out to them. Nevertheless, the limp, boneless position of her limbs, the pallor of her skin, made Brigid rush to check her pulse.

"Pulse is good." Her eyes were fixed on Jackson, who loomed above. "We don't even know what happened."

Jackson leaped up the stairs, nimbly dodging the two women. "I'm going to check Roman. Get her out of here. There could be intruders..." his voice trailed after him as he disappeared onto the second floor.

Intruders?

She hadn't considered that, but Jackson was right. Earlier, in the car, after Farrah had hung up on them, Brigid had called 911 while Jackson drove. But because they'd been pulled off the road less than a minute from the Benedetti's home, they'd beaten the police and the paramedics to the scene. So now they were in a house—a possible crime scene—a possible *ongoing* crime scene, on their own.

She stared down at her shaking hands, and then her gaze traveled back to Farrah, collapsed and half-nude, apparently unable to keep it together.

Overhead, she heard footsteps, the sound of a door opening, Jackson moving about.

Brigid's breath, her lips, her chin—*everything* trembled. But she had a choice, either lie down next to Farrah and give in to her anguish, or be the person Jackson and Farrah... and Roman... needed her to be.

She tugged her hair, and then took a long, deep breath. "Can you sit?"

Walking out of this house was the ultimate goal but the first order of business was to get Farrah upright.

"You're doing great," Brigid coaxed in a calm, quiet voice as Farrah lifted, first her head, and then her shoulders off the stairs. "Now, we're going to get up and walk outside. Do you think you can make it?"

Moaning, Farrah tugged the straps of her gown in place—a sign she was coming back to herself.

Brigid climbed to her feet. "Grab onto the rails if you feel like you might fall."

Farrah did, and a minute later, Brigid had managed to guide her out of the house and onto the front lawn. "Wait here."

She hurried to the car to retrieve a blanket from the trunk, and ran it back to wrap around Farrah. The night was warm, but Farrah's skin was cool to the touch, and she shook like she'd been pulled from an icy river. "Is that better?"

"Thank you," Farrah said, her voice, suddenly stronger, steadier. Apparently she'd found an inner strength, like Brigid had, in order to get through this. "I feel much better."

Brigid pulled her in for a hug. "Help is on the way. Jackson's with Roman, and I'm sure if there's anything that can be done... Farrah, what happened? Are you sure Roman is dead?"

Wordlessly, Farrah slipped out of the embrace.

Brigid's mind was racing with questions.

Did you try CPR?

Why didn't you call the paramedics?

Why did it take half an hour after we dropped you off to call us?

But she was here to support a friend—the authorities were on the way, so it was up to them to ask the questions, except...

"I can't believe he would do this to me." Farrah's huge blue eyes were moist, but no tears fell down her ghost white cheeks. "He *promised* me he would take care of me. Now he's left me alone to deal with everything."

He'd promised Brigid something, too. That he'd call her if he was feeling low. "Farrah, I just talked with Roman yesterday. And he shared some problems with me—but he seemed confident everything was going to work out. He didn't seem... If you don't want to talk about anything, of course, I understand, but Jackson is in that house alone. Can you at least tell me if there was an intruder or—"

As much as her heart ached for Farrah, another part of her was taking a mental step back from her friend. The whole situation wasn't adding up.

I can't believe he would do this to me.

Farrah's distress was obvious, but was she devastated for Roman or for herself? Her words implied that Roman had taken his own life. And if something different happened, like a burglary or a heart attack, Farrah would've said so by now. "What do you mean about his promise? Had he been talking about hurting himself, because he told me the incident at Supper Club was a misunderstanding, that he hadn't planned to use that gun on himself or anyone else, and that he never would."

"He told me the same thing. But he lied to both of us, because he just shot himself."

Brigid squeezed her eyes closed and willed herself to open them again.

Do not shut down. Do not hide from this.

"How do you know? What happened, Farrah?" And then, Brigid softened her voice, tried to catch Farrah's gaze. Was it possible he'd done it in front of his wife? *"When* did it happen?"

Farrah threw her arms wide, letting the blanket drop away and pool at her feet. "You think I did this. Well, I did *not.*"

"Oh, no, Farrah. I'm just trying to understand. My mind is spinning. I'm worried with Jackson inside a house where I have no idea what happened—except you said, now, that Roman's been shot. How do you know it was by his own hand?"

She blinked several times. "I-I wasn't thinking about that. I'm sorry if I didn't explain. I thought I did. I will."

Brigid's shoulders lowered, and her chest loosened.

"When you dropped me off, I went straight upstairs—to our bedroom. But Roman wasn't there. I assumed he was working in his study, so I got ready for bed, but in the bathroom, I saw he'd gotten out his bottle of little blue pills. The lid was off and there was an empty water glass, so I knew he was in the mood. I waited in our bed... I don't know how long. Then, finally, I went looking for him—to tell him I was sleepy, so if he wanted sexy time, he better wrap up whatever he was doing and..." Farrah jerked her gaze around the yard. "You called the police, right?"

"We did. I'm sure they'll be here any minute."

Farrah turned ever so slowly in a circle and waved. "Hey, neighbors. It's me, Mrs. Benedetti. I'm in the yard in my night-gown. Enjoy the show."

She's in shock.

"Where's Jackson?"

"Upstairs," Brigid reminded her.

"In the study? That's where Roman did it. I went looking for him. Did I say that already? I saw the light on under the door to the study. And I found the note."

Brigid couldn't prevent her gasp—so this was real. He planned it.

"The note was on the door. It said 'Farrah, I'm sorry I let you down. I love you. Do not open the door.'" She laughed, a weird, crying laugh. "And so I opened the door because of course I would and there he was in his chair. A gun on the floor beside him and blood. Blood, blood, blood. All over the desk. All over him. On the wall. He was gone. Gone. Gone. Gone. So I ran downstairs, and I called—"

"Here's Jackson," Brigid whispered.

His face blank, he descended the front steps, and then picked his way across the yard to them.

"My Roman. My poor sweet Roman." Farrah ran at Jackson and flung herself against his chest.

Jackson's arms went around Farrah. Holding Farrah, looking over the top of her head and into Brigid's eyes, he said, "There was nothing I could do. Part of Roman's skull... there's nothing anyone can do. I've been on the phone with nine-one-one. They want everyone to wait outside on the lawn for the police. We're not to go back inside. And we should be prepared to answer questions—at the station."

TWENTY-SIX

A man in a rumpled white shirt with the sleeves rolled up, ducked his head, swaggered into the cramped interview room at the Cielo Hermoso police station, and then dragged an armless chair to within a foot of Brigid. With one hand, he swiveled it so that its back faced her. "I'm Detective Javier Vargas, Mrs. Templeton. I know you've had a rough night, and I promise I'll get you home soon. I hear, from Mr. Templeton, you had a tumble down the stairs earlier. Do you need a doctor?"

"No, thank you. I slid down a few steps, but I'm fine."

He lowered himself onto the backwards chair, facing her, his long legs straddling the seat, propped his bare forearms on the top rail and rested his chin on them, which brought his gaze in line with hers.

The effect was disconcertingly intimate.

She resisted the urge to shrink away and fought back by taking a long, direct look at him: a lined forehead, blue-black hair, lightly gelled and swept back off his face—as if to say nothing, not even that thick head of hair, cut just long enough to curl behind his ears, was going to come between them.

She wiped her palms on the fancy silk gown she wore.

"Pushed or slipped?"

"I thought we were here to talk about Roman."

"We're here to talk about whatever I want to know. You're under no obligation to answer anything, and you're free to go at any time."

"You want to know if someone pushed me down the stairs tonight."

"Did they?"

"I honestly don't know. I thought I felt a shove, but there was no one around."

"All right. I'll bear that in mind. You and I were supposed to talk, later this week, about Mr. Benedetti and the incident at dinner. Sorry we didn't get to that sooner, but I heard you were in no hurry. From what I understand, you agree with the other parties involved that your injuries resulted from an unfortunate accident. Are you fully recovered now?"

"I agree it was unintentional, and I've been cleared by my doctors."

"Good. But, now, you see, that makes two unfortunate accidents for you, and one death—for Mr. Benedetti. Any thoughts on that?"

Her shoulders jerked forward. "I'm not sure what you're asking. Are you suggesting foul play? I might have been pushed, but Roman took his own life."

"We don't have an official manner of death yet, Mrs. Templeton, and until we do, it's my job to gather all the pertinent information from both the scene and the witnesses."

She nodded, took a sip from the water bottle they'd brought her while she'd been waiting on the detective.

"I saw Roman yesterday. Sorry, the day before." It was well into morning now. "I met him at the Balboa Park Rose Garden. He wanted to explain more about why he'd brought that gun to Supper Club."

Detective Vargas lifted one eyebrow. "What did he have to

say? Mr. Templeton thinks it was a suicidal gesture, one that finally escalated into the real thing."

"When I spoke with him yesterday—day before—he wasn't suicidal. That's why I'm so..." she paused and pressed her fingers against her eyelids, took a few breaths "... surprised. He promised me he'd call me... he had a lot of money problems. He'd had his identity stolen. Someone moved money from his bank to an offshore account. The FBI and the IRS were involved—"

"We're aware of the financial issues." Vargas straightened in his chair, and it was a relief to get a break from his eyeball to eyeball interrogation technique.

"Good. He thought he had it under control. I should mention, though, that Roman suspected it might have been one of our friends who stole his identity and messed with his bank accounts. I don't believe that."

"And yet you're prepared to accuse one of your friends of pushing you down the stairs."

"No. No, I'm not." Her knee was bouncing, and she crossed her legs to quiet them. Did he think there was a connection between someone pushing her down the stairs, which seemed unlikely now that she'd had time to reflect, and Roman's death? "But say someone did push me. That would actually rule them out as a suspect in Roman's death—if you're saying that death is suspicious."

"Possibly."

"They were at the museum. In fact, the whole group from Supper Club was there, except Roman, so none of them could've been involved."

"Makes a convenient alibi. How far is the museum from the Benedetti's home?"

"Fifteen minutes by car, if there's no traffic."

"So someone could've left and returned. And then there's Mrs. Benedetti, who was in the house for half an hour alone with him."

"I can see how some might think Roman and Farrah's marriage was one of those..." her spine stiffened "... Farrah wouldn't kill Roman. I simply don't believe that. And if he were alive, he'd want to be sure someone was sticking up for her. He left a note, right?"

"Did you know that only a minority of suicides leave notes? And this one was typed, making it even rarer. Do you know anyone, besides his wife, who had motive to harm Roman? What about you or your husband?"

"What? No!"

"He did cause you serious bodily harm, and by your own admission he was suspicious that someone from your club had stolen his identity."

"I was at the museum all night, along with my husband and *everyone* from Supper Club."

"Okay, take it easy. I have to ask."

"Because you don't think it was suicide? Is that only because the note wasn't written in his own hand, or do you have some other reason?"

He cleared his throat.

Brigid shifted in her seat. "Don't keep me in suspense."

"A bottle of erectile dysfunction pills was left open on the bathroom counter next to a glass containing a small amount of water. I don't think most men who are about to blow their brains out take a little blue pill first. It seems to me Roman Benedetti had very different plans."

TWENTY-SEVEN

In the weeks since Roman's death, Charity had not seen her Supper Club friends, and for a social creature such as herself, that had made a sad time all the more difficult. Roman's funeral had been held in his hometown of Essex, Connecticut. A closed casket, family-only event. Given the circumstances of his demise, Farrah, and Roman's brother, Lorenzo, said they preferred to keep it private.

Naturally, Charity wanted to respect their wishes.

But Roman didn't only belong to Farrah.

He was a good friend, and the group needed closure.

So tonight, Charity had invited the gang from Supper Club to gather at her home, not to party or show off her truly fabulous furniture, but to support one another in their grief, and to honor Roman in a respectful way. She was serving hors d'oeuvres and sweets, and she'd instructed each member of the group to be prepared to share a favorite story about Roman. All very dignified and tasteful; not a dinner party—that would be gauche.

Nevertheless, Farrah wasn't coming, despite the fact Charity had bent over backwards to get Farrah's input and work around her schedule (what schedule?).

The trouble Charity had gone to!

She'd hand-selected a variety of gorgeous, fragrant flowers for the evening, including Roman's favorite roses, Marmalade Skies (which meant a trip into San Diego to her *go-to* florist) and she'd even managed to procure several bottles of Donnafugata 2019 Sherazade Nero d'Avola—a wine from a Sicilian vineyard where Roman's parents had once toiled.

Then, last minute, Farrah texts her regrets, pleading a migraine?

Charity didn't buy it.

"Do you think we should all just go home and wait until Farrah is feeling better? It seems wrong to do this without her." Rollin pushed the bridge of his wire-rimmed glasses—a chronic habit of his.

"No, sweetie—" Aiden captured his hand "—Farrah doesn't really have a headache. And she's okay with us getting together without her. Personally, I think it's too soon to expect her—"

"Agreed." Charity picked up a pen and scribbled, to get the ink flowing, on the personalized notepad she always kept handy. Before her parents had died, and along with them her hopes of higher education, Charity had fancied the notion of becoming a journalist—not the boring kind, of course—the television kind with a huge fandom. "She doesn't have a headache. She has a heartache, and our job is not to wait it out; it's to help her cope."

"How can we help her if she's not here?" Darya chimed in, smoothing a hand over her dark hair, which, tonight, she wore sleeked back into a high pony. "I think this whole 'go around and tell a story about Roman' plan is too much. I bet that's part of the reason she's not here. I loved Roman, but I think it's corny and creepy at the same time."

"If I'm being honest," Rollin said, "it reminds me of the way my stepfather wouldn't let me get up from the Thanksgiving table without saying how grateful I was for everything he did for me. I'd have to invent something I knew would please him, or else he'd take it out on my mother."

"Oh, honey. That's so sad. I love Thanksgiving. And going around the table counting our blessings is my favorite part. You should have told me this before now." Aiden squeezed Rollin's hand.

Charity's first instinct was to pack up the beautiful cannoli she'd made from scratch from Roman's family recipe and go home, but seeing as how this was her house... Her second instinct was to cite examples from popular films where scenes such as this played out, thus proving hers wasn't a numbskull idea, but rather a time-honored tradition—at least in the movies. But her third instinct was to turn lemons into lemonade. She'd take their sour grapes and sweeten them with a plan everyone could get behind.

No one was better at brainstorming a plan to pull people together than she was.

"We're veering way off track," Darya said. "Sorry I brought it up."

"I don't think it's off track. I think what Rollin is saying—" Charity clicked her pen "—is that he wants to show respect, but not in a phony way. There's nothing wrong, or right, about going around the group and saying what we'll miss about Roman. But what Rollin brings up makes me want to find something more meaningful. Something we can *all* feel good about, that will honor Roman without being too sentimental or sad."

"But I am sad," Brigid said.

As if they weren't all sorry to lose a friend. And that wasn't Charity's point. She simply wanted to make everyone feel better, but, so far, this evening was a bust in that regard.

On the other end of the couch, Nash sat staring off into space.

Jamal had his head between his hands.

Neither had said a word since she'd brought out the hors

d'oeuvres. Then there was Jackson, who wouldn't make eye contact with her, but of course, that was because Brigid was here, and heaven forbid they make her uncomfortable.

Never mind how Charity felt.

"So let's scrap the 'go around and recite a memory'," Charity said, in a tone she hoped would end the discussion. "Who has a better idea?"

"Roman liked the lake." Jamal, at last, seemed interested.

"Yeah. Lake Tahoe. Remember the time we all went up there for Brigid's—" Darya started.

"Per some people, we're not to speak about old times," Charity interrupted. "But let's riff on this. What can we do at Lake Tahoe, in the near future, that will be meaningful?"

"We could take a walk around the lake together," Aiden suggested.

"That sounds nice." Jamal reached for a cannoli. "We can silently commune with nature, and then hit a nightclub and get blasted."

Charity frowned. "Be serious."

"Oh, but I am—quite," he said. "Come to think of it, one of my fondest memories of Roman is him getting wasted in Tahoe and galloping around the dance floor, belting out the lyrics to 'Senza Una Donna' while the band was on break."

Darya tilted her head. "He was always the life of the party. I think he'd want us to celebrate rather than go around hanging our heads. But clubbing in Tahoe doesn't feel, to me, like the right tribute, considering the way he died. He was struggling with demons we didn't know anything about—if only he'd gotten help."

"I have an idea," Charity said, climbing to her feet. Then she grabbed an open bottle of Donnafugata 2019 Sherazade Nero d'Avola and circled the room to top up everyone's glass. "One of the things that made me feel better after Hope died..." she paused, suddenly short of breath, but quickly recovered, "was when Nash and Brigid... of course, they were married then—" she cleared her throat "—Nash and Brigid donated ten thousand dollars to Mothers Against Drunk Driving after Hope's accident. I've always been grateful for that. Since Roman took his own life, what if we all make a big donation to a mental health organization in his name?"

"Is that certain, though?" Brigid said. "They haven't officially stated the manner of death, as I understand it."

"I'm sure that's just a formality, or they wouldn't have released his body for burial," Jackson said. "Brigid and I would be happy to donate—anywhere the group decides is fine with me. Right, Brigid?"

Brigid swished her wine in its glass. "Of course, but we don't know for sure that he intentionally... and *Tahoe*? Isn't there some other place?"

"We might be a little short on cash at the moment." Rollin exchanged a glance with Aiden. "Nothing to worry about, but..."

"It's the bookshop. We're *not* in danger of closing. It's not as bad as before, but the economy hasn't been great for a small business like ours lately, as I'm sure everyone knows." Aiden put in. "We're working on straightening it all out, but it's been a strain. We haven't said anything because we've got it under control. It's just not a good time for us to have to come up with cash."

"I'm sorry," Charity said. "I'm not trying to pressure anyone to do something they can't afford. It *is* a tough economy. Nash is feeling the effects in the real estate business, too. So how can we come at this another way?"

"Oh, I've got it," Nash said. "Let's do our walk around Lake Tahoe, like Aiden suggested, and we'll collect pledges for every mile. No matter how much money we get, it will raise awareness and it will be a genuine tribute to our friend."

"That's the best idea I've heard," Darya said. "Count me in."

"Does it have to be Tahoe, though?" Brigid shifted in her seat. "There are lots of nice areas around Cielo Hermoso and, frankly, the memories of our group adventures in Tahoe are a mixed bag for me."

"This is about *Roman*, and he loved Tahoe, especially in October," Charity said. "This is the perfect time for fall colors. Show of hands for a fundraising walk around the lake."

Every arm popped up except Brigid and Jackson's.

Majority rules.

Charity mentally clapped herself on the back. She'd managed to turn the evening around, and she was certain Farrah would welcome the idea of an outing to Tahoe. It would allow her to have some fun without appearing to be anything less than a dutiful widow.

The only drawback was that Brigid was an experienced fundraiser—she'd likely out-raise Charity with her connections from the museum, but so be it.

Charity wasn't petty.

She could sacrifice her own glory for the good of the—

The front door chimed, interrupting her thoughts.

Oh, good.

Maybe Farrah had decided to join them after all.

Charity wandered in the direction of the front door, but before she made it halfway down the hall, Tish barreled into her arms.

"Sweetheart, are you okay?" Charity patted her back.

Tish's loud sobs drew the others out into the hallway.

"What's wrong?" Nash turned Tish away from Charity and tilted her tear-stained face toward his. His rising voice, his flashing eyes, told the tale. This was his little girl, and whoever made her cry would have him to deal with.

Charity clenched her fists, bracing herself for Tish's

response, because, obviously, the person most likely to have made Tish cry was—

"Christian," Tish wailed.

Nash's face reddened, and his Adam's apple worked in his throat. "Did he hurt you, honey? What's he done?"

"No. H-he..." More sobbing, and then, at last, she gulped in a deep breath and said, "He's gone. Christian is gone for good, and it's my fault."

TWENTY-EIGHT

The first time Brigid had been inside the Cielo Hermoso police station, she hadn't noticed the yellow leaves on the tree shoved in the corner of the waiting area. But now, when a slender woman in uniform approached it with a watering can, Brigid called out, "Excuse me. I think you're overwatering the schefflera."

The officer drew to an abrupt, military-style halt and then swung around, splashing water from the can onto her black leather boots. "Is that why it's dropping its leaves?"

"You might want to move it closer to the window," Tish put in. "Scheffleras need adequate light, and I think my mom's right about too much water. The yellow leaves are a dead giveaway."

The tightness in Brigid's shoulders eased.

Other than terse responses to pointed questions, Tish hadn't spoken since they'd arrived at the station. Now, her attention to a wounded tree, something that would ordinarily draw her interest, gave Brigid hope she might not be as detached as Brigid had feared.

"Thanks. I could see it was in trouble, but I thought more water was the answer." The officer dragged the tree in front of a panel of tall windows—it was dark out tonight, but the morning light would bring a fresh start. "Detective Vargas will be with you shortly."

"We'll be here," Brigid said. Turning to Tish, she noted her cheeks had a bit more color. "Are you feeling okay?"

"No. I'm starting to get really angry with Christian for putting me in this position. At first, I was so worried, so scared for him, that I couldn't be mad. When I came home and found that note, and then, the look on Charity's face when I had to tell her Christian was gone... I blamed myself. All I could think about was poor Charity and how I was the one responsible for Christian leaving... how terrible it will be for her—losing another family member. But the longer I sit here..."

Brigid reached over and swept a hank of hair out of her daughter's eyes like she used to do when she was a little girl. For Tish to tolerate, seemingly even welcome, such a motherly gesture from Brigid was a small miracle. Brigid whispered a *thank you* to the universe for returning her daughter to her. Whether or not their reconciliation lasted remained to be seen, but things had been so much more promising recently. Tempting as it was to rush to criticize Christian, Brigid refrained. Instead, she dug deep for the self-control to wait, to listen.

"I feel awful for Charity. When she asked me not to report Christian to the police, it was hard to say no. But, Mom, she's asking me to cover up a crime. In my heart, I know that would be a disaster for everyone. Do you think I made the right decision?"

Brigid squeezed Tish's hand. "I think you're doing the right thing, and in this case, the right thing is so hard, so heartbreaking. I hope you know I'm incredibly proud of you."

"Detective Vargas will see you now." The policewoman was back, this time without a watering can.

Brigid and Tish followed her down a long corridor and into

a tiny room that might've been the same one where Vargas had interviewed her the morning after Roman's death. At least the beige walls, square table, and hard-backed armless chairs seemed the same.

The waiting was also familiar.

The first time Vargas had interviewed Brigid, he'd kept her waiting because he'd been interviewing Jackson before getting to her. This time, he left Brigid and Tish cooling their heels in this cramped, poorly ventilated room for unknown reasons, but it worked out for the best. By the time Vargas swaggered across the threshold, Tish's back was ramrod straight, and her sweet, blue eyes blazing. Between the time she'd burst into her father's house sobbing and now, she'd transformed, right before Brigid's eyes, from a sad little girl into a strong, determined woman.

A woman who was mad as hell—and understood she had every right to be.

Like last time, Vargas ducked his head as he entered the room, then drew up a backwards chair too close to Brigid's.

Good.

She'd much rather he crowd her than her daughter.

"Which one of you ladies wants to go first? I recommend we do the interviews separately, but—"

"I'd like my mother here with me while I make my report. I hope that's okay."

"You're not a minor," Vargas said, "but this is not an interrogation—you're coming to me with information, and I appreciate it. That said, in my experience, it's better to talk one on one."

"I still want my mom here."

And only her mom. Nash and Charity had volunteered to come along, but Tish had refused. Brigid's chin rose. She hated being right about Christian, but she loved the way her daughter had turned to her, was trusting her.

"If you feel more comfortable, I'm not going to refuse your request. I do appreciate you coming down to the station,"

Vargas said. "And then, Mrs. Templeton, I understand you want to speak to me privately once your daughter has finished?"

"I do. Tish's father is waiting for her call. He'll pick her up when she's ready."

Vargas looked from Tish to Brigid and back again, cleared his throat. "Excuse me, ladies." He jumped to his feet, swiveled his chair around and sat down on it like a normal person, facing them. "So, Ms. Clarence, you're here to report a potential crime and a possible missing person."

Tish nodded.

"Fire away." Vargas took out a notebook. "Just take your time, and tell me your story in your own words. I'll jump in if I have questions."

Brigid tried to send her daughter a reassuring glance, but Tish wasn't looking her way.

Tish sat tall in her chair, staring the detective straight in the eyes. "Yesterday, while my boyfriend, Christian Drury, was taking a shower, I looked at his phone—I wasn't snooping—I was trying to find a selfie he'd taken of us so I could post it on Instagram."

"How did you get into his phone?"

"He uses the same passcode for everything—Hope's—his niece's—birthday. Anyway, after I found the photo I was looking for, I kept scrolling because I saw some other cute pictures, and then another album popped up. The first image was the front of a credit card. It caught my attention because of the name on the card."

Vargas's pen hung in the air. "Whose name was on the card?"

"Drew Samuels."

Brigid's stomach clenched, just as it had the first time she'd heard this, when she'd helped her daughter make the difficult decision to file a police report.

"And do you know a Drew Samuels?"

"Yes, he's our landlord. So I clicked on the album and found more photos of credit cards. Lots of them. Fronts and backs, all names I didn't recognize—except Drew's. At first, I was in disbelief. I thought Christian would have a good explanation."

"What happened next?"

"I was nervous, and so I waited until after dinner. By then, I'd worked up my nerve to tell Christian I'd been on his phone, and I asked him about what I'd found."

"And how did he explain it?"

"He blew up. Yelled at me. Said I had no business spying on him. He was so mad he knocked a plate off the table—"

Brigid half-rose from her chair. "Did he hit you?"

"No, Mom."

She relaxed back into her seat.

"He didn't hurt me—he never laid a finger on me. But we argued a long time, and he went into the bedroom and slammed the door. I left him alone, and then, about an hour later he came out, and he was crying. He told me he was sorry. That he'd been stealing people's cards for extra cash. He promised to stop—to never do it again, and begged me to forgive him."

"Honey, did he steal your credit card, too? Is that why it was declined when—"

"He swears he didn't. But I guess that's another one of his lies." Tish turned back to Vargas. "I said I thought he should turn himself in to the police. I told him my dad would help him get a lawyer. Christian is my stepmother's brother, so I know my dad would've helped him."

"And did Christian agree to turn himself in?"

"He said he would. I can't believe I was gullible enough to trust him, but I did. He asked me to wait. To give him one more day so he could meet with my dad about getting an attorney before turning himself in. This morning, he told me not to worry, that it was all going to be okay, that he'd arranged to meet my father. I offered to go with him, but he didn't want me to. I had a job inter-view lined up for this afternoon, so... When I came home, I found a note from Christian. It says he loves me but he doesn't want to go to jail. He says he's sorry, and that I should move on with my life."

Tish passed a crumpled note to Vargas.

"Do you have his phone?" Vargas asked.

"I'm sorry, but no."

"That's okay. You've done really well, Ms. Clarence. Do you happen to remember any of the other names on the credit cards?"

Tish shook her head. "I didn't recognize the other names, and I'm afraid I didn't write them down."

"What about Roman Benedetti?"

Brigid clutched the edge of her chair, held her breath.

"Oh, no. I would've said so right away." Tish's eyes were wide, but dry; her voice soft but firm. Whatever fault Brigid had found with her daughter's choices, she had to admit Nash had been right about one thing: Tish had a damn good head on her shoulders and she deserved their trust.

"If you think of anything else, you'll let me know," Vargas said.

Tish nodded. "Are you going to arrest him?"

"Without the phone, and without any hard evidence, I'd have to say not at this time."

"But you'll look for him?" For the first time since she'd started her tale, Tish's voice faltered. "What if he—do you think he might try to hurt himself?"

"Did he threaten to hurt himself or anyone else?" Vargas steepled his fingers.

"No."

"Good. I know that you must care about this young man very much. I'll put out a BOLO, file a report—we'll have you come back to sign a sworn statement tomorrow. I'll talk with

Mr. Samuels to determine if he's had any unauthorized charges to his cards."

"Sorry to interrupt," Brigid said, "but is it okay if Tish goes now?" Her daughter had been through enough. She didn't want her confined in this hot, cramped room any longer than necessary.

"If she's said all she has to say, then I'm good."

Alone with the detective, Brigid shook out her hands.

Vargas stood, stretched his legs, then sat back down and took out his notebook.

"Whenever you're ready."

Don't bury the lead.

"I think Christian Drury might be guilty of more than credit card theft," she said.

Vargas folded his hands behind his head. "Like what?"

Like murder.

It was a terrible accusation to make—even worse to make it about Christian—but she had to be open with the detective. "You'll draw your own conclusions, but I'm concerned that he might have been involved in Roman's death. You're the one who told me there were some things that might not add up to suicide. And Roman had his identity stolen."

"Don't think I haven't thought of that. But your daughter was clear she did not see Roman Benedetti's credit card photographed on Christian's phone."

"Yes, but—"

Vargas put up one hand. "Let me give you some information that may put your mind at ease. Your friend's death *was* a suicide. The medical examiner made her official determination yesterday. His financial problems obviously contributed to his death, so whoever stole his identity bears indirect responsibility, but he wasn't murdered."

"I don't understand. What about the erectile dysfunction pills?"

"He did take them. The undigested medication was found in his stomach contents, so it must have been very shortly before death. But all the forensics are consistent with a self-inflicted gunshot wound to the head."

"So you're just ignoring the inconsistency of the pills?"

"We have an explanation. You remember that Roman told you he was cooperating with the Feds? It turns out they were more interested in *him* than anyone else. And while he might not have known that when he met you in the rose garden, he did know it before he died. A representative from his board of directors called him, informing him that because the FBI suspected him of bank fraud, he would not be getting his old job back. Based on the timing of that call, and his estimated time of death, we believe he was preparing for an evening with his wife, hence the little blue pills, when he got the bad news. Then, rather than face up to the consequences of his actions, knowing his luck was not turning around like he'd hoped, he typed that note and took his own life."

Brigid let out a long sigh. It was a relief, but a heartbreaking one. "Thank you. I know you didn't have to tell me all of that."

"Hey, I've got a daughter of my own. Anything else?"

She hesitated. How many unsubstantiated theories was she prepared to fling around in a single day? "I think I might have witnessed a murder a few years ago at Lake Tahoe. I saw a person, I'm not sure if it was a man or a woman, but I saw someone drown a woman in the lake."

"Tell me more," Vargas said, with the cool of someone who'd been down this road many times with many witnesses.

Still, he didn't seem dismissive. If he thought she was crazy, he was doing a good job of hiding it. "I thought it was just a dream, until I returned to Lake Tahoe with Jackson, and I saw the beach in my dream—except I've never been there before."

He leaned in, still no hint of disbelief on his face. "I'm confused. If you've never been there, how can you have dreamed about it?"

"That's exactly my point. If I've never been there, I couldn't dream the details of the location, so that's how I know it's a memory disguised as a dream. My psychiatrist thinks..."

"You're seeing a shrink?"

"Since my accident. I've been having some problems with my emotional memory."

"You mean like amnesia?"

"We're calling it emotional amnesia."

He kicked back in his chair. "Brigid... may I call you by your first name?"

"Yes."

"Brigid, I want you to know how much I appreciate you and your daughter coming down to the station. You've been a big help, and I'm going to do my best to find Christian. I'll travel down any path that case leads me without hesitation. In a small town like this, I've got precious little to investigate. I also want you to know that I take your concern about a possible murder at Lake Tahoe seriously. Even though it's not my jurisdiction, I can certainly pass things on to the relevant authorities."

"But?"

"I'm not one to discount a witness simply because they are seeing a psychiatrist. Believe me, I don't find most eye witnesses half as credible as I find you."

She took a breath. "Thank you, but I can hear what you're *not* saying. Even if you want to believe me, you don't."

"Here's what I think: I believe you dreamed you witnessed a murder. I believe you've now been to the actual location from your dream. But I also believe in evidence. And here, we have none. I haven't heard of any bodies discovered in Lake Tahoe, and I've been a cop in this state for decades—"

"Decades?"

"In most cases, we have a victim, and then we try to find a witness to the crime. Here we have a witness but... You see the problem?"

She did.

She was the witness, but *who* was the victim?

TWENTY-NINE

Lake Tahoe, California

Charity had shown true grit, Brigid thought, by organizing this fundraising hike in such short order—and under such difficult personal circumstances. She'd been putting on a brave face since Christian had fled to parts unknown, but Brigid noticed the way her eyes were uncharacteristically quick to water, and how fleeting and fragile her smiles had become. So when Charity volunteered to man the sign-up table for the hike, Brigid decided to hang back with her, offer moral support.

Be a friend.

Given the clear indication that Christian was a credit card thief, the strong suspicion among the group was that he might've been the one who'd stolen Roman's identity, and Charity's role in Super Club had shifted from beloved leader to something much more tenuous. The official club stance was that Charity and her brother were two different people, and no one blamed her for his crimes.

But despite talking the talk, whenever Charity walked in a room, you could sense people tightening their grips on their purses and patting their pockets for their wallets.

As unfair as that might be, it was hard to blame them.

For her part, Charity acted as if she didn't notice that Darya and Farrah hadn't invited her to lunch at Café Francois, or that the men hadn't included Nash in a round of golf since the night Christian skipped town. Charity seemed to be going along with the group mantra—*everything is perfectly normal.*

A fiction designed to put everyone at ease.

But for Brigid, who was struggling to overcome her own tendencies toward denial, the pretense was painful.

Beside her, Charity toyed with a pen, and studied the sign-up sheet in silence.

With the exception of the time period surrounding Hope's accident, Brigid could not recall an instance where Charity had not assailed her with effervescent comments on how pretty the day was, how much she loved the way Brigid had done her hair (which would have been fixed in the same style as always), how excited she was about an upcoming movie or dinner or concert.

Tugging her shorts and shifting her legs, Brigid tried to get comfortable in her saggy-bottom canvas chair and wondered if staying behind with Charity had been the right choice. Brigid might as well have been invisible, sitting here, and she could've been enjoying a lovely time with the others. The Fallen Leaf Lake trail they'd selected for their hike was an easy four mile out-and-back with great views of a small, but beautiful lake adjacent to the big lake. The crowds would be at Lake Tahoe proper, so this little gem of a trail was perfect—like the day with its sunshine filled skies and soundtrack of birdsong playing in the background.

It had been easy to recruit a number of locals and tourists to join the event for a small entry fee, and many had made generous donations on top of that. Each member of Supper

Club had donated five thousand dollars that came either out of their own pocket, or from pledges collected from friends. So far they'd raised over fifty-thousand dollars for a local crisis line— Roman would have been pleased.

Now, Charity put down the sign-up sheet and began picking her nails.

Brigid sighed, tried to focus on the idyllic day.

Think of all the good we're doing.

Forget about the dream.

Being at Lake Tahoe, again, had Brigid jumping at the mere rustle of a branch crackling underfoot, or the soft whoosh of the wind in the trees.

She took a sip of bottled water and cast another glance at Charity. She'd hoped they might distract one another, but Charity was no more help to Brigid than Brigid was to Charity. The silence had passed "awkward" a long time ago, but Brigid wasn't ready to give up yet. "Should we close up shop and get hiking? It's almost noon, and I'm not sure how many more people are going to be signing up at this point."

"I'm expecting someone," Charity said.

"Oh, okay. Want some sunscreen? It's time for me to reapply."

"Pass."

"It's important to apply sunscreen year-round, you know."

"I guess I'm not quite the staid stickler you are."

So much for small talk. "Who are you expecting?"

"If you must know, he's a friend of Christian's. They volunteered together at the soup kitchen."

"I didn't realize Christian kept up with volunteering."

"You don't realize a lot of things."

Brigid applied a squirt of sunblock to her arms and cheeks and set it on the sign-up table in front of Charity. "If you change your mind about the sunblock…" Maybe the problem wasn't

Charity. Maybe it was the small talk itself. Maybe the lack of candor was bothering Charity as much as it did Brigid.

This was the first time in years they'd been completely alone together.

Brigid had wanted the day to be meaningful. This could be her chance. "Charity, would you mind if I brought up a difficult topic?"

Charity stared straight ahead. A few beats passed and then she said, "Honestly, I'd love it. I'm so tired of the hearts and flowers everyone is blowing out their butts. I wish, for once, we could just be real with each other."

How about that? Charity was sick of being fake, too. "I'll be real if you will. In fact, even if you don't reciprocate, I'd be honored if you'd allow me to tell you what I'm honestly feeling."

Charity arched an eyebrow. "I always say what I'm feeling. Well, I used to."

"I'm sorry."

"For what? I hate it when people apologize just to move on, when nothing's actually been resolved."

"I'm sorry about Christian. I know that you love him, and you must be worried sick."

"I do love him. You've got that right."

"And I'm also sorry about the way I behaved on my thirty-sixth birthday."

At last, Charity pivoted to face her. "That's quite a change of subject. Why bring it up now?"

"Because we're here, in Lake Tahoe—the scene of the crime so to speak—and because we're being real. The truth is, I don't remember much about that night."

"No kidding. You were drunk off your rear."

"I was. But that's no excuse for flirting with Jackson."

"At least it sort of explains it—but what's his excuse? You and I were drinking but Jackson was sober. And anyway, it was all innocent, I suppose."

"I hope so."

"Meaning what, exactly?"

"Meaning I don't remember much. Maybe Nash has told you already, but later, I went wandering around on my own and came home in the wee hours of the morning. He had to clean me up and call for a late checkout so I could sleep it off. I have no idea where I went that night, and it's frightening to think of what might have happened. I have nightmares about this place, and I don't know if they're real or just some wild stuff I dreamed up."

"They say you won't do anything when you're drunk that you wouldn't do sober."

"Who says that?"

"Liars, I guess." Charity laughed.

"Jackson was with you that night, right? He didn't happen to wander off, did he?" It was a fear she hadn't voiced until now, not even to herself.

"You'll have to ask him. I went straight to sleep when we got back to our hotel. I was *almost* as wasted as you. But I'm sure he would've told you if something had happened between you that night—if that's what you're worried about."

In part, but that wasn't her main concern. "I guess you and I would have each done the other wrong, in that case. But what I am wondering most of all is whether there was some kind of trouble that night. In my dream... someone drowned."

Charity's brow drew down, as if considering her response carefully. "Why not check with the local cops? Something like that would be a matter of public record."

Brigid's camping chair tipped precariously. "You don't think it sounds crazy?"

"It's not important how it sounds. If it's bothering you, you should check with the park rangers, too. If someone went missing it would've been reported." Then, as a man hurried toward them, Charity rose on her haunches.

"Thank you, Charity. That's a great suggestion. I'm going to stop by the police and the ranger's station as soon as we check this gentleman in. Sorry, but I'm going to skip the hike—I'll need to catch them during business hours."

The man, heavy-set with a beard, reached them, huffing and out of breath. "Am I too late?"

"Not at all. Thanks for coming, Nick—that was a long way from San Diego."

"Any excuse to visit Tahoe, and in a way, I'm acting as Christian's proxy. I believe, in my heart, he'd be here himself, if only he could."

"I believe that, too," Charity said. "I truly do."

THIRTY

Brigid's visit to the South Lake Tahoe police had yielded nothing... except the suggestion to try the ranger at Emerald Bay State Park. Said ranger, Bart Costas, standing before her, now, represented both her last hope and her worst fear. If, in truth, she'd witnessed a murder the night of her blackout, if she actually had been on the beach at Vikingsholm, then a killer was out there—somewhere.

And he was all the more terrifying because her mind had inked out his face.

If he was real...

He could be anyone.

Anyone.

"Maybe." Ranger Costas planted his hands on hips and widened his stance.

The left side of his mouth remained frozen in place when he grimaced as if he'd had a stroke or an injury of some type— there was a tiny white scar below the eye on that same cheek, so maybe an injury was correct.

"The circumstances ring a bell?" She dreaded the answer —either way.

"I remember an incident a few years ago. Somewhat similar to the dream you just described. But, ma'am, if you don't mind my saying, there haven't been any drownings. I'm confident of that. And you said yourself, it's a dream. Dreams aren't real—mine can get pretty wild, but then I wake up and it's all okay."

She smoothed her hair behind her ears and took a breath. "I know how it sounds. And thank you, so much, for taking me seriously." Was he? "But I believe a specific memory triggered this dream. I admit it sounds..."

Let's jettison the concept of crazy: she heard Dr. Tanaka's admonishment in her head.

"... unusual. Do you think you've seen me before? Could I have been involved in this incident?"

"I won't say it's not you. But the woman was wild-eyed. Drenched, frantic, and it was a long time ago. And the man..."

"You remember a man?"

"Yeah. He was very cooperative. I don't mean to offend you, but you—if it was you—were the belligerent one. High as a kite."

"Drunk or high?"

"Not sober, that's for damn sure."

"I'd like to know more about the incident. It's very important to me."

"Because you have nightmares."

She decided not to press the point that there might've been a murder. The ranger had shut that down right away, and she wanted to enlist his cooperation. "Yes. Do you keep incident reports? Records of any kind?"

He stuck out his lower lip, and it had the same funny droop on one side. "I keep a log. And I made a detailed report after the incident. Just in case anything further ever came of it. But, I couldn't begin to tell you the date. So it would be hard to dig out. Unless you've got a warrant, I'm not inclined to read through the entire log."

"I appreciate that. But if I could pinpoint the day, will you check?"

"I thought you said it was a dream? How can you know the date?"

The only time she could possibly have been to Vikingsholm beach and not remembered was the night she'd gotten blackout drunk. "Because it was my birthday."

"And that was?" He opened a drawer and yanked out a tattered journal with a photograph of a bear taped to the cover.

Could it be this easy? "Four years ago. July twenty-fifth."

"July twenty-fifth. Right here it says high temperature ninety degrees—man, that was a scorcher. Wind fifteen miles per hour—conditions on lake choppy—warning level for boating and swimming. Black bear spotted at Vikingsholm Beach." He pushed his hat up and glanced at her. "I guess you got the wrong day—but you'd know your own birthday. So that means the belligerent woman wasn't you, and the dream isn't real. But hey, it's good news, right? You're not a drunkard and nobody got murdered—like I said before."

"What about July twenty-sixth? If it happened after midnight you might've logged it under the following day."

"You're determined to find out something bad—most people would take the win, but okay." He flipped the page, and then began dragging his finger over the entry, his face losing color.

"You found it? What does it say?"

"See for yourself." He passed her the journal.

July 26

Time of entry 5:45 a.m.

At approximately 12:30 a.m. I responded to an alarm at Vikingsholm Castle. We've had several bear incidents in recent days, and, as anticipated, this turned out to be another, although there was an additional situation, which I was able to resolve on my own.

Upon my arrival at the castle, I turned on both the interior and exterior lights and cleared the premises. I found a broken window with evidence of bear tracks leading to and from the area, an overturned kitchen table, and what looked to be claw marks on the cabinetry. While I was photographing the prints and damages, I heard a woman scream for help.

The screams seemed to be coming from the woods and moving closer to the castle. I went back outside, and at that point, I unholstered my taser and called out to the woman. I identified myself as a park service ranger and instructed her to remain where she was until I could locate her and render aid.

However, the screams continued to grow louder, and as I made my way toward them, a woman rushed out of the trees. Her clothing and hair were wet. She was barefoot and covered in sand. I thought she might have been chased by a bear, but I did not see a bear in the vicinity. When I approached her, she stopped screaming, pointed toward the beach and began babbling, mostly incoherently, although I did understand her to say the word 'murderer'.

After about a minute, a man emerged from the trees. I instructed him to put his hands behind his head and get on his knees, and he readily complied with my instructions. He then explained to me that it was the woman's birthday, and that he had planned a romantic evening. He said he'd brought her by boat to the beach where they'd had a late-night picnic. He said he had not imbibed because he was operating the boat, but that she had drunk almost a full thermos of martinis and initiated a sexual encounter, after which they'd both fallen asleep. He further stated that upon awakening, he'd found her missing and begun searching the beach. He heard her yelling and spotted her in the water. Fearing that in her inebriated condition she might drown, he ran after her into the ocean, but she swam to shore, and then bolted into the woods, hysterical.

I patted him down and determined he did not have any

weapon on him, and I allowed him to get up off the ground. When I questioned the woman, she flailed her arms as if wanting to strike me and asked, "Are you a murderer?"

After we calmed her down, the man admitted the woman (who identified herself as Brigid Clarence) was married to another man. I suggested we take her to the local hospital, but he requested that he be allowed to take her back to their hotel so she could sleep it off, since an emergency room visit would alert her husband to the affair.

I checked her pulse and respiration, which were normal.

He helped me bring her up to my boat where I keep an emergency first aid kit. I took her blood pressure and oxygen saturations there, and made the determination that she was not in any medical danger.

The woman fell asleep, and after observing her for fifteen minutes or so, she woke up, and stated that she was confused, but otherwise felt fine. I asked if she would like to go to the hospital, and she said she wanted to return to the hotel with her companion. I asked her if she felt safe with him, and, appearing surprised by the question, she answered 'of course'. I ferried them to their own boat after taking down his name and address, which he readily provided: Jackson Templeton, 415 Woodland Drive, Cielo Hermoso, California.

I cautioned him that I was noting the incident, and that any further disturbances would be investigated thoroughly, and warned them both to stay out of trouble. He wanted to take her home in his boat, and I agreed that I would allow it as long as I could escort them. I followed their boat and verified that they made it safely back to their hotel. I then returned to Vikingsholm Castle for cleanup.

THIRTY-ONE

Tonight's the night.

Brigid was on a mission to mine the secrets buried in her brain. After speaking with Ranger Costas, she had no more doubt that her recurring nightmare had been triggered by an actual event. How far that dream strayed from reality, she couldn't say. But she believed she'd witnessed a murder by drowning that long ago night, and she refused to go on protecting herself—and a murderer—by pretending it was nothing more than the fanciful concoction of a broken mind.

Brigid *couldn't* go back to the hotel without answers.

Jackson had been with her on the beach that terrible night, and he'd lied about it. He'd probably told himself it was better she didn't know.

It wasn't.

And while she might be able, eventually, to forgive him his secrets, she would not allow him to keep her away from the truth even one more day.

A woman had been murdered, and no one seemed to care. That woman had a family, maybe a husband, maybe a child. Brigid had to bring the truth to light for their sake. She wasn't trying to catch a killer on her own—she wasn't that foolhardy—but she needed more information in order to get the police to take her seriously. And if she was being honest with herself (wasn't it long past time for that?), she no longer knew who she could trust.

So, tonight, she was planning a reenactment.

If she could recreate the events she'd read about in the ranger's report, if she were lucky, if she found the courage to face the truth, then perhaps the distorted events in her dream would merge with the reality.

Perhaps she would *remember* what really happened.

And so, after much reflection, she set out on her own late-night picnic.

The concession hut on the beach, where one could rent canoes, closed at dark. But Brigid called the concierge and, with the help of a $100 "thank you" for both him and the young man who manned the boat rentals, she convinced them to open the stand and help her get her canoe into the water.

THIRTY-TWO

I'm monumentally bad at murder.

Actually, I'm being too hard on myself. The truth is I *used* to be bad at murder, but I'm getting better.

I had no trouble getting rid of Roman.

So I guess practice makes perfect.

Who knows how many people, like me, bungle their first attempt?

A lot—maybe even most.

I learned my lessons the hard way, but at least I did learn.

The most important thing I've discovered is this: If at first you don't succeed, try, try again.

Second lesson: If you want a job done right, do it yourself. Accomplices are great until the chickens come home to roost and then you have to get your hands dirty just to get rid of a problem you created for yourself by being soft-hearted and bringing them along in the first place.

Poor Christian.

He turned out to be far worse an accomplice than I'd hoped.

If only I could've overlooked his mistakes. But he proved

himself to be downright incompetent, getting himself caught—after everything I taught him.

He left me no choice but to get rid of him... but I'm getting off the subject of lessons learned.

Third lesson: The best-laid plans aren't plans at all. They're opportunities found and seized.

Like tonight.

I can hardly believe my luck, but I'd be a fool not to take advantage—just like I took advantage of having a perfect alibi for Roman's murder on the night of the concert.

I mean, here's Brigid, paddling off in a canoe into the dead of night, all alone with no one to keep her out of trouble, right before my eyes.

The concessionaire helping her launch her canoe will make a great witness, proving she struck out all alone.

Chances like this don't present themselves every day.

I don't know, just yet, how I can get rid of her—but *tonight's the night*.

THIRTY-THREE

Moonlight, augmented by the high-beam lantern Brigid had secured to the bow of her canoe, paved a path across the water and into the secluded cove.

"Easy does it. Get yourself sideways on approach. You're almost there." Speaking aloud over the flapping of the wind, Brigid gave herself instructions, repeating words her father had used when he'd taught her how to beach a canoe. She'd operated one on her own plenty of times, but never in the black of night in lonely waters.

Her teeth rattled as the canoe's hull scraped the shore.

Though she knew how to approach and disembark safely, talking herself through the process soothed her and provided a distraction from the swirling thoughts that threatened to destroy her calm determination. She climbed from the canoe and dragged it up on the beach, her waders sinking in the sand. "This looks like the most likely spot for our picnic."

From the ranger's incident log, she knew she and Jackson could not have been picnicking directly in front of Vikingsholm —the ranger said she'd run out of the woods, not straight up the beach. That meant they'd moored their boat out of sight of the castle, but close enough that she'd been able to reach it on foot.

Now, she grabbed the lantern and tied it to the branch of a cedar tree. Next, she spread a blanket and sat down cross-legged to eat. In her dream she'd reminisced about her parents picnicking on pimento cheese sandwiches. So she'd brought one with her tonight.

"Maybe in real life you were eating pimento cheese sand-wiches with Jackson in a cove like this, but you dreamed you were walking on a beach, thinking about your parents eating them."

According to Freud, the psyche distorts fears and wishes and daily life through dreams in varied ways.

"This is complicated." She sighed, and nibbled the sand-wich. It tasted good, and reminded her of her happy child-hood when her parents were still alive. So at least there was that. She took another bite, then closed her eyes, concen-trating on the smell of cedar, the way the wind felt on her hot skin.

From somewhere nearby, wings flapped.

A duck taking flight.

Her mouth went dry, and she took a sip of bottled water, aware of her heartbeat gaining speed.

"It's okay to let yourself remember. There is no killer here. You're safe."

She opened her eyes and blinked away moisture, acutely aware that all alone in the dark, she felt safer than she had since the day of her accident—because she no longer knew who she could trust.

"You can trust yourself," she said.

Dr. Tanaka would think she was crazy talking to herself like this... No, that wasn't right. Dr. Tanaka would tell her to forget about that and keep going.

"What's next?" she asked the wind.

In her dream, she'd been wading in the lake, barefoot, when she'd spied the man forcing the woman under the waves.

She yanked off her waders, followed by her socks and sneakers. After that, she gathered up her trash, put it in the picnic basket, folded the blanket and stowed everything in the canoe. "Stop stalling. What are you so afraid of?"

Whatever happened that night was terrible—an event so awful she'd repressed the memory and changed it into something less threatening. But if the dream scenario was *less* threatening than reality, then, impossible as it seemed, whatever actually happened was... "Worse than witnessing a murder."

She placed a hand over her pounding heart.

Sand squished between her toes as she waded gingerly into the lake, trying to recreate the only version of that night she'd dared remember thus far. "Just let the dream take control."

My bare feet sink in wet sand, while wind-generated waves stir around my ankles, cooling my scorched skin. Lifting the skirt of my sundress, I pad on until the water reaches my thighs. My gaze stretches across the lake, past a small island, to find the blue-black shadows of mountain peaks, and then descends onto moonlight shimmering atop the water like sequins on a ball gown.

I follow the path of light, until I see movement.

An arm darts above the water; ghostly white against inky waves.

"Help! Help me!" Brigid covered her mouth to stop her own screams.

The moon drifts behind the clouds, leaving me in utter darkness.

The midnight lake feels bottomless.

I see a figure dressed in black. The night has disguised its form well, but its movements...

Wrapping her arms around her waist, she rocked, back and forth, resisting, squeezing her eyes closed with all her might.

This was it.

The thing too terrible to remember.

Dr. Tanaka had said a lack of oxygen could make the brain more vulnerable, the mind less able to cope.

Dissociation.

"It's like it happened to someone else. Like I'm watching a movie," Brigid said aloud. "I am the witness, but who is the victim? Like it happened to someone else... who is the victim?"

She shivered, so cold it seemed her core was a solid block of ice... like she was immersed in frigid water.

"Like watching a movie starring someone else... but it *didn't* happen to someone else. It happened to *you*."

It happened to me!

She fell to her knees in the shallow water, threw her head back, pounded her chest with her fists.

She'd dreamed it as if she was watching someone else when, all along, *she* was the one drowning.

Gasping for air.

Fighting for her life.

And above her, holding her down beneath the waves, his face hidden from her memory until this very moment...

Nash!

He looms above me, waist deep in the lake, hunched over, forcing something...

"Me! He's forcing *me* underwater. My head juts above the surface, and Nash wraps his elbow around my neck."

Silence.

Even the birds go quiet.

I have to act quickly.

I have to stop him before it's too late.

My chest is frozen, my heart paralyzed beneath my ribs. I feel the absence of its beat, a burning in my shriveled lungs. I am desperate for oxygen.

I gasp in a trickle of air and will my legs to kick.

"He releases his choke hold, grabs my shoulders, pushing me down."

I disappear below the black water.

I'm out of time!

"I kick. Harder and higher until I'm spinning around and my foot finds his neck and he grabs his throat. My toes grip the bottom. I lunge out of the water."

Eyes... glowing, fix on me, transforming my anemic heart into a full throttle engine.

"I run."

With powerful strides, he charges through the water—coming at me—coming for me.

"I set my sights on the shore and the forest beyond."

The wind-churned waves are my enemy. I fight them, slipping and struggling back toward the beach, not daring to look behind me until, at last, I stumble face first into sand that seeps into my pores, my mouth, my eyeballs... I catapult off my knees and bolt. When I reach the edge of the trees, rocks and sticks shred the soles of my tender, bare feet, but they do not deter me.

I keep running.

I am fleeing for my life.

"Murderer!" Brigid screamed, and the word echoed in the darkness.

The "murder" she'd witnessed was her own!

The man whose child she'd carried and nurtured had tried to drown her.

Nash had wanted her dead then, but what about now?

She didn't know the full extent of the things he'd done, but the *why* wasn't hard to figure out. Like a lot of people, Nash had suffered enormous losses in the stock market that year, and his real estate business had taken an even bigger hit. Brigid had a substantial life insurance policy and the beneficiary converted to Tish once she turned eighteen. When Brigid got drunk, she was practically incapacitated, and Nash must've seen a golden opportunity to cash in before the policy converted and it was too late.

An accidental drowning with no witnesses.

It was the perfect murder until Brigid ran out of the water and wound up in Ranger Costas's incident report.

Now *she*, the intended victim, was the witness.

Nash Clarence was a black-hearted sociopath and a *liar*.

Brigid remembered it *all* now.

A midnight picnic on the lake, darling. Just the two of us so I can lavish all my attention on you just like you've been begging me to do.

Nash had *lied* to the ranger when he'd asked his name. Jackson hadn't been there at all. How very clever of Nash. But not clever enough, because now Brigid knew the truth.

Adrenaline raged through her blood.

Nash is a killer.

And not *just* a killer—a cold-blooded merciless one. A heartless monster who'd put her into a choke hold and held her underwater, watched her gasp for air, minute after grotesque minute, cruelly waiting for the life to leave her body. And after she'd escaped, and he'd missed his chance to get away with *murdering his own wife*, he'd taken her home and dined with her, laughed with her, made love to her, as if nothing had happened, lulling her into a false sense of security.

Her pulse was pounding so hard she could barely think, but think she must. Was he done with her? Would he strike again?

Of course!

He already had: It was *Nash* who'd pushed her down the stairs the night of Jackson's concert. *He's probably worried I'll remember the truth.* Clutching her heart, she struggled off her knees and waded back to shore, and then suddenly pulled up short.

Charity.

If Nash would seize an opportunity to kill the mother of his own child, what would stop him from trying something with Charity? The way he'd been spending lately... Brigid had to ask herself where all that money was coming from. Was he expecting a windfall? Did he have a fat life insurance policy on Charity like the one he'd had on Brigid?

She jerked on her waders and rushed to the canoe—dragging it back into the water, leaping inside so quickly it nearly capsized.

Take a breath. Stay calm.

Her hands shook, tears nearly blinded her, but she kept moving.

She had to warn Charity that she was living with a murderous monster.

That she wasn't safe around him.

Thrusting her paddle into the lake, she heaved against the waves with aching arms. The wind buffeted the canoe, turning it, charting a course in the wrong direction, toward the castle and away from the safety of town where Charity was, *please Lord*, still safe among the friend group.

Brigid struggled to bring the canoe around, but then her heart jolted in her chest.

On her left was the main shoreline, the beach and the path leading to the castle, and on her right, Fannette Island, with its old, unroofed teahouse.

From the windows of the teahouse, on that deserted island in the dark of night, lights flickered—candles in the wind.

Someone was having a late-night rendezvous.

THIRTY-FOUR

Opportunity. Risk. Reward.

These are the words I live by, in business, and also in life.

"Careful, my love, I don't want you to slip."

Charity clings to my hand, and I'm tempted to finish it right here and now. It would be so easy to give her a shove and watch her tumble down the rocks as we make our way up the incline to the old, abandoned teahouse. But a fall, as I've learned, isn't always a good bet.

You win some. You lose some.

Which is no problem as long as you've done the math and have got the risk-reward ratio right.

As long as you haven't put all your eggs in one basket.

Still, one doesn't like to lose.

I've had enough of solving one problem only to find I've created another for myself.

What a headache my life has been since the night I tried to drown Brigid—the consequences falling like dominoes from there. I can see how, from a certain perspective, it might look like I've been more bungling fool than criminal mastermind, but appearances can be deceiving.

The best-laid plans are not laid; they're opportunities seized.

My crimes never leave a trail back to me precisely because they are designed, not by my hand, but by fate's—and then I simply give fate a little push.

Like I did Brigid, down the stairs, when the opportunity presented itself.

That didn't work out, unfortunately.

Nor did the other time, a few years back, when Brigid's and my marriage *and* our bank account were in deep trouble.

Then, on her birthday, Brigid got blinding drunk. I saw an opportunity, and I took a calculated risk for the insurance payday.

That's when the dominoes began to fall.

She got away from me, and a park ranger wrote up an incident report—and the risk-to-reward ratio flipped. Although I was quick thinking enough to give the ranger Jackson's name, instead of my own, and to come up with a good story, I knew, if I tried again too soon, the chances of my being found out and going to jail far exceeded my chances of walking away with a big purse.

So I followed my rules—backed off and diversified.

I married Charity, whose divorce settlement was just enough to bail me out, and later I set up a credit card scam to keep the expensive gifts and vacations flowing. Then, when Christian discovered my scheme, the best risk-reward scenario was to bring him along... until it wasn't.

Poor Christian.

Oh well, there are always going to be ups and downs and collateral damage.

"Is it much farther?" Charity asks.

"Just a few more yards. You're not tired so soon?"

"Just hungry. And ready for that martini you promised."

"Me too." Perhaps we'll have a little fun and games on a blanket under the stars before the real festivities begin.

One for the road, as Charity might say—that woman loves her clichés and I swear it's rubbed off on me.

I've got a headlamp on my cap, my gear in a backpack, and Charity soldiering on in great spirits. I do wish it hadn't come to this. My second wife is beautiful, she's great in the sack, and she damn sure knows how to have a good time.

What other woman would be all in when her husband suggests a midnight picnic on Fannette Island? It's a dangerous climb in the dark, and there's nothing but an old relic of a teahouse at the top. The view might be stunning during the day, but at this hour there's nothing to recommend it but the isolation.

I thought it might be difficult to convince her. I could barely persuade Brigid to go on a late-night picnic in a secret cove—and that was romantic as hell, no climbing involved, and Brigid was high as a kite at the time.

But I needn't have worried about any resistance on Charity's part.

My Charity craves adventure.

She didn't issue a single word of protest—fortunately, because who knows when, if ever, I'll stumble upon another chance to kill two birds with one stone.

Brigid going out alone in a canoe set up a unique opportunity.

Fannette Island is the perfect spot for a murder.

If Charity tries to get away—and she's so spunky, I'm certain she will—there's simply nowhere to run.

No forest.

No castle beyond the trees.

No park ranger nosing about to spoil my plan.

If, years ago, I'd brought Brigid to Fannette Island, instead of the cove by the castle, I would have gotten away with it: my beloved wife who'd had too much to drink drowned in the lake.

A tragic accident.

There would've been absolutely no way to prove what really happened out there in the dark—until that ranger mucked things up.

But tonight's venture is brilliant, if I do say so myself.

When I saw Brigid get in that canoe, my first thought was to follow her and capsize her boat, drown her like I'd planned before. But that would be messy—plus *no money* in it for me anymore, now that Tish is Brigid's beneficiary.

So I came up with a lower risk way to get *both* Charity and Brigid permanently off my back: eliminate Charity, collect on *her* insurance, and then let Brigid take the blame.

There's a solid witness who will testify Brigid went out in her canoe alone tonight, whereas I've taken great care to be sure no one saw *me* launch a vessel with Charity on board.

I sent Charity to rent the canoe herself, and while she was gone, I ordered a takeaway meal for one at the hotel. I also made a big fuss about how my wife had left poor me on my own for the evening in order to meet up for an island tea party with her best girlfriend, Brigid.

In case anyone doubts I was at the hotel, I left my phone back in the room, so it won't be pinging anywhere near this island.

Tomorrow morning, I'll report Charity missing.

I'll say she planned to paddle her canoe to meet up with Brigid. Once Charity's strangled corpse is found in the lake, it won't take the police long to figure out who had motive, means and opportunity to do away with my poor darling Charity.

Certainly not me.

I'm devastated.

With so much bad blood between them, I was a fool to let Charity meet crazy, unstable Brigid all alone.

I should have seen the potential for a deadly argument, but alas I did not.

I'll never forgive myself—damn it!

THIRTY-FIVE

Charity stretched out on her back on the blanket that Nash had spread in the center of the ruin. Decades ago, wind and rain had unroofed the structure, and now, only remnants of the stone walls remained, offering just enough shape to confirm that this had once been the site of tea parties hosted by an eccentric old widow who'd owned the island before the park service took it over.

Charity shifted and rolled onto her side to face Nash, who lay propped on one elbow, so near she could feel heat wafting off his skin. The wind lifted his hair, revealing a fine sheen of perspiration on his forehead. Above them stars twinkled, clouds drifted, and the night whispered its secrets in her ear.

She smiled at Nash as he slid closer, leaving only inches between his body and hers.

He was everything she'd ever wanted, everything that Jackson was not.

When she'd first met Jackson, she'd thought he was someone else. Not Stone Songbird. She wasn't so naïve as to confuse him with a character he played on television. But she had believed him to be someone who, like her, enjoyed the spotlight. She'd envisioned a life filled with premieres, paparazzi and caviar. Women would swoon, but Jackson would turn away from them and place a hand possessively on the small of her back, signaling to the world that she belonged to him, and he to her.

But, as it turned out, Jackson didn't crave attention at all—he shrank from it. And Charity soon realized he had no possessory interest in her, nor a desire to accumulate wealth. Whenever she encouraged him to rekindle his star, his rote reply was that he was a fortunate man who had far more than he'd ever wanted.

Then, when they lost Hope, the grief became a gulf too vast.

Unlike Jackson, Nash dreamed big.

Her second husband was the kind of man who, however much he possessed, fiercely desired more. And he wasn't shy about going after what he wanted. He would do whatever it took, smashing any conventions that stood in his way.

Tonight, when he'd proposed they sneak off to an island in the dead of night for a romantic picnic, it hadn't surprised her. And she hadn't hesitated to accept his invitation, hadn't worried about rough water or capsizing in the lake with no one around, or how they would manage the rocky slope up to the teahouse in the dark and then back down again.

Nash wanted to be alone with her, and she with him.

He reached out and feathered his palm across her collarbone, dipped his fingers into the cleft between her breasts.

She sighed, invitingly.

"Are you ready for a martini and some cake?" He withdrew his hand and wrangled himself into a sitting position, lifted the thermos and shook it—she could hear liquid swishing inside.

"So ready." She got onto her knees and, catching his gaze, undid the first few buttons of her top to reveal the red lace push-up bra beneath. "But only if you join me."

"Hold on. I want to set the mood." He retrieved his back-pack, removed a half-dozen candles, and then went to set them ablaze in the teahouse "windows".

Now, flickering lights encircled them, creating a devastatingly sensuous mood.

He joined her back on the blanket, poured martinis for them both into paper cups.

"Very romantic, but surely the wind... oh, never mind. I see. You've thought of everything." The slender candles were made of hard plastic, and the light they gave off was imparted by batteries.

"I try."

She broke open a container of pink-champagne petite fours iced with white buttercream, gobbled one up, and then fed him cake.

He greedily sucked the icing off her fingers and slugged his martini.

In between nibbles and sips, she made little noises designed to let him know she was enjoying herself and ready for more—much more. "You know what one of my favorite things in the world is? Besides buttercream frosting and martinis?"

"I'm eager to find out," he said.

"Skinny-dipping." She ducked her chin and glanced up at him through her lash extensions. "Are you in?"

"You're not worried the water's too cold?"

"You'll keep me warm."

"Let's have another drink first."

"I've already had two." Actually, she'd knocked her first one over onto the rocks while he was busy setting out the candles. The path down to the water was steep, and she wanted to keep her wits about her. "You go ahead and have another. I'll watch."

He was on his feet. "No more for me. I'm driving. Don't want to get pulled over for drunk paddling."

"I don't think there's a ranger around this time of night, but you're right, better not to overindulge. I'm counting on you to keep me safe."

"Always, my love. Skinny-dipping it is."

Once they'd climbed all the way back down to the bottom of the trail, he hopped over a small boulder and helped her scramble over it.

She eyed the canoe they'd dragged up onto the shore earlier. "I brought a little present for you, darling."

"What? When did you do that?" he asked.

"Since you sent me to rent the canoe, I took the opportunity to sneak into one of the tourist shops. I wanted to surprise you. Your gift is in my bag in the boat. You go ahead and strip down, while I go get it."

"I'll come with you."

"Stop." She held up her palm. "I said it's a surprise. Now then, get naked, mister, and close your eyes."

He grabbed her wrist.

"Let me go. You're spoiling the surprise."

He tightened his grip, shaking his head. "No."

"Nash, what's the matter? You're hurting me." She tried to make her voice sound confident, but her heart was pounding, her stomach twisting. He didn't know. He *couldn't*. If he'd seen her sneak that pistol into her bag, he would've killed her already.

Nash dragged her over to the canoe and retrieved a pistol from a waterproof bag under the *bow* seat—a different bag, not the one that she'd stowed under the *stern* seat.

"Is this my surprise?" Yanking her by the arm, he pulled her toward the water. "Do you think I'm stupid?"

"Do you think I am?" She jerked her arm, and he released it, letting her fall backwards onto the rocky beach. Her hands stung as she pushed herself up off the gravel, eyeing the canoe.

"It's not there, my love."

He thinks he's smarter than you.

"Nash, this is crazy. What are you even talking about? Why did you bring a gun?"

"I didn't. I took this pistol—" he waved it in her direction "—out of *your* bag and put it in the bag under my seat instead. So, the question isn't why did I bring a gun; it's why did you?"

Think, Charity. "For protection. I hear there are bears."

"Good try. But I don't believe you, and even if I did, it wouldn't make any difference. I'm not doing this to get back at you. I quite like you, in fact. And I'm going to miss the good times we had. I was planning some incredible goodbye sex before sending you off. Sorry I didn't deliver on that, but when you offered to skinny-dip it seemed like the path of least resistance to get you back down to the water. You can leave your clothes on if you like, but you're going to get wet." He flicked the barrel of the pistol toward the lake. "March."

She clamped her jaw. Took a breath. Commanded her hands to stop shaking. If she couldn't control her emotions, she'd be dead within minutes, maybe less. But if she harnessed the adrenaline jetting through her, she might still be able to make it home alive. "Not a chance." If there was one thing Charity knew how to do, it was to suppress her feelings. "I'm not walking myself into the water so you can say I got drunk and drowned."

"You will, because if you don't, I'll shoot you. And by the way, why aren't you tipsy?"

"I had one martini, and dumped the other. And you can't shoot me, because then that won't look like an accidental drowning."

"Interesting. How were you planning on getting around that problem when you shot me, I wonder."

"Easy. I'm a small, helpless woman and my diabolical husband tried to murder me. I shot him in self-defense. I can sell that with one hand tied behind my back, but you will never get away with arguing self-defense. Especially after you just had me change the beneficiary on my life insurance policy from Christian to you."

He took a step closer, cocked the pistol. "I'm not bluffing, Charity."

"That is what it's all about, isn't it? Money. What will you do now that you can't live off stolen identities... you stole Roman's, didn't you? And then your own daughter's! Now you're going to kill your second wife for profit. But then what? How long will that tide you over? Who'll be next? *Tish?* I know you have life-insurance on her, and I'll never let you hurt her. *Never!*"

"I wouldn't harm a hair on Tish's head. And I had nothing to do with any credit card scam. That was all Christian."

"Oh, please. I love my brother, but he's not smart enough to pull off a scheme like that on his own. And for your information, he left me a letter."

"Get in the water or I will shoot you. I was planning on death by strangulation—you and Brigid argued, she became enraged and so on—but premeditated murder might work even better since you've done me the favor of providing a pistol."

She couldn't see his face well enough to read his expression, but his voice rang with fury. He was on the verge of losing it.

"Then do it."

He raised his arm, hesitated, and she lunged for him, butting his chest with her head. The pistol flew from his hand onto the rocks at the water's edge.

She dove for it, and her body landed hard.

A sharp sting.

Blood dripping onto the ground near her face.

The pistol just out of reach.

Don't give up.

She stretched her arm, reaching with her fingers.

His boot stomped her hand, but she managed to get hold of

his ankle with the other. He slipped, and in the process kicked the gun into the lake.

Nash rolled onto her, and with his hands clamped around her throat, got to his knees, straddling her. "Bitch! You want to know a secret? Christian's dead! I killed him."

She spit in his face, and he jumped up and kicked her in the stomach, sending pain radiating through her. Her skin incinerated as he dragged her on her back across the gravel, then towed her into the lake.

Cold, black water, swirled around her. Her lungs ached from holding her breath as he held her under. She was going to die tonight but she no longer cared.

As she struggled for air, she reached up and dug her nails into his cheek.

"Bitch!" He lifted her head by the hair and punched her in the face.

Again and again and again.

She managed to claw his neck.

There was no real chance of escape, but she could make sure the cops saw the marks on him. They'd find his skin under her nails, she hoped, and if he beat her badly enough, they'd know for certain that a powerful man, a monster, had done this. Brigid would be cleared, and Nash would go to prison.

Tish would be safe.

Hit me again, you bastard.

Hit me again.

THIRTY-SIX

Brigid released the canoe's paddles. She'd been gripping the wooden shaft so tightly her hands had gone numb, and now that the sensation was returning, her palms burned as if she'd been holding a pair of lava rocks in her hands.

She lifted them in front of her face, staring, disoriented, unsure how she'd gotten here. What was she doing sitting in a canoe in the middle of the lake at night? Ahead, she could see Fannette Island, lights blinking from the windows in the teahouse ruins atop the hill.

Her head ached.

Her ears buzzed.

Her thoughts flickered like the lights.

No. No. No.

She could feel her mind disconnecting, and she could not, she would not let it happen again.

Make a different choice.

When she was a little girl afraid of monsters hiding in her closet, it had served her well to simply close her eyes and tell herself over and over and over again: *there's nothing to be afraid of.*

But when the monster is real... closing your eyes doesn't work. The only way to stay safe is to open them.

Look that monster dead in the face.

Take action.

Stop hiding. There's no safe place.

She pulled in a long breath, let her hands drop into her lap and stared at the island.

Nash.

Her own personal monster.

Nash had tried to drown her. He was a murderer, and no one in his orbit was safe.

"I will never forget again," she spoke the words into the wind. "I will keep my eyes open, no matter how terrified I am."

The teahouse!

Those flickering lights.

Someone is on a late-night excursion.

But that doesn't mean it's Nash and Charity.

Don't jump to conclusions.

Fannette Island was completely deserted.

The old ruin wasn't protected with a security system like the mansion-turned-museum.

It was the perfect place to get away with murder.

She shivered, counting her blessings that Nash hadn't been clever enough to take her there that night. Her chin quivered, and she bit her lip—relishing the way the pain cut through her nerves.

It could be a coincidence, and yet her gut told her it wasn't. Nash had brought her to this same area on the pretense of a late-night romantic picnic, and then tried to drown her. If he ever wanted to get rid of his second wife, like he'd wanted to get rid of his first, he would know better than to go back to the beach near Vikingsholm, where the castle was alarmed, and Charity might be able to draw the attention of a ranger.

Brigid's canoe rocked in the waves, the cool wind blew

against her skin, and with each breath, each small movement of the boat, she felt more and more anchored to reality. A light flashed near her feet.

My phone!

Her mobile lay at the bottom of the canoe. She must've dropped it as she pushed off from shore.

Carefully, deliberately, she picked up her cell.

One bar might be enough.

Please. Please. Please.

Charity's phone sent her straight to voicemail, like it was turned off or out of range.

Keep calm.

It seemed risky to leave a message, but even more dangerous not to. "Nash tried to kill me. He might try to hurt you, too. If he's taken you to the island, hide. Keep away from him. You probably don't believe me, but I'm begging you to trust me. Hide." She took a deep breath. "I'll get help."

Brigid hit end and started to call 911, but changed her mind. It would only waste time. The operator would have to figure out who to send to an island in the middle of the lake, but Brigid already knew who would be nearby.

She scrolled rapidly through her contacts and found Ranger Costas.

No more bars.

Her boat had drifted out of service.

She tucked her phone in her pocket, grabbed the oars, and paddled furiously toward the island. A minute later she dropped the oars to check her service.

No bars.

She paddled until her arms ached, and checked again.

Okay.

With steady hands and a shockingly clear head—the adrenaline bursting through her body seemed to be working in her favor now—she called Ranger Costas.

As the phone rang, she came up with a plan.

Costas knew her as an unstable, unreliable woman.

She needed his help, but if she told him the truth, that her ex-husband was a psychopath who *might* have taken his second wife to Fannette Island for a death picnic, that she was fearful history would repeat itself, the chances of him sending help were low. The whole thing sounded far-fetched, even to her, but she wasn't willing to risk Charity's life if there was the slightest chance she was in trouble. For once, she wasn't going to "be reasonable". Not with every fiber of her being crying out to her that Charity was in danger.

"Mrs. Temp...?" He must have her on his caller ID since he knew it was her right away, but his words were breaking up.

"Help!"

"Can you... me?"

"I'm on the island. Fannette Island."

"Your husband, Mr. Templeton, is looking for you. You say you're on Fannette..."

No point in trying to answer questions or have a real conversation with the connection likely to drop any moment. She had to just keep talking, and hope he heard enough through the broken air waves to send help. But if Jackson was worried, and already had people searching for her, that was a good thing. "I'm drunk." That, Costas would believe. "I don't want to get in my boat."

"Stay where you are. Don't... boat."

"I'm in the teahouse. I'm drunk."

"I'm coming."

She released her breath. How could she get more help? Not just him. "I'm bleeding! I need medics."

"You're hurt?"

"Need medics. Bring more people!"

She left the line open, but stuck the phone in her bra, and kept paddling.

Her fingers were numb, her arms burning when she, at last, sidled her canoe up to the shore of Fannette Island. Then, she leaped into the water and towed her boat onto the sand, just feet away from another vessel.

Maybe it wasn't them.

Maybe she had it all wrong.

It was entirely possible some other, utterly foolish, couple had planned a late-night rendezvous in an abandoned ruin of a teahouse.

"Bitch!" Nash's voice, unmistakable to her, carried on the wind, erasing all doubt.

Thank heavens she'd trusted her gut. It sounded as though he had Charity out in the lake, somewhere nearby. Her first thought was to call out, to run, but that would give him warning. Better to think, to plan, even if only seconds ahead.

Listen.

She held her breath so that even that soft sound would not, like the rushing of the wind, distort the location of his voice.

"Bitch!"

They were somewhere to her left. She could move faster on the shore, but she had a better chance to take him by surprise from the water. She couldn't see him anywhere on the horizon, so this was her chance.

She kicked off her waders, tossed her phone onto the shore, and strode into the lake.

Nash might kill both her and Charity, she knew that.

But she had to try. She couldn't stand by and do nothing while he hurt another person.

She didn't want to die, to leave Tish... and Jackson.

Suddenly, her heart expanded.

Knowing she might never see her husband and her daughter again, every molecule of air she breathed seemed filled with love—love that had always been there, hiding inside, along with a newly discovered love that deepened with every step she took into the night.

Into the lake.

Frigid water nipped her ankles, and then slid up her thighs to her waist.

The moon broke through the clouds, and her gaze followed its light to a hand darting above the water, a figure standing in the lake.

Just like her dream. Except this time, she knew who and what she was facing.

Brigid swam, mostly underwater, keeping only her nose and eyes above the surface of the waves.

His arm drew back; his fist slammed forward.

"Hit... me..." Charity's voice sounded weakened with pain, broken by the wind, hard to recognize, but Brigid knew it was her.

Once again, his arm drew back; his fist slammed forward.

Brigid dove underwater, swimming blindly toward her monster, guided by some inner radar, or maybe the struggle between Nash and Charity was sending physical clues—a slight warmth in the water, an effervescence beneath the surface. It was impossible to know how she found them underwater in the dark lake, but she did.

His leg, like an underwater tree, was suddenly there, in front of her.

Grabbing his thigh, she bit down hard, kicked his crotch, then felt him slip out of her grasp.

She was moving again, arms churning through black water, her body colliding with a tangle of slime—she was swimming in weeds.

Soaring to the surface, she saw bubbles.

From behind, Nash grabbed her shoulders, forcing her back under water, until her lungs screamed in her chest. Then her scalp exploded in pain as he ripped her head by the hair above the water.

Her lips connected with air, and she gasped.

Nash stood over her, one arm around her chest, one hand jerking her head back, her neck in full extension, staring into his eyes, seeing for the first time, his black, black heart. His mouth was moving, like he was trying to tell her something.

Killing her wasn't enough.

He wanted more.

He wanted to triumph over her.

But that was impossible now. She loved Jackson, and though Nash might destroy her body, he could never take that from her, again.

His face was so close now, first his breath was on her, then his lips.

He'd pulled her out of the water to kiss her goodbye!

What a fool.

She opened her mouth, drawing in as much oxygen as she could and then bit down hard on his devil's tongue.

He yelped and let go of her hair.

Her feet found the bottom and she lunged back, saw his hands lift, his fist coil, and then... a form looming behind him with an oar held high.

A loud crack, and his head jerked to the side.

His body sank beneath the surface, and Charity grabbed him by the hair and pulled his head up.

Brigid heard whirring, grower louder, closer.

A bright white cone of light shone down, spotlighting crimson blood leaking from Nash's scalp.

"Are you okay?" Charity shouted over the whirring of the helicopter. "I tried... stop him, I wanted to kill... what he did to Christian."

Brigid pointed to her ears. "What did you say?"

"Christian's dead!" Charity cried out. Her arms were under

Nash's limp body, supporting him as he floated, keeping his face above water.

"Oh, no. No, no, no. I'm sorry." Brigid splashed over to Charity. "But how did you know?"

"Christian left letter... friend Nick..."

Brigid could only hear snatches of sentences above the din of the helicopter. She pointed to her ears again.

"Christian's friend... soup kitchen... brought letter to the hike!"

The chopper was circling closer. They were on solid footing in the shallows of the lake, now, and could easily make the shore, even with Nash in tow.

"... bastard... confessed!" Charity screamed above the noise. "Let him drown?"

"Too late!" Brigid gestured at the chopper.

If it weren't directly overhead shining a bright light down on them, what would they have done?

She'd never know, but she took comfort in knowing Nash wouldn't get away with this. Not with testimony from Charity and from her... not with a letter from Christian.

THIRTY-SEVEN

Sis,

If you're reading this, I've gone to my eternal rest, and I know that hurts you bad. That is my first thing to say sorry for. I wish I could say I'm with Mom and Dad and Hope smiling down on you and Tish, but I don't like my chances. Nick, the friend I left this letter with, told me God forgives sinners as long as they're sorry.

I am.

So you never know, I might be in the good place after all. When Mom and Dad died you were the best sister any kid ever had. I wouldn't have made it through all that stuff we went through without you, so don't blame yourself for my mistakes. I did a lot of wrong things, but you got to know I tried my best for you and for Tish to be a better man.

Where I went wrong ~~no one is to blame but me~~ *I blame Nash.*

It is going to hurt to hear this, and I thought a long time about if I should leave you a letter. But like I said, if you're reading this then I'm worm food, and that means you're in danger, too. Nash swore to me he would never hurt a hair on your head, and when I asked him to swear he would never hurt Tish, he punched me in the nuts. I thought she was safe from him. I still think she probably is, only now I'm not one hundred percent sure because of everything he's done, and if he has killed me he might hurt you too.

So here goes.

I'm going to tell you everything, and you'll have to fix it. I'm sorry, but I know how strong you are. I believe in you.

Nash has a LOT of secrets.

When you two got married I thought he was a good guy like Jackson. He paid for that real estate course and gave me money without me asking. He taught me about stocks and investment strategies too. He didn't mind me hanging around his daughter, and he didn't ask for anything in return. I guess it was the first time any man, except Jackson, treated me like I was worth a damn. That made me feel real good, which is part of why I went along with his plans at the start.

It wasn't for the coin. I didn't want to steal from anyone. But working for Nash I could see he didn't care about the law. He taught me you have to know the rules so you can break them, and that all good businessmen know how to get around taxes and regulations and how to dirty trick the competition.

He said everyone does it, and I looked up to the guy.

So I hoovered up everything I could learn from him. And then one day I saw some stuff I shouldn't. He left a drawer unlocked that had the safe combination in it. I opened the safe and I found a phone with pictures of credit cards and checks. I was standing there with my dick in my hand, so to speak, when he comes in and catches me catching him.

Then he takes me out for a long ride in his car, and I wonder will he off me just for knowing he's a thief. We drive and drive without him saying nothing, and then finally he stops the car and tells me he's calculated the risk-reward ratio and decided it is too risky and not enough reward for him to kill me. So from now on, me and him are going to be partners. Or if I don't want to he can kill me instead.

This is not a hard choice for me.

I don't have to do any math to decide.

That's when the lessons start up. Identity theft is easy if you keep it simple. Nash likes to take advantage of opportunity when it knocks. If you are getting your coat from the closet at Supper Club or your stuff out of the dry bag on the yacht, and it happens that no one is around, then that's when you lift a wallet and start taking pics with your phone.

He says I can be a big asset and take pics of his real estate client's credit cards while he distracts them. That way we are in détente because of mutually assured destruction. Détente is another risk strategy, he said.

Life is about understanding opportunity, risk, and reward.

Nash lives by risk strategies.

I am worried I will die by them.

So, to get on with the story, one day Tish gets her identity stolen, and I know it's Nash.

He stole his own daughter's identity.

When I finally see who he really is, it makes me ashamed that I ever wanted to be like him. I tell him I'm finished, and he laughs and says we are like a mafia family, and I can't get out because I know too much and he'd have no choice but to kill me.

I wasn't scared of him that much just then. I would have moved to Mexico where he couldn't get me thrown in jail, but I didn't want to leave you and Tish. I tried to talk Tish into moving to Tijuana but that made her suspicious, and she wasn't going to leave dear old dad ever. Even if I told her all the rotten things he did: stealing her identity, making me lie to her by saying Brigid and Jackson cheated, she'd never take my word over his.

She'd hate me, and I couldn't stand that so I kept my mouth shut.

Me and Nash kept the credit card scam going until one day he spied on Roman and Brigid in a rose garden and found out Roman was talking to the FBI and the IRS. Then Nash says we have to stop the identity theft because the risk-reward ratio is no longer in our favor. He says it's time to put his eggs in a different basket.

Without the credit card scheme, Nash's easy money is gone, so what will he do next to get more?

That thought makes me scared.

For you. For Tish. And for Brigid too.

I know he keeps life insurance on you and Tish.

And Nash kept running his mouth about Brigid going to that psychiatrist. What is she telling her shrink? What is she telling her shrink? He started searching up repressed memories and memory recovery on his computer. I can see he's afraid Brigid might remember something he doesn't want her to.

The night Brigid fell down the stairs, I saw Nash disappear around a corner, and I'm pretty sure he pushed her.

By then, I hated him, and I hated myself even more for being his pawn. But I kept on because it was the only way I knew to keep me and you and Tish safe.

Until Tish found my phone with a bunch of credit card pics on it and said I should turn myself in.

I shouldn't have told Nash, but I didn't know what to do. He says don't worry. He says he is going to get me a hotshot lawyer and a smoking plea deal. He says if I can just do a year or two behind bars he'll smooth everything over for me with Tish and make sure I get a piece of some offshore accounts he's got. He says I should calculate the risk-reward ratio and trust him.

All I know is that I love Tish and I want to live.

You and her are all that matter to me.

I don't care about money. I don't care if I have to do time. I need you two safe. So I'll take a chance with Nash and hope that he'll fix it so Tish takes me back, and you'll both be okay until I get out.

All I want is a normal life. A family of my own.

I wish I had never done any of this illegal stuff. I don't know what happened to Roman, but I've got a bad feeling Nash had something to do with it, and it makes me sick.

Nash isn't like us. He doesn't care who he hurts, and I do not trust him.

He might break his promise and kill me, and if he does that means he'll kill ANYONE to get money and stay out of jail.

And that's what keeps me awake at night.

That's what keeps me playing his game.

But I'm giving this letter to Nick in case Nash does his worst. You'll have to do whatever it takes, then, to protect yourself and Tish.

If you're reading this, that means it's up to you.

Tell Tish I'm sorry and that I love her.

Love always,

Your baby brother

EPILOGUE

FIVE YEARS LATER

Cielo Hermoso
North San Diego County, California

As the morning sun rose higher in the sky, the pale-pink horizon changed to bright blue. In the distance, where Brigid's eye created an optical illusion of ocean meeting sky, cottony white clouds appeared to rise from the water before climbing into the heavens. She closed her eyes, believing Hope was among the angels looking down on them this morning.

That she was nearby, watching.

Sometimes, calling up the past brought tears to Brigid's eyes and an ache to her chest, but more often it lifted her up. Either way, these days, she didn't hide from the emotion.

Brigid's bout with emotional amnesia changed the way she looked at life.

It had taken almost losing her ability to love for her to understand that, while it's possible to forget your heartache, you can do so without abandoning your joy.

Now, she inhaled deeply. "I love the scent of eucalyptus. It brings back my memories of Hope so vividly. Puts me right back in the moment."

"Don't take this the wrong way, but you sounded like Charity just then," Jackson said.

Arms full of sunflowers, she shrugged. "Tish thinks Charity and I, like most ordinary people, are alike in more ways than we're different. So maybe it's true."

"Not so sure I'd call either you or Charity ordinary, but I take your point." He tilted his head. "Speaking of memories, you see that tree, that rainbow eucalyptus, with the neon colors —it reminds me of the day Hope painted a landscape filled with them. I can picture her now, her mouth tightened into a determined line, furiously dabbing the purples and greens onto the canvas. The memory hurts like hell, but I'll never let go of it because it keeps her alive in my heart."

Walking side by side, they reached Hope's grave.

It wasn't Hope's birthday, just a normal day when they'd been thinking of her, and talking about her, as they often did. Jackson spread a blanket, sat cross-legged on it and started up strumming Hope's old guitar—the one with the scratched soundboard.

Brigid knelt and began to weave the long stems of the sunflowers into a giant garland, one large enough to drape over the headstone. "We should all come out here, together, soon. You and me and Tish and Charity."

She meant that.

Brigid and Tish's relationship had never been stronger, and Brigid was no longer just *playing the role* of friend to Charity. The resentment she'd felt for Charity had long since evaporated. Not only because they'd literally saved each other's lives —but because it gutted her to think about how much Charity had lost in such a short time. First Hope, and then, just a few years later, her younger brother, Christian.

Plus, the fact that it had been Nash who'd murdered him. That had to be almost unbearable. "It's amazing the way Charity's come through all of this. I'm so proud of her—although I guess that sounds weird, since—"

"No. I get what you mean. I'm proud of her, too." Jackson set his guitar down gently. "The perfect time to visit here together might be when Charity heads down from L.A. for our Supper Club 'special event' next month."

"I almost forgot about her season premiere." Nash's trial and his many crimes had not only made headlines, they'd hurt a lot of people in the group. But their friend circle, amazingly, had weathered the storm, rallying around one another rather than casting blame where they easily might have. Not only that, they'd planned a big party to watch the season premiere of *Crime on the Coast* next month.

Charity, apparently, had been hiding a talent for alchemy, and turned infamy into gold.

She'd made such an on-camera splash during Nash's trial, they'd offered her a gig hosting a true-crime television pilot. The series got picked up, so Charity moved to Los Angeles and finally planted her heels on the red carpet she'd always wanted to walk.

"Has she said anything more to you about the show's big reveal?" Jackson asked.

"Only that she told Tish the secret ahead of time, and that Tish is taking it well, whatever that means. Charity also said we should be prepared for the most dramatic season ever."

"Tish isn't coming down for the viewing party? I suppose she's awfully busy, what with graduation coming up, planning a wedding, looking for a job."

Christian's death had devastated Tish, but she'd eventually gone back to USC and buried herself in the books, found a counselor recommended by Dr. Tanaka who'd helped her tremendously. And then, junior year, she'd met "the one". "Slow down there, buddy, Tish and George haven't set a date. I think they want to wait at least a year—they just got engaged last month. And, as you point out, they're both graduating soon and looking for jobs."

"Then what are all those bride magazines I saw in your study?"

"I'm just getting some ideas... but it's Tish's wedding and I want her to take her time. Don't out me, please. I don't want her to feel pressured to get married and give me—"

"Grandchildren? I'm sure she has no idea you're interested in such matters."

"For your information, although I will welcome any additions to the family with open arms, you make me so happy, I don't feel like we're missing a thing in our lives."

"Come here." Jackson spread his arms and she leaned into them, buried her face in his chest. He brushed a kiss on the top of her head. "For me, everything we've been through, you struggling to find your love for me, has only strengthened our bond. I love you, Brigid... I won't say nothing is going to change my love, because I believe love changes every day."

"It has to... or else it dies." She pressed her cheek to his chest, relishing the sound of his heart beating against her ear. "Never again will I go looking for the love we had yesterday. I think I'm lucky I had emotional amnesia—if I hadn't forgotten those old feelings, I might never have understood that marriage isn't only about the love you feel in the beginning; what's most important is the love you recreate every day."

* * *

Tijuana, Mexico

Widening her eyes, Charity looked over her shoulder, directly into the lens, and motioned.

"Follow me!" she enthused to the camera crew the station had sent along with her, and to her viewers. Even though the season premiere of her true crime series wouldn't air for another month, she pretended they were filming in front of a live audience.

And they more or less were, since a crowd was trailing them, being held at bay by a handful of off-duty Federales hired as private security. They'd just crossed into Mexico and were headed on foot into the bustling border town of... "Tijuana! A mere eighteen miles south of San Diego, California."

Charity marched toward a giant metallic arch. "We arrive at the famous Avenida Revolución—the main downtown drag, an easy walk from the border crossing, and a feast for your eyes."

She circled her hand in a gesture that communicated to the crew she wanted plenty of shots of the flags waving on wires above the streets, and the colorful umbrellas shading carts loaded with touristy wares. Too bad the cameras couldn't capture the smells of hot sugar and buttery bread blowing on the breeze.

"Are you hungry? I am. Lucky for me our secret guest will be joining me at Tia Tacos. I wonder if he... or she... is already there, waiting. Who wants to know the identity of my super-special top-secret guest?"

A series of whoops and applause from onlookers followed.

She winked. "All in good time."

As they approached the archway leading to Tia Tacos, her heart began pounding above the music of the mariachi bands.

"Big day," she whispered into her mic. "Just another block."

And then she spotted him. A "gringo" with electric blue eyes, jet-black hair tied into a man bun, and a sleeve of tattoos showing beneath the yellow collared T-shirt he wore with slacks so new they still had their pre-wear creases. She lifted her hand to return his wave, before striding, with as much professional restraint as she could muster, toward her baby brother.

"Christian!" They embraced.

Then took seats across from each other at a square plastic table. It took a few minutes for the crew to beat back the crowd and get a mic on her brother, and set up the cameras' positions. Charity used that time to quickly recap the process for Christian while the owner brought over plates of complimentary fish tacos and sides of roasted corn on the cob topped in a creamy tan sauce.

"Are we supposed to eat on camera?" Christian asked.

"Maybe take a bite for this guy's sake. Great publicity for him." Even though the show didn't air in Mexico, Tia Taco thrived off the business of tourists from the US side of the border. In fact Tijuana had declared itself to be the most visited city in the world, and if there had been any successful challenge to that claim, she didn't know about it. She reached under the table and quickly squeezed his hand. "Nervous?"

"Yeah."

"Me too. But we'll get through it, and once we do, imagine the relief."

"I don't know, Sis. Life on the lamb has been pretty good. I'm not sure I want to go back to—"

"That's good stuff. From the heart. Save it for on camera. Oh, wait—we're on? Okay, don't worry about a thing. Editing is magic." She adjusted her mic, gave a nod to the pretty young woman in the baseball cap, and then squared her gaze with the lens. "Welcome to the season five premiere of *Crime on the Coast*. I promise you, this is going to be the most dramatic season ever as we kick off with an exclusive interview that is deeply personal to me. We're here today, in Tijuana, Mexico, with a man who has been labeled 'missing and presumed dead' by the authorities for the past five years: My brother, Christian Tanner, formerly known as Christian Drury."

"Thanks, Sis."

When she met his gaze, genuine tears pooled in both their eyes, which was good stuff for the cameras, but caused her throat to squeeze so tightly she couldn't speak. No worries. They could edit out that long pause, or maybe leave it in to amp up the emotion. "Thank you. Shall we begin with the obvious question? Where have you been for the past five years and why have you been in hiding?"

Christian took a bite of fish taco, and then inhaled the rest, before wiping his mouth. "Tastes great. Tia Taco is my favorite place to chow down in Tijuana."

No matter how old he got, she'd always see him as her kid brother, scarfing up whatever was put in front of him, grateful to have a meal at all. "You've made mistakes, but you're my brother. I know you have a good heart so just take your time and tell us in your own words. What really went down?"

"Five years ago, I got involved in an identity theft scheme. My partner in crime was your ex-husband, Nash Clarence."

"Okay, we're going to insert a video here. Many of our viewers know about Nash—his story is how I got my fifteen minutes of fame and parlayed that into a career—but we will give them a rehash, a detailed monologue where I summarize the basics and then they will see a clip of Nash hearing the guilty verdict in the Roman Benedetti murder trial. Verbiage will roll across the screen informing the audience that based on footage deleted from Roman's doorbell camera that was later recovered from the cloud, as well as incriminating financial records, Nash was convicted of Roman's murder and sentenced to life without the possibility for parole. And, in a subsequent trial, he was ordered to pay restitution to his other identity theft victims. His assets were sold off to accomplish that, and I, personally, paid an extra two hundred thousand dollars to cover any stolen goods or monies my brother may have received. But you never took anything close to two hundred thousand dollars.

How about you pick it up for the camera with how much you actually stole?"

"My share from the identity theft scheme was, I think, about five grand over the course of our grift, plus my legitimate salary as Nash's assistant in his real estate office, which added another twelve thousand dollars—bringing the total to around seventeen thousand dollars. I want to state, for the record, I am —I mean I *was* a thief—however, I did not take part in planning or carrying out the murder of Roman Benedetti."

"To be clear, did you have anything to do with Roman Benedetti's death, either before or after the fact?" she asked coolly, as if she were interviewing an ordinary criminal and not her own flesh and blood.

"Nothing whatsoever. I worried that Nash was involved, but I had no evidence. I was scared to ask him, because if he knew I suspected him, I feared he'd harm me or my family."

"And by family, do you mean me, his own wife?"

"Yes, and I also feared for the life of his daughter."

"I see. But if you suspected this man was dangerous, maybe even a murderer, how could you just run away and leave us?"

"Like I said, I was scared. I made a mistake, and I'm sorry for it. What happened was someone, my girlfriend, found evidence of the identity theft on my phone. She's an honest person through and through and she wanted me to turn myself in. I told Nash, and he promised to get me a lawyer, but in the end, I knew I couldn't trust him. So I left a letter. You weren't supposed to get it unless I died, but my friend decided it might be important and gave it to you after I skipped town. I think you later showed it to the cops."

"That's right. I turned it over and it was used as evidence in the trials of Nash Clarence and helped secure his convictions. Viewers will find a link to the letter on our website if they'd like to read it. Was everything in the letter the truth?"

"One hundred percent. It's all true. Like the letter says, I was going to go along with Nash's plan for me to do time for the credit card theft. I gave that letter to my friend, Nick, to give to you only if Nash killed me. I was going to stick it out and do jail time like Nash wanted me to do."

"So what changed?"

"I thought, why am I waiting around to see if Nash is going to keep his word and get me a lawyer or not? And what if he did kill Roman Benedetti, and he tries to pin it on me?" Christian sighed. "So I went to plan B. I ran to Mexico. When I went missing, Nick didn't know what had happened to me and gave you the letter."

"And I thought you were dead—" her voice shook from the anger she still couldn't escape "—because my ex-husband, Nash, who is now a convicted murderer, told me he killed you. It was a horrible, horrible thing you put me through."

"I'm sorry. I didn't know he'd be so sadistic as to try to make you believe he'd murdered me—"

"While he was attempting to murder *me*! The rat bastard." She closed her eyes.

"Do you need a break?" her cameraman asked.

She shook her head. They were about to get to the good part. There was more drama ahead. "So you ran to Mexico, and you let the cops, and your loved ones, believe you were dead."

"Yes, because I didn't want to go to prison. I was guilty of identity theft."

"You know that's a financial crime, and with a good attorney—"

"Nash is smart. I didn't know what heinous crimes he'd committed and what he might try to frame me for. All I knew was that he wanted me to take the fall for the credit cards. And let's face it, I didn't want to accept any consequences for my actions. It was a horrible thing to let you believe I was dead, and I'm even more sorry to my former girlfriend. Sorry, Tish. But she has a loving family to support her, and I thought she was better off without me in her life. I wanted her to move on… but you had no one, and I couldn't let *you* go on believing I was dead."

She took both his hands. "Tell the viewers more about that."

"About six months after I ran, I emailed you to let you know I was alive."

"And did you tell me where you were?"

"No. I didn't want to make you guilty of obstructing justice or anything. I didn't want to put you in legal jeopardy. Later, you emailed me to say you'd spoken to a lawyer, and he said, since no one ever charged me with anything, I wasn't a fugitive. He said if the police asked about me, you would have to tell the truth—that I was in email communication with you, and let them take it from there."

"But they never did. So a couple of years later, after Nash was convicted for his crimes, you told me where you were. That you were laying low in Tijuana, and that you had a family."

"A wife, Maria, and a son, Mateo—he's three years old, now."

"Then you and I decided, together, that I would pay restitution to your victims. An amount far exceeding what you took from them. That two hundred thousand dollars I paid on your behalf wasn't actually my money, even though I told everyone it was. The money came from you. How did you get it?"

"I traveled back into the United States, where you helped me legally change my last name and open a brokerage account."

"I know what happened, but for the viewers… no one tried to arrest you?"

"No. I entered the country with my own passport, and then I changed my last name to Tanner, legally, and got a new passport. I had no problem getting that or a brokerage account. I was presumed dead, and the police weren't actually trying to find me. You weren't trying to make them find me because—"

"I knew you were alive. But I think people may still be wondering how you got all that money to pay your victims."

"In the stock market. Nash Clarence taught me about investing strategies. He taught me to evaluate the risk-to-reward ratio and how to diversify—to make sure I didn't have my eggs in one basket. I did real well for myself, all on the up and up. I pay my taxes. It's one hundred percent legal."

"Have you ever stolen anything since the credit card scheme with Nash Clarence came to a tragic end after the death of Roman Benedetti?"

"No."

"So why are you telling the public about this *now*? Why are you coming out of hiding at this particular time?"

"You want me to be honest?"

"Of course."

"I've wanted to tell the truth for a long time. Keeping such a terrible secret is hard on a person, but I have a family to consider. So I waited until the statute of limitations was up to come clean. Now that the time for my crimes has expired, I can't be charged with them, even though I'm guilty. I used the system to my advantage. If you want to judge me for that, I don't blame you."

"I'm sure a lot of folks will. But it must feel good to get that off your chest, and it's been a great show." She tapped her nails on the table. "Before we go, I have one last surprise in store. I believe there's someone else who deserves a chance to say her piece."

Christian tipped back in his chair, nearly falling over, and then jumped to his feet.

He sees her.

A young woman stepped out from behind a camera and swept off her baseball cap, setting loose a riot of short blonde curls.

"Tish!" Christian took a step in her direction and then

stopped short. "I-I... it's so good to see you. I'm sorry, so sorry for—"

"Letting me think you'd been murdered? Allowing me to believe I'd had a hand in your death because I found incriminating evidence on your phone? My mother was right about you. She warned me to be careful, and I wish I'd listened. My mom has been my rock."

His face crumpled. "I-I made a lot of mistakes. I'm sorry for anything I said or did that might have driven a wedge between you."

Tish's blue eyes blazed as the camera zoomed in on her fierce expression. "You haven't come between us. We love each other too much for *anyone* to succeed at that. And the truth is, I've known for a long time that you were alive. Charity understood how devastated I was over your supposed death—the guilt I felt. She told me you were alive the same day you contacted her, and that, along with my mother's unconditional love, has enabled me to move on with my life." Without dropping her gaze, she pulled a cream-colored envelope from her jacket pocket and tapped it into Christian's outstretched hand.

"What's this?" he whispered.

"An invitation to my college graduation ceremony. You can come to my wedding, too, once we set a date."

His hand shook as he opened the envelope and traced the engraving with his finger. "I know this is an 'in your face' kind of gesture, but I'm honestly happy for you."

"You can take it that way if you want, and I won't pretend I wasn't furious with you. But there's something I've learned from my mother. I used to think she was phony for being so nice to people who'd wronged her—now, I realize she's a genuinely kind person, who believes in giving people second... and third chances. So this is yours. As far as I'm concerned, you're still a part of this family."

"Tish, thank you. If you feel up to it, my house is a few

miles from here. I'd love for you to meet my wife and my boy." His face reddened and tears began to stream down his face.

Charity's chest tightened at the sight of her brother's heart cracking wide open in front of the world. She rose and went to stand beside him, then threw one arm around him. "Tish, Christian, thank you both for being here and for an amazing show. I think when I promised our viewers the most dramatic season opening yet—I delivered. Is there anything else either of you would like to say before we sign off?"

"I love you, Mom." Tish lifted her hand in a brief wave.

There was a long pause, and then Christian looked up, his face wet, his expression somehow contrite and defiant at the same time.

"Is there something you want to say to the viewers?" Charity gave him another opportunity.

"Just that I'm sorry and... I suppose it's obvious, but I want to own it—I'm not a perfect person."

"Yeah," she said, turning to shrug into the camera. "I'm not either. Until next time, this is Charity Drury reporting from Tijuana, Mexico for *Crime on the Coast*."

A LETTER FROM CAREY

Dear Reader,

Thank you! I'm honored that you have taken time from your world to join Brigid and Charity in theirs. I truly appreciate your reading *Second Wives* and bringing your own perspective to the story. I loved creating these characters, and I hope you enjoyed getting to know them and taking their journey as much as I enjoyed sharing them with you.

If you'd like to be one of the first to know about my next book, please sign up via the following link. Your email address will never be shared and you can unsubscribe at any time.

www.bookouture.com/carey-baldwin

If you loved this story, I would be very grateful if you could leave a short review. Reviews are one of the best ways to help other readers discover my books. They don't need to be long or clever. You can make a big difference simply by leaving a line or two. And guess what? I actually read every review!

Building a relationship with readers is one of the best things about being a writer. I love hearing from you, so please stay in touch by connecting with me on Facebook, Twitter, and my website, and following me on BookBub. I've posted the information below for your convenience.

Thank you very much for reading and don't forget to stay in touch!

Love, Carey

www.CareyBaldwin.com

facebook.com/CareyBaldwinAuthor
twitter.com/CareyBaldwin
bookbub.com/authors/carey-baldwin

ACKNOWLEDGMENTS

Thank you so much to my fantastic agent, Liza Dawson, the terrific Lynn Wu and everyone at Liza Dawson Associates. I want to thank my wonderful editor, Laura Deacon, who not only gives me brilliant insights into how to make the story better, but is also a joy to work with. Laura, you are truly my dream editor, and I thank you, so much, for sticking with me. Thank you, thank you, thank you, to publicists extraordinaire Kim, Noelle, Sarah, and Jess. Thank you to the directors and publishers as well as all the individuals in marketing, art, audio and the entire team at Bookouture who champion every book by every author they publish. Thank you for treating each of us with so much care.

Thank you to my dear friends and brainstorming, critiquing, beta-reading geniuses: Suzanne Baldree, Leigh LaValle, Tessa Dare, Lena Diaz, and my newest buddy—Lenora Bell. You are always there for me whether I need to cry, celebrate, or fix a plot hole. I don't know what I'd do without you. Nancy Allen and Kristi Belcamino, I treasure your friendship beyond words. To my family—Bill, Shannon, Erik, Kayla, Sarah, Junior, Oliva, and Marlene—I love you truly, dears.

Printed in Great Britain
by Amazon

22160313R00179